No Ordinary Day

The stunning story that introduces the brilliant new series of romantic suspense, intrigue, and humor, *Extraordinary Days*, by novelist Polly Becks, making her debut in women's fiction.

Set in 1991, *No Ordinary Day* tells the tale of an epic tragedy that changes life forever in a small town in the wild, mystic Adirondack Mountains of upstate New York, especially for eight special women, and the mystery that surrounds it.

Kindergarten teacher Lucy Sullivan has an Irish temper, a love for her students, and a growing fondness for fellow teacher Glen Daniels—until plain-spoken soldier Alex "Ace" Evans comes into her life, quite literally saving it. As they struggle to rescue five little girls caught in a flooding school, will these two opposites find the love missing in both their lives—or even survive?

Publication Date: January 5, 2015

Each book in the *Extraordinary Days* series makes a direct cash donation to a different charity or non-profit organization. Your free download of *No Ordinary Day* benefits **The American Red Cross.**

The *Extraordinary Days* series
[set in present day]:

Monday's Child/ FAIR OF FACE

Where has supermodel Briony, the one-named wonder of the fashion world, disappeared to? That's what style magazine maven Katherine Bruce desperately wants to know—and she's manipulated Pulitzer Prize-winning investigative journalist and war correspondent Erik Bryson into chasing that story down. A serious writer, he's resentful about being stuck with the fluffy task—and utterly unprepared for what he discovers.

Publication Date: Monday, February 2, 2015

Tuesday's Child/ FULL OF GRACE

Grace Fuller, the youth pastor in her father's church, is guarding several painful secrets that threaten her future. Will she find a happily-ever-after with Steve, the confident, handsome assistant pastor with whom she's vying for her dream job, or will the mysterious bad-boy biker who has just come to town, darkly guarding his own painful past, steal her from her chosen path?

Publication Date: Tuesday, March 3, 2015

Wednesday's Child/FULL OF WOE

Life in the fast lane has never been an easy place for twitchy high-society event planner Sloane Wallace, a woman born to privilege and pristine family lineage. But when a freak snowstorm and auto mishap leaves her stranded in the freezing mountains in her designer heels, a burly mountain man, unimpressed with her pedigree, shows up in time to save her couture-covered backside— and completely mess up her world.

Publication Date: Wednesday, April 1, 2015

Your purchase of *Monday's Child: Fair of Face* benefits **The American Cancer Society**.

Your purchase of *Tuesday's Child: Full of Grace* benefits **Tuesday's Children**, a non-profit organization founded to promote long-term healing in all those directly impacted by the events of September 11, 2001.

Your purchase of *Wednesday's Child: Full of Woe* benefits **Wednesday's Child**: **Dave Thomas Foundation for Adoption**, Finding Forever Families for Children in Foster Care

Four more books will follow, beginning in fall of 2015:

Thursday's Child: Far to Go
Friday's Child: Loving and Giving
Saturday's Child: Works Hard for a Living
Sunday's Child: Born on the Sabbath Day

No Ordinary Day

Polly Becks

Book 1 in the EXTRAORDINARY DAYS series

FLOWER IMAGERY

The flower featured on the cover is an
American Beauty Rose,
long a symbol of romantic love, deep and true

Your free download of this e-book provides a direct cash
donation to
THE AMERICAN RED CROSS
dedicated to helping people in need throughout the
United States and, in association with other Red Cross
networks, throughout the world since May 21st, 1881

For more information about The American Red Cross,
go to:
www.redcross.org

Monday's child is fair of face,
Tuesday's child is full of grace,
Wednesday's child is full of woe,
Thursday's child has far to go,
Friday's child is loving and giving,
Saturday's child works hard for a living,
But the child who is born on the Sabbath Day
Is bonny and blithe and good and gay.

This rhyme was first recorded in A. E. Bray's *Traditions of Devonshire*
(Volume II, pp. 287–288) in 1838

To
Bill and Greg
with love

Prelude

APRIL 27, 1991

Obergrande, New York, at the heart of the Adirondack Park

T HE STREETS AT the center of the small city in the mountain wilderness were swollen with seemingly endless rain that spring, gushing in torrents every now and then, or sometimes running in thin rivulets through the gutters.

Making it difficult for people to meet on street corners.

Particularly when it was critical that they not be seen meeting together in public.

So on this night, the three people who met did so under the enormous tree atop a hill in the center of town, the towering, centuries-old tree for which the town was named.

Obergrande.

The rain had paused for a few moments, which should have made umbrellas unnecessary. The stoppage should also have been helpful to the meeting participants remaining unnoticed. The enormous tree's branches and leaves, sheeting water with every passing breeze, however, repeatedly baptized the three with unpleasantly cold precipitation, soaking their raincoats and clothes.

As if it were trying to tell them something urgent.

All the secrecy barely mattered; no one else was out in the dark and the heavy fog anyway.

As the three reached the summit of the hill, and the base of the tree, the first person looked around, then back at the second.

"You found someone to do it? You're certain?"

The second person nodded reluctantly.

"And it's done? Is it done already?"

Another nod.

The first and the third exhaled simultaneously, then exchanged a nod as well.

"All right, then," said the first. "Get home safe. Get and stay dry if you can—it'll be your last chance to for a while."

Like drops of mercury beading, then skittering away from a broken thermometer, the three walked quickly down the hillside in separate directions and disappeared into the thickening fog.

None of them having any idea of what they had unleashed.

Chapter 1

A FEW WEEKS LATER

A primitive riverside campsite, between Newcomb and Obergrande, New York, in the Adirondack Park

IT HAD BEEN a difficult week, Bram thought.

He had just come back inside the tent, soaked to the skin from the relentless rain, after one more failed attempt to get a fire going under the tarp. He shook the water from his hair gently so as not to assault anyone else with it.

The baby had been screaming for most of her waking hours, sending his wife, Anjolie, over the edge and repeatedly into tears, as she struggled to calm their child amid the pouring rain that only let up for a few moments at a time before it returned, full force. Whenever she had gotten the almost-one-year-old to sleep, a rolling clap of thunder would echo through the surrounding mountains, violently shaking their tent and the ground beneath it.

Waking the baby, who immediately returned to wailing.

He had to admit that the female members of the family were not the only ones in their small tent that the weather was frightening.

Bram was a young Dutchman, tall, lean, and strong, an experienced hiker and camper. He was visiting the United States for the first time with his wife and infant daughter with the intention of looking for employment there, though at the moment he was merely on vacation with a visitor's visa.

The school at which he taught in Eindhoven, Holland, had let out for the summer the previous week, and Anjolie, his childhood sweetheart and spouse of almost three years, had a generous vacation policy at her otherwise-low-paying job as a ceramic engineer, so they had undertaken their first trip to the United States with their relatively new daughter in tow, as they had all her young life in Europe.

They had flown into Montreal in the sunlight, taking a bus into Lake Placid, New York, from which they planned to hike their way down to the heart of the Adirondack Park, camping all along the way. Rain had greeted them shortly after leaving Lake Placid, and had not let up entirely since then.

While Bram was under no misconception about his own value in the American job market, he had been advised that Anjolie's prospects were much better in the U.S. than in Holland. But, in addition to the better salary a job for her with an American firm would provide, Bram had a potential financial windfall of his own in the works as well.

An odd inheritance from his recently deceased and long-beloved grandmother, known to him all his life as

Mutti.

Once he and his little family had made it to a small town called Obergrande, he would have a better idea if that inheritance had any value at all.

He looked over in the dim light of the oil lantern at Anjolie, who was on the verge of tears again, and hurried to her side.

"Here," he said quietly in the tongue of their homeland, "let me take her for a while. I think the thunderstorm is passing; lie down and try to rest."

His wife, too exhausted to argue, handed him the baby and slid gratefully into the zipped-together sleeping bags.

"There, there, little one," Bram said, putting the infant up on his shoulder. He rubbed her back and spoke in a low, melodic voice. "The weather is nasty, and I know the thunder frightens you. But we are here all together, you, your mama, and I. Together, God willing, we will make a lovely life in this beautiful place of mountains for you to climb, lakes for you to swim in, and bright stars to light the darkness for you—once the rain finally stops."

After a slew of hiccups, the baby settled down and rested her head against his neck. He caressed that tiny head, covered with waves of the finest, softest auburn hair, its color just like that of her mother.

Bram began to sing to her, a low, wordless tune from the back of his throat and sinuses, the lullabye that always caused her to fall asleep sooner or later.

Thankfully, this time it was sooner.

Once he was certain she was sleeping soundly, he laid her down on her little sleeping bag surrounded by their backpacks, covered her with the blanket, dimmed the oil lantern even more, then turned back to where his wife lay, her large eyes open, gazing glassily at him.

"She hates me," she murmured as he removed his wet shirt and jeans and lay down beside her.

"She adores you," Bram said, smiling. He pulled himself into the sleeping bag and took Anjolie into his arms. "She hates that her baby food is cold because her idiot father can't get a simple campfire going."

"Satan himself couldn't get a fire going in all that rain."

"Don't speak such names in a thunderstorm," Bram said, kissing her neck up to her ear. His fingers caressed, then unbuttoned, the fastenings on her pajama top.

"What in the world are you doing?" Anjolie said crossly as he slid the top carefully off her shoulder within the confines of the sleeping bag.

"Is that a rhetorical question?" Bram teased, running his fingertip around the rosy nipple he had exposed, then following his finger with his lips.

Anjolie squirmed away as far as the bag would allow.

"No. I'm wondering if you are in your right mind. The baby's been howling most of the day, it's been raining since we got here a week ago and shows no signs of letting up. I haven't had a good night's sleep in almost two weeks. I'm exhausted. My hair is always wet. And I look like a hag."

"You have never looked anything but beautiful in your whole life," Bram said quietly as he kissed the hollow of her throat. "Exhausted as you are, sodden as our tent is with rain and mud, you are still the most gorgeous woman I have ever seen—not to mention my soulmate and the mother of our beautiful little girl, who is *finally asleep*."

"And I see no need to risk waking her," Anjolie said, but her tone had softened.

"We'll be quiet."

"Bram—"

"Shhh," he said as he fumbled with the drawstring of her pajama bottoms, then caressed her gently, ardently as he found his way inside them. He continued until he saw the look in her eyes change from annoyance to the beginnings of passion, and brought his lips back up to her ear again.

"I know this has been a miserable week, not the best introduction to the place that soon might be our new home," he said quietly, interlacing the fingers of his other hand through her smaller ones, causing their wedding rings to click metallically. "But we cannot allow something as meaningless as this bad weather to dampen our happiness."

"Dampen—ha. Funny."

He kissed her mouth warmly, taking his time.

"We came to America to find a better life here, leaving very little behind," he whispered after their lips parted. "Treasure hunts are always full of misdirection and obstacles. We have to keep going if we want to win the prize."

Anjolie rolled her eyes, but heat was rising to her face and chest as desire was building inside her.

"Why do we need to hunt? I thought Mutti had already given you the prize—the treasure," she said huskily, taking him in hand and mirroring his caresses, causing him to shiver violently.

Bram glanced over his shoulder at the baby, who was still sleeping soundly, then returned his attention to his wife.

"No," he said, pulling her closer and smiling at her in the dim glow of the lantern. "Mutti's gift may or may not bring us fortune in the place our ancestors found it. But make no mistake, Anjolie; I am well aware that our treasure sleeps a few feet away, and that mine will sleep in my arms tonight. And those are the only treasures that really matter to me."

Her eyes took on the glow of the lantern-light as she smiled in return.

As the storm blasted through again, they were soon lost in each other, making love in time with the falling rain, surging and dancing passionately but quietly within the warmth of the sleeping bag as the wind howled around their tent, rattling the trees.

Chapter 2

In an old cabin, south of the town of Obergrande

SAM HATED BEING left alone in the cabin, especially on rainy nights.

It had been bad enough when Jeremy had first brought her here, babbling about the joys of fishing and scuba diving and outdoor sex beneath tall trees and starry skies. He was proud to have saved enough to rent this hell-hole cabin far from the lake's actual shore, a run-down shack that looked nothing like what the photocopy ad had shown when they saw it on a diner wall in Johnstown. It had no electricity, and therefore, no TV, so it was even harder to pass the endless, often rain-filled days.

But for the last week or so, having him with her was much harder than being alone.

Something had happened on one of the many occasions Jeremy had left her during the day, going to 'work,' whatever that was. He had never held anything but day jobs that she knew of in the past, though she believed him to be a hard worker and, while not exactly smart, he wasn't stupid either, and could follow directions most of the time.

Whatever had happened had put an end to most of that.

Now each day he would sleep late, though not well, unlike the days when he had been working, would rise numbly and wander off without any explanation of where he was going or what he was doing. Occasionally he would give her money if she asked for it to buy something to eat from the small store more than two miles down the road, but he wasn't willing to ride her there on his motorcycle as he had always been before.

And now he always came home after dark, leaving her alone in the horrible cabin among the scary night sounds and the threatening hum of mosquitoes and mayflies.

Sam had come to the end of her patience. She was past ready to go home.

Except she didn't really have anywhere to go home to.

In her own way, Sam loved Jeremy. Before whatever happened had taken place he had told her routinely that she was beautiful, had left her raunchy notes under the peanut butter jar or in her pocket when he left for work about what they would do when he came home, and usually followed through, even when he was tired.

He had been pretty excited with this place when they first got here, and was especially fascinated with the massive tree on the hill in the middle of town. Back when the weather didn't suck, they had spent some time picnicking underneath it, watching the sun go down, like much of the rest of the town. It had been early spring, still barely past winter when they arrived, so their time outside was limited even then.

When the warmer weather came around, he had shared his excitement of fishing off the public pier in the melting ice of the lake with her, something she found disgusting, but hadn't said so, because she was glad to see him happy, especially since scuba diving equipment rental had turned out to be far beyond their limited means.

As promised, the outdoor sex had been great until they had accidentally rolled onto a nest of stinging ants and spent three days itching ferociously in places that hurt a lot, especially for Jeremy.

After that, it had been awkward and quiet.

But not like it became after whatever had happened a few days before this one.

In addition to being alone all day, for a week or more Sam had been trapped inside the cabin by the constant rain drumming on the roof, leaking a little near the pit toilet and bottle of hand sanitizer in a closet that served as the bathroom, again, nothing like the flyer had advertised. The books she had bought at the grocery store and brought along and had read a dozen times were no longer working to help her escape her reality.

Every night when he finally came home, Jeremy was a little more agitated. He would pace the floor of the cabin, running his hands nervously through his sweaty hair, as if he was trying to solve a puzzle that his brain wasn't up to. Often he would go outside and stare up at the sky through the trees, but never seemed to find whatever he was looking for.

Now, as she was musing about her problems, she heard the roar of a motorcycle shifting down outside the cabin.

She stretched out on the lumpy mattress and waited.

After a longer time than she expected, the door of the cabin creaked open and Jeremy came inside, soaked from the rain. He took his motorcycle helmet off and shook his hair, which was drenched, spattering her with droplets of it.

"Eeeggaagggghhkkk," Sam muttered, recoiling. "Thanks, Germ."

He set his helmet down and ran his fingers through his wet hair, not looking at her.

"Got a hole in your helmet? Your hair's all wet."

She got no response.

"Where ya been?" she asked, sitting up and hanging her legs over the side of the bed.

"Ridin' ." The word was more mumble than speech.

"No kidding. I thought you hated riding in the rain."

Jeremy turned in her direction as he unzipped his jacket, but didn't meet her eyes.

"I do, but in upstate New York, you ride in the rain or you don't ride. That's just how it is. Especially in the Dacks." He glanced around the small cabin. "What've we got to eat?"

Sam rose from the bed and sauntered over to him, trying to look sexy. "Each other."

He rolled his eyes and turned away, looking into the single empty cabinet and along the small counter that together served as a kitchen. "Seriously—what've we got?"

She rolled her eyes as well, then went to a drawstring sack she carried as a purse and fished out half a candy bar, which she tossed unceremoniously at him.

"Here—choke on that."

Jeremy caught the half-eaten bar in the air, looking at her in surprise. "What's the matter with you?"

"You're kidding, right?"

Jeremy tore back the wrapper and bit into the bar, then looked at her for the first time since he'd entered the cabin. He scarfed down the candy bar as he watched her, then lowered his gaze and swallowed.

"Sorry," he said. "I know it's sucked here. We should never've come."

Sam watched him as he sat in one of the rickety chairs at the even more rickety table. He had turned toward the door as he did, and let his head fall to the table on his arms.

Sam's brows drew together.

For the first time since he had come into the cabin, she noticed he was shaking.

"You gonna tell me what's wrong?" she asked as she rose and came to him, pulling his wet motorcycle jacket carefully from his shoulders. She hung it over the back of the other chair.

"No. Not ever."

Sam blinked. "Why?"

Jeremy lay with his face on his arms for a long time. She waited in silence, sensing that whatever was upsetting him was far worse than she had imagined. Finally he spoke.

"Because I love you. Can you let it go now?"

Sam waited in silence for something to change—for

him to stop shaking, or raise his head, or change the subject, but he did nothing, just lay with his head on his forearms on the table.

Trembling.

Sam did not have a lot of tools at her disposal at the moment for comforting a man with very little imagination. She waited for a long time, then took hold of the bottom of his wet T-shirt and slowly pulled it up and over his head and shoulders.

He pulled away. "What are you doing?"

"Taking off your shirt."

"Why?" His voice sounded almost threatening.

Sam contemplated the good sense of going forward, then decided she had nothing to lose.

"Because *I* love *you*," she said matter-of-factly. "And you're wet. Don't want ya to catch cold. Now turn around."

Jeremy, now sitting straight up, rotated ninety degrees until he was facing her.

It was all Sam could do not to gasp at the look on his face in the dull gleam of the kerosene lantern.

His jaw was clenched like a vise, and his eyes were shining.

She wasn't certain, but she thought that it might be fear gleaming in them.

Her voice broke. "Aw, Germ," she whispered.

She straddled him and sat down on his thighs, looking at him thoughtfully. Then, slowly, she pulled the clips from her hair and let it fall from the messy knot she had tied it up in atop her head into the long brown waves she knew he had a soft spot for.

Sam took Jeremy's hands in hers and placed them on the ends of her longest locks, closing his fingers around the strands of her dark hair, then pushed the rest of it up against his chest, rubbing it sensuously against his nipples.

She could feel the muscles in his thighs tighten beneath her. The muscles of his chest and shoulders did so as well; Jeremy was a skinny young man, hardly more than a boy, really, but what little flesh he had was nicely sculpted along a ribcage on which she could count every bone.

Beneath her open legs, even through her jeans, she thought she felt some of his other muscles tightening, too.

One of which was impressively oversized for a man of his slight build.

Sam ran her hands up his chest to the back of his neck and interlaced her fingers, then applied her lips to the hollow of his throat, warmly, as tenderly as she could.

Feeling his throat quiver beneath them, whether from panic or, perhaps now, heat.

"Aw, Sam, baby, no," he whispered as her lips made their way up his neck, kissing it softly, but she could tell his resolve was crumbling. "I'm tired. C'mon."

"Heck, I'm working on that," she whispered in his ear. "You're just not helping much." She decided to try humor. "You're the one that told me the best reason for coming to this gross place was that everybody gets laid in the Adirondacks, that there was sex everywhere around here."

"There—there is—"

"Yeah? Well, there hasn't been any around *here*—" she took hold of one of his hands and pulled the ends of her hair from it, redirecting it between her legs—"not for almost two weeks."

Jeremy leaned his forehead against hers and sighed. "I'm sorry."

"Don't be sorry—just *do* me. Or let me do you; I don't care, just let's do *something*—I've been so bored and dry, you're making me feel like an old woman—"

Jeremy seized her face and kissed her hard.

Caught by surprise, and by the blind intensity of his kiss, Sam opened her mouth and let him in, his tongue probing, caressing hers, stealing her breath. She let go of him and quickly began to unbutton her camp shirt, pulling it from herself without making him need to release her or stop the wildness of his kiss.

The kiss that was sending waves of hot desire through her entire body.

The kiss that continued as his hands left her face and were immediately on the clasp of her bra, springing it open like a pro.

"Dry, are you?" he said as he pulled back from her mouth, which was now open and panting. "We'll see about that—stand up."

Shaking now herself, Sam stood, her legs astride his on either side of the chair.

Jeremy had already tossed her bra aside and turned his attention to her breasts, gleaming with the sweat of unexpected excitement.

"You're so pretty, baby," he said, his voice low and husky, as his fingertips, then his warm mouth addressed the first, then the second one, blowing a stream of warm breath over her tingling nipples, holding her around the waist so she wouldn't fall over. "I gotcha—open those jeans."

Her head swimming now, Sam obeyed, her hands trembling.

Distantly she could hear the rain beating on the metal roof, filling the ugly little cabin with a pounding thrum that drove her excitement higher as he roughly pulled her jeans off.

She was anticipating a different pounding thrum momentarily.

An anticipation that was met and exceeded a few minutes later, perched on the table in front of the kneeling Jeremy, his head between her legs, her fingers wound through his hair.

And then again on the floor in front of that table, atop him.

And then once more on the lumpy mattress of the uncomfortable bed, beneath him.

Once he had finally partly-pushed, partly-carried her, scrambling through the discarded clothes on the cabin floor, to that bed, and was driving his impressive self into her again, gripping her backside instead of her thighs this time, Sam forced herself to open her eyes and think long enough to focus her swimming gaze on his face, hovering over her in the darkness.

And immediately wished she hadn't.

She'd been having sex with Jeremy for fairly close to two years, but had never seen a look on his face like the one she saw now.

His eyes, usually closed as he approached climax, were open wide, staring blankly above him.

His teeth were still clenched as they had been before, but now in an ugly manner that made the shivers of impending orgasm that were sweeping through her turn cold for a moment.

Making her suddenly afraid.

Then, caught between fear and passion, instinct took over.

Sam planted the soles of her feet firmly on the terrible mattress and slid her hands from Jeremy's back down to his backside, which she gripped as hard as she could.

Sending him, and, a moment later, her, completely over the edge into hot, black oblivion, fireworks shooting behind their eyes.

They lay for a long time afterwards, panting and clinging to each other, trying to recover their breath.

Rather than resting his head between her breasts, as he usually did, or running his fingers through her hair, Jeremy remained with his eyes open, still staring above him.

He almost seemed to be looking through the wooden walls and the metal roof to the black, rain-filled sky beyond them.

Sam closed her eyes, unwilling to watch.

Finally, he lowered his head and kissed her nose.

She was awake, but she didn't respond.

He brought his lips closer to her ear.

"Betcha don't feel dry no more, now, do ya?" he whispered teasingly.

When she remained still, unmoving, he rolled off her and laid his hand on her stomach.

"That's too bad," he said seriously. "Because, pretty soon, you're gonna be grateful to be dry."

Sam lay still until Jeremy began to snore beside her.

Then her eyes opened wide in the darkness of the cabin, staring at the ceiling.

Wondering what he meant.

IN THE MORNING, they got up, got dressed, got packed, got on the bike.

And got gone from the beautiful Adirondack mountains and the pretty town of Obergrande.

Never looking back.

Chapter 3

THE NEXT DAY, Thursday, 2:35 PM

Obergrande Elementary School, Obergrande, NY

"RAIN, RAIN, GO 'way, come again some other—no, never mind. Just go 'way."

Lucy Sullivan, the newest of the school's three kindergarten teachers, was sitting cross-legged on the floor of her classroom, up to her elbows in paste and children. She choked back laughter.

Then looked up to see five-year-old Dominic glaring out the classroom's wall-to-wall back window at the sodden playground and gray-black sky where the clouds hung down almost to the ground. His arms were crossed over his chest and his small, rotund face was set in a scowl, making his cheeks even more deliciously chubby than they normally were.

"I hear ya, Dominic," she said in agreement. "Come back and finish your collage, please."

Nicola, a tiny girl with long, golden ringlets similar to Lucy's own, and enormous eyes, came over to her side.

"S'been waining a bewy, bewy long time," she agreed, moving so Dominic could come back in the circle.

"You are certainly right about that, Nicola," Lucy said, nodding for the little girl to sit down next to her. "Can you use your r's that you and Mrs. Mastrantonio just learned?"

Nicola swallowed hard, her little face puckered with anxiety.

"S' been rrrrrraining a berrry, berry, long time," she said carefully again.

Lucy's alabaster face lit up, and she smiled at the little girl. She leaned close to her.

"Beautiful," she said. "Beautiful r's. Good job. Will you please pass Dominic the paste, then sit down and join us?" She handed Nicola the jar.

Beaming, the child complied.

Lucy exhaled. The project was almost done, a mosaic mural of construction paper collages that would be graced with dried flowers, if the rain would stop falling and the sun would ever come out again long enough to gather them.

Given that the edge rains of Hurricane Clarence, a seemingly mild tropical storm that had roared unexpectedly into a Category 4 off the East Coast a few days before, were predicted to dampen the area of the central Adirondacks later in the week, that possibility didn't appear particularly likely.

So Lucy had procured an impressive stash of tissue paper in a glorious variety of colors to make into small folded flowers if the naturals ones were unable to be dried in time for the Mother's Day Tea.

She looked with secret pride and not-so-secret fondness at her eighteen students, grouped in two big circles, one with her, the other with her aide, Kelly Moran, all working intently on the art project that would decorate the walls of the Playroom for the big event that their mothers and grandmothers had been invited to come to next week.

The class had made ribbon decorations for each of the ladies' chairs and cookie presents for each guest of honor, had learned a poem to recite together entitled *Mothers Are Very Nice People,* and were practicing several mother-related songs with their vocal teacher, Mr. Daniels, during music class.

There had been impressive cooperation, only a few spills of art supplies, and surprisingly little fighting, mostly because all of the energy the kids usually put into bothering each other had been directed at the annoyingly endless rain.

She glanced at the clock. The warning bell would ring any moment.

"All right," she instructed as she rose. "Let's pick up the supplies, get cleaned up and ready to go home. Collages on the window shelf. Mrs. Moran will help you. What day is it tomorrow?"

The entire class pointed in unison to the enormous calendar on the wall near the door where the word THURSDAY was impossible to miss, even if many of them still couldn't read it.

"Friday!" they shouted. The approach of the school day's end had sweetened their mood, and hers.

"En Español?" she asked.

There was a pause. "Miércoles!" half the class called half-heartedly.

Lucy shook her head disapprovingly. She turned to a little girl in a lacy white cotton dress, odd among the jeans and T-shirts of the rest of the class.

"Elisa, can you help us? Mañana—qué dia es?"

"Viernes," the little girl said shyly.

Lucy turned back to the class as the warning bell sounded.

"Repita?"

"Viernes!" they shouted, even louder than before, in unison.

"What language will we use for the calendar tomorrow?"

"German!" the most-awake kids called as the rest of the class was beginning to dissolve.

She clapped her hands, catching their attention, and the class followed suit.

"Whose turn is it to feed Sebastian tomorrow?"

Dominic's hand shot up excitedly. "Oh! Oh! Oh! Me! Me! Me!" he shouted, hopping up and down, his hair flapping like batwings. "Meeeeeeee!"

Lucy let loose a belly-laugh in spite of herself.

"All right, everyone, say goodnight to Sebastian."

The class turned in the direction of the aquarium that housed the class turtle, sitting on the window shelf next to the framed picture of Lucy's cat, Sadie, and waved vigorously. "Goodnight, Sebastian!"

Sebastian, a small Red-eared Slider, stared back, emotionless.

"Clean up, folks," Lucy directed. "We leave for the buses in five minutes."

2:57 PM

ON HER WAY to the main office, Lucy came speedily around a corner and almost collided with Glen Daniels, the vocal music teacher whose windowless, interior classroom was around the corner and down the hall from her exterior one, causing the tower of sheet music he was carrying to pitch violently from side to side. Amid a good deal of awkward motion between them they managed to right the tower and avert a catastrophe.

"I'm so sorry," Lucy stammered as she patted the papers back into place. She pulled a few strands of her long, curly hair that had escaped the up-do back out of her face and tucked them behind her ear.

"No need to be," said Mr. Daniels, smiling uncertainly. "I was hoping to run into you anyway; this is as good an opportunity as any, I guess."

"Oh?"

"Yes, I'd like to come and snag a couple of your students tomorrow for some extra practice for the Tea," he said. "There are a few featured parts in some of the songs."

"That would be great," Lucy said, standing up straight again. "Drop by any time; we have a pretty flexible schedule tomorrow."

"Will do." He cleared his throat. "Would—would you perhaps like to grab some supper tonight in town?" His face flushed red; Mr. Daniels, a tall, fair-skinned, attractive-enough man with blond hair, had a reputation among the female teachers for being almost painfully shy and awkward.

Lucy blinked. "Uh—well, I'd love to, but I'm planning on attending the Town Board hearing tonight." She saw his face fall, and felt her stomach cramp, so she sighed inwardly and threw herself on the bonfire of kindness. "Can we eat early? I have to be at the Town Hall by six o'clock."

Glen brightened. "Sure. I was going to suggest Charlie's, but that can take a while. Do you want to go to the Lebanese place, Pita Gourmet, down by the lake? Pretty fast service there."

"That'd be nice. I need about an hour to get cleaned up and ready for tomorrow—does that work for you?"

"I'll stop by your classroom—see you in an hour."

Lucy smiled at him awkwardly and headed into the main office.

She greeted Karen Ridley, the long-time general secretary.

"Hi Karen—any chance Mrs. Cox is in?"

"She is," came the voice of the principal from behind her.

Lucy spun around and smiled.

Mrs. Cox was a smart, placid woman several inches shorter than Lucy, with a full head of beautiful white hair. "What can I do for you, Lucy?"

"Can we step into your office for a moment?"

"Certainly." Mrs. Cox dropped the papers she was holding onto Karen's desk and led Lucy down the hall into the principal's office, closing the door behind her.

"What's up?" she asked as she went behind her desk and sat down, indicating the chair in front of it to Lucy.

"I have a concern about three of my students regarding the Mother's Day Tea," Lucy said directly as she sat. "I'm worried that they might be compromised by it."

"Who?"

"First, Ashleigh Winters." Lucy's throat tightened; the little girl's mother had died just before Christmas, after the birth of her second child, Ashleigh's baby brother.

Mrs. Cox nodded. "Already got that one handled," she said. "I spoke to Ashleigh's father, and he plans to take the day of the Tea off from work and spend it with her. He's arranged for a sitter, and it should be some nice father-and-daughter time."

Lucy exhaled in relief. "That's great."

"Who else?"

"Elisa Santiago. I sent an invitation to Mrs. Santiago home via backpack express, but I haven't heard back from her."

Mrs. Cox jotted a note on a small pad of paper. "I'll check into that one," she said. "Did you use the English version of your invitation as a guide?"

"Yes. Why?"

"Well, I noticed you put 'RSVP' on the bottom of the English version—and since those letters are abbreviations for French words, perhaps it's not in their culture to know what they mean."

"Of course. How stupid of me."

"Stupid is a twenty-five-cent word," Mrs. Cox said,

not looking up from her note-writing, but pointing with her other hand toward a large mason jar full of spare change and the occasional dollar bill with a wide slit in its metal lid on the window shelf behind her. "Tomorrow, make sure you contribute to the Don't Be Unnecessarily Negative jar."

Lucy dropped her head and chuckled. "Yes, ma'am."

"And finally?"

The kindergarten teacher exhaled deeply. "Garrett Burlingame."

Mrs. Cox looked up, exhaled herself, and nodded.

Garrett's older brother, Devin, had been the only child at the Tea two years before whose mother had forgotten about it. The little boy had entered the Playroom, looked around, then burst into tears when he realized she was not there.

Mrs. Cox had been called to come down from the office and stand in for Mrs. Burlingame. She sat in the carefully be-ribboned chair next to him during the various events in the program, trying to substitute for his parent without any success whatsoever. Devin could not be coaxed into any sort of happy state of mind, but just sat through the entirety of the Tea, weeping silently.

Lucy had gone after about fifteen minutes of agony to the kindergarten-through-3rd-grade office nearby and had called his house, only to be informed by her husband that Mrs. Burlingame was running errands, the Tea having slipped her mind. Lucy's fair-skinned face had gone completely red with rage, and she needed to go into the teacher's restroom and splash water on it, cursing quietly under her breath, trying to cool her Irish temper, without much success, before she returned to the Playroom.

"I've sent her three invitations now, but still have received nothing back," she said, trying to keep her voice calm. "At least with Devin she sent a response in. Garrett insists he's given the invitations to her, and reminded her to RSVP, but to no avail. Their answering machine is full. I swear if she misses the Tea by going to the bank, or Hardware Heaven, or the liquor store again like she did two years ago, I'm going down there and drag her back here by her hair. I can't bear to watch another one of her sons sob through the Tea. It'll kill me."

"Understood," said Mrs. Cox. "I think I'll call Mr. Grimes at the hardware store and Chris Weiler, the owner of the liquor store, and ask them both to keep a lookout for her. They would be willing to remind her what she's missing quietly and non-judgmentally if she shows up there."

"That's it? What if she goes somewhere else?"

The principal looked levelly at her.

"There's only so much we can do, Lucy," she said sensibly. "I'll ponder the situation and see if I can come up with some other preventive action. But, while I appreciate you being so devoted to and protective of your students, there are some lines we just can't cross. No hair-dragging. The school doesn't need the lawsuit."

Lucy sighed. "All right. I guess I'll just send a fourth invitation home tomorrow."

"Not a bad idea. Anything else I can do for you?"

"No," the young teacher said as she rose from her

chair. "Unless you want to stand in for me at my dinner date with Glen Daniels in an hour. That would put me in your debt forever."

Mrs. Cox winced. "Yeah. Uh, no. Sorry."

"You can't blame a girl for trying. Aw, c'mon—he's treating—I think. Is your husband perhaps working late? You like Lebanese food, don't you, Mrs. Cox?"

"Mr. Daniels is actually quite a nice man, Lucy," Mrs. Cox said. "You really should give him a chance—"

She stopped and broke into laughter at the sight of Lucy's face.

"All right," she said. "I won't even try."

"Yeah, it's a waste of your time," Lucy said as she took hold of the door handle. "Thanks. I know he's nice, and nice looking. I just, well, I just can't—"

She shook her head and walked out the door, Mrs. Cox's amused snort following her.

Chapter 4

3:31 PM

Windsor Gardens nursery, near the center of town

SUSAN WINDSOR MANEUVERED her station wagon around the other cars in the small parking lot of her family's garden center, careful to avoid the customers who were loading large bags of mulch or heavy potted plants into the back end of their own vehicles.

The rain that had been tormenting the town all spring had been especially heavy for the last week. At this moment, however, it had quieted into a mild shower, so all the power gardeners were out, trying to make up for lost time.

She pulled into a parking space near the little shop in front of the greenhouse, turned off the engine, leaving the auxiliary power on, and unbuckled her seat belt. Then she turned around and looked into the back seat at her three favorite things in the world.

Two of which were asleep.

Her oldest daughter, Sarah, a five-year-old kindergartner, was sitting between her two ten-month-old twin sisters in their car seats with a skeptical look on her little face that made Sue Windsor burst into laughter.

"What's the matter, honey?"

Sarah sighed. "How come they can cry at the same time, be hungry at the same time, sleep at the same time, but every time you change one, the other one poops when we's in the car?" She raised her little hands in a grown-up gesture of surrender.

Sue leaned over the seat. "I ask myself that every day, Sarah." She unbuckled the little girl from her car seat and put her hands out to her.

Sarah reached out and climbed over the front seat into her mother's arms.

"You don't have to *sit* between them," she said moodily.

Sue kissed her daughter and hugged her tight.

"You're such a wonderful big sister," she whispered. "I know it's not easy."

The passenger side door opened, and a handsome man's head crowned with dirty-blond hair the same color as his daughter's popped into the car.

"There's my girl!" Dave Windsor, owner of Windsor Gardens, called rowdily. "C'mere, you! Where's my hug?"

"Daddy," Sarah said indignantly, "shhhh! You'll wake the baobabs."

Dave's tone quieted immediately.

"Ooops, sorry," he whispered, pulling Sarah out of the car and into a hug. "Let me get a kiss from Mommy, and we can go water your plant."

"Plants, Daddy," Sarah reminded him as he carried her around the front of the station wagon on his way to the driver's side door. "Blythe and Bonnie need they's plants watered, too."

"You got it, Sweet Pea." Dave crouched down in front of Sue, a fresh-faced brunette who had worked as an art teacher before the birth of the twins, and planted a warm kiss on her lips. "How was your day, Beautiful?"

"Not bad. The babies didn't sleep much, so if you and Sarah are going to water the plants, I'm gonna take a quick nap with them in the car."

"OK. We'll be back in a while." He kissed her again, then locked and closed the door quietly.

Susan watched them walk away across the parking lot, smiling. Then she turned the radio on. Nirvana's *Smells Like Teen Spirit* screamed out of the speakers; Susan quickly hit the second station button, switching away from a song she really liked but did not want disturbing the twins.

On the second channel, Whitney Houston's *All the Man That I Need* was playing softly. She settled back against the seat's upholstery and closed her eyes, singing along softly to an intermittently wailing saxophone.

How appropriate, she thought dreamily as she drifted off, her head drifting to the same side as both her baby daughters. *She might just as well be singing about you, Dave.*

She was asleep before the second verse.

"HOW WAS *YOUR* day?" Dave inquired of Sarah as she took his hand and trailed along with him back to the open gardens where the rare plants, trees, and vines stood, light drops of rain falling as they walked.

The kindergartner regaled him with all the events of her school day as they traveled across the wet garden center to the place where a small flowering vine was growing up against a trellis.

Dave snatched the watering hose and brought it to Sarah's hand.

"There you are, my love," he said as he wrapped her small palm around the trigger. "Give 'er a nice drink."

Sarah looked doubtfully into the sky.

"I think the rain did that already," she said.

"Yes, but when you water her, it's special," Dave said. "You and she have the same name—at least the same middle name—and so you're special to her. Go ahead, give her a splash."

Sarah smiled and turned the hose on the plant, spraying it generously.

"She's little," she said as she let up on the hose. "Is she going to get bigger?"

"Oh yes. She will be high as the sky in a few years. Just as I suspect you will be. Come on, let's water the plants for the baobabs."

A FEW ROWS away were the plants that belonged to the baby twins.

"Daddy," Sarah said as they pointed the hose at the pots and carefully added water, "why's Blythe and Bonnie's plants different? Aren't they s'posed to be the same?"

"Nope," said Dave, shaking water from the leaves. "Each of you has a different middle name, even the twins, and the plant's name is the same as the middle name. Each girl has a different plant that's special to her."

The little girl's forehead wrinkled in thought.

"Are they baobab plants?"

"No," Dave said, coiling the hose back up. "Baobabs are huge-mongous, gi-normous trees, and they grow on the other side of the world. They grow *very* tall and are *very* special—some people think they are magic trees, because they can do all kinds of amazing things."

Sarah picked up the very end of the hose and helped him carry it back to the storage hook. "Like what?"

"Well," Dave said as they walked, "a baobab can hold as much water in its trunk as a big swimming pool."

The little girl stopped in her tracks. "Really?"

"Really. Keep walking." Dave turned around so she could not see the grin on his face at her adorable expression of shock. "They can feed animals and people with their fruit, and they can be used to make clothes, and all kinds of other things. They are sometimes called Trees of Life, because they can keep a whole village alive—people *and* animals."

"Is Oba-gran a baobab?" Sarah offered him the end of the hose as he hung the coil up.

Dave took it and smiled, then looked seriously into her eyes.

"No," he said. "But it's a Tree of Life." He took her little hand. "Maybe someday we will all travel the world, you, your mama, the twins, and me, and go and see some real baobabs."

"I think our baobabs would like that."

"Good. OK, let's take a stroll inside, then head back to the car—I have to get back to work soon."

AFTER THEIR WATERING chores were done, Dave took Sarah for a longer walk inside the greenhouse and store, out of the rain, quizzing her about the plants on the tables while he occasionally rang up a purchase for a customer. Every so often he glanced out the window to make certain that the station wagon was not being disturbed. Finally, he took his daughter's hand again and they made their way back to the car.

He unlocked the door quietly and opened it slowly, then held up Sarah so she could wake her mother with a kiss.

Sue's eyes blinked open, and she smiled.

"Good nap?" Dave inquired.

"Any nap is a good one at this point," Sue said, sitting up behind the wheel. "So who's going to go to the Town Board meeting tonight?"

"Not me," Dave said, helping Sarah crawl over her mother and sit in the front seat, something she considered a privilege when the car wasn't moving. "I've got fire training tonight."

Sue exhaled. "I suppose that means that no one from our family is going, then," she said, a little tersely. "I don't have anyone to watch the girls."

"There will be plenty of people there to argue our side of the debate," Dave said. "No one is listening to anyone at this point, anyway. We're inducting a few new members tonight, but otherwise it shouldn't be too late."

"It never is." Sue's tone was sarcastic.

Dave shrugged. "My term as chief ends in July," he said. "Only a couple more months."

"Thank goodness. Can you get Sarah back in her car seat, please?"

"Absolutely." He obliged, then kissed his wife good-bye.

"Have a restful evening, ladies," he said to the two awake females in the car, then looked over the seat at the babies who were still asleep. "You two too."

"Have a good meeting," Sue said. "If you finish early, drop by the Town Hall and see if anything interesting is going on. I suspect their meeting will run a lot longer than your training."

Dave rolled his eyes. "I have no doubt you're right. I'd rather stick forks in my eyes, however."

"Daddy," Sarah said seriously, "don't do that. That's not what forks is for."

Her parents chuckled as he pulled back out of the car and shut the door again.

Chapter 5

3:57 PM

Obergrande Elementary School

AS PROMISED, GLEN Daniels came to her classroom exactly an hour later to find Lucy just finishing up her lesson plans for the next week. He waited patiently out in the hall until she was ready, then walked with her to the door of the school that led out into the faculty parking area, where he opened a large black umbrella and held it over her.

"Thank you," Lucy said appreciatively. "I am sick of this rain, but nowhere near as sick of it as my students are."

"I don't blame them," Glen agreed. "They have few enough hours of daylight in the spring as it is. The snow is finally gone, and now they can't even play outside. It pretty much sucks."

Lucy laughed in spite of herself at his final word, which was something she was far more likely to say outside of school than she thought he was.

"Normally I would offer to drive, but it seems to me that if you need to get to the Town Hall for the hearing, you might want to leave directly from Pita Gourmet," he said as they made their way in the strafing rain across the parking lot. "If we drive separately, you'll have your car there when we're done and can get a space near the Town Hall."

"Thanks," Lucy said again. She was beginning to feel badly about her earlier attitude, especially in the face of Mr. Daniel's thoughtfulness.

He held the umbrella over her while she got the car door open and into the front seat. As soon as she had started it, he peered out from beneath the umbrella himself.

"Do you know where the restaurant is?"

"Oh, yes."

"All right, then I'll meet you there."

Lucy nodded, closed her door, and watched him dash off across the parking lot. She reached up to the rearview mirror, where the rosary that had been her mother's and grandmother's hung, and caressed the crucifix, murmuring a quick prayer, as was her tradition.

Then she put her car in gear and headed over to the near side of Lake Obergrande.

THE LEBANESE RESTAURANT was one she normally avoided. It was owned by a family that, while not directly unpleasant, had not made customer service a priority, at least in the times she had been there, though the food was excellent. But when she and Glen Daniels entered, the faces of the grumpy grandfather manning the ovens and the sullen, middle-aged blond waitress behind the cash register both lit up in delight.

"Bonsoir," Glen greeted them.

"Bonsoir," they replied in unison, smiling, or approximating it.

"Bone swa?" Lucy added in her best French accent, and failing.

The two restaurant staff stared at her in an ugly way.

"I'd be happy to order for you if you tell me what you'd like," Glen said as they were led to the nicest of the small restaurant's tables. "You get vastly better service if you order in French. Unless, of course, you can order in French yourself. Or Lebanese."

"Not a prayer," Lucy admitted as he pulled out her chair for her. "Except for Spanish, which I can carry off pretty well, I only know enough other foreign languages to teach my students the days of the week, the numbers from one to ten, 'hello,' 'goodbye,' 'please' and 'thank you.' That's about it."

"That's more than sufficient for kindergarten, I would guess," Glen said, taking his own seat. "Your students are lucky to have you."

"Thank you," said Lucy once again. "Which ones are you planning to 'snag' tomorrow?"

Glen opened his menu. "Hmmm. Let's see; Grace Fuller, Sarah Windsor, Corinne Byrnes, Sloane Wallace. Oh—and Elisa Santiago—she has a lovely singing voice when she can be coaxed into using it."

"None of the boys?"

"Not this year, no. I've worked with a few of them in class to learn a Mother's Day rap, which is hilarious, so they will have their moments in the spotlight. The young gentlemen in this class need some time to mature a little before we can teach them harmony and solos like the girls. But that's OK—they get to sing all the other songs, and their moms will be really proud."

"Good. Is one of them Garrett Burlingame?"

"Yes, why?"

Lucy sighed. "I just hope his mom remembers to come this year."

Glen exhaled deeply. "Oh, right. I remember what happened with Devin. I hope so, too."

The waitress approached, looking sourly at Lucy, then turned to Glen, her face morphing into a more pleasant expression.

"Ready to order, sir?" she asked in accented English.

"Oui, merci," Glen replied. He proceeded to order *mezza,* an array of little colorful dishes similar to *tapas,* with flat bread to dip in hummus and baba ghanouj, white cheeses, sliced melon, artichokes, yogurt with cucumbers and garlic, grilled meats and fried fish, marinated skewers of chicken, stuffed grape leaves and Kalamata olives, kibbeh and tabbouleh salads in French for them both, per Lucy's request. Then he asked the waitress, Lucy thought, about the availability of baklava and a special type of flaky pie he had mentioned on their way into the restaurant.

The waitress replied in French, then took their menus and left the dining room.

"What did she say?" Lucy asked.

"They have plenty of baklava, but the pie is gone, except for a piece she was saving for her father."

"Oh well."

"No, she says he can do without it, he's apparently 'too fat to fit into his belt,' whatever *that* means. We can split it."

Lucy laughed. "All right."

"And they always bring a roasted onion at the end of the meal. I haven't figured that out yet," Glen said, opening his napkin.

The rest of the dinner went off without a hitch. Glen Daniels had a low-key sense of humor that had her giggling in a way she found almost embarrassing, though harmless, throughout the meal, which was over far too soon.

The waitress brought out a small, bald, roasted onion which she set near Lucy, then gave Glen a magnificently plated piece of pie on a ribbon of chocolate with a single fork. She placed it before him, and looked pointedly at Lucy before she left the table, causing them both to laugh out loud once she was gone.

"Nah sveetz fah youh," Glen said in an intentionally bad accent as he pushed the pie plate in front of her, chuckling. "Voman getz zee onion—zat's it—no chocolate fah youh."

Lucy almost choked, laughing.

"I'M GLAD I hung on to my fork," she whispered to him as they left the restaurant later. "That pie was phenomenal. Thanks for sharing. I'm not sure the waitress would forgive you if she knew you let me have some."

Glen just smiled.

The rain had stopped, at least momentarily, as they made their way to the street parking at the bottom of Tree Hill, the town park in which Obergrande, the enormous historic Northern Red Oak tree stood, spreading its vast limbs protectively above the little village.

"I hope your meeting goes well," Glen Daniels said as he approached his car. "You should have plenty of time to make it to the Town Hall, even if you walk."

"Why aren't you attending the hearing?" Lucy asked curiously. "I thought everyone in town was itching to be there tonight."

"Maybe, but I don't live in town," Glen replied. "I come over from Schroon Lake."

"Ah. Well, the rain has paused. I think I'll climb the hill and say goodnight to Obergrande. I'm very fond of that tree. It's a tradition I've tried to observe since I moved here."

"Well, if you don't mind, I'll go with you, then," said Glen. "I have the same tradition."

"Really?" Lucy commented as they started up the hill in the fading light. Dusk was setting in below the heavy gray clouds, making the sky even darker than it normally would be.

"Yes." Glen lapsed into silence until they had reached the summit of the hill where the magnificent tree stood.

"Did you know this tree is registered as a national landmark?" he asked.

"Really?"

"Yes; it's certified to be over four hundred years old. There are documents formalizing treaties signed beneath it between the Iroquois Nation and the French, British, and Dutch settlers that were living around here at the time. This tree was a meeting place, a place of negotiation and the signing of peace treaties, a place of judgment. A very historic place."

Lucy nodded. "It was also a place where lovers traditionally met. I've heard a lot of weddings were and are performed here—I see them all the time in the summer. Every class that graduates from the high school gets its picture taken around and beneath the tree, and a lot of families take photos of their kids in its branches, or used to. I'd be nervous to do that—the first limb is pretty far off the ground."

Glen nodded in agreement. "This whole place was a very important region in the French and Indian War, I hear. Lots of interesting stories from that time."

"Why do you know about the French and Indian War? You're a kids' music teacher."

"Probably the same way you, a kindergarten teacher, know about music."

"Well, you're wrong there. I have a solid tin ear."

"I doubt that. Let's test it out. Close your eyes."

"Why?" Lucy asked suspiciously.

"Humor me for a moment," said Glen, amused.

Lucy exhaled sharply, then closed her eyes nervously.

"Listen for the sound of the river rushing by, the water wheel, the sawmill—it's closed now, with dusk coming, so you can't hear the machinery, but if you listen closely, you can hear the creaking of the wood. Listen for the bells, which are about to toll the hour, and then play the hymn *All Through the Night.* It's a shame there are no kids out, but you can listen for the patter of the rain instead." He fell silent, and Lucy could hear the sounds he had just described.

"You're right," she said. "I *can* hear it."

"Now open your eyes," said Glen Daniels, "and take another look at your town."

Lucy did so, and took in an unexpected breath as she did.

The Adirondack mountains rose up on both sides of the river valley, their purple and green peaks wreathed in heavy fog that also frosted both the Hudson River and Lake Obergrande to the east. In the heavy pall of rain, Lucy took in the sight gratefully, so much more lush and beautiful than the mid-West dustbowl where she had grown up.

Even swollen with rain, the air atop the hill was sweet and clean, with the lights of the little village shops and restaurants just beginning to glow. *Such a pretty place,* she thought, looking at the quaint buildings that lined the streets around Tree Hill, each corner lighted by a traditional street lantern atop an historic pole. *I'm so glad I live here.*

Making the need for strong advocacy at the Town Board meeting tonight even more crucial.

"It's amazing how much a place in the world is made more beautiful by its natural music. I love listening to the music of this place." Glen's voice broke the silence, but it wasn't a disruption as far as Lucy was concerned. It blended in with the sounds from all around that she could hear beneath Obergrande's vast branches, the new leaves sprouting on the vast network of twigs amid countless empty nests left over from years before, nests that would soon have new occupants and a cacophony of new birdsong.

"Me too," she said aloud, resting her hand on the massive trunk, running her fingers through the deep rivers in the bark. "It's like the tree is singing."

"Not just the tree—the whole place," Glen said, pulling his jacket a little closer around him as the rain began to drizzle again. "The symphony of this area is amazing—the percussion is the rattle of the wheels and the machinery of the mills, the splashing of the water of the river running through them as it grows stronger, swelling into the massive force that is the Hudson."

He inclined an ear to the western side of the village, where the churches stood.

"The melody of the song is the carillon in the tower of Our Mother of Sorrows, singing to the evening sky. Our Lady of Lourdes, the church in Schroon Lake, has a carillon, too—I'm told it's a French-Canadian tradition. The descant—"

"The which?"

"The descant—the musical term for the high part floating over all that rich sound—is the laughter and noise of the children playing in the park when it hasn't been raining forever. And the bass is the never-ending rumble of Route 87, the Northway, in the distance, that brings me to this place each day, that takes me home at night. The tree is the conductor of the symphony. Can you hear the music? Close your eyes again, and listen."

Curious now, Lucy obeyed.

"You're right," she said after a moment, opening her eyes again. "I *can* hear it—and it's beautiful. I never thought of it that way before. Thank you for taking the time to show me."

Glen smiled slightly. "Speaking of time, we both better get going. I have a lot of stuff to take care of tonight, and you have a meeting to catch."

"Yes. Well, thank you for dinner."

He bowed slightly. "It was my pleasure. Thank you, Lucy. Here—you hold on to the umbrella. You can give it back to me at school tomorrow."

He turned toward the street parking where he had left his car.

Only to stop when Lucy caught his sleeve.

"Glen?"

He turned around again. "Yes?"

She let her hand encircle his wrist, pulling him gently back under the umbrella, then stood on her toes and, to his surprise and hers, kissed him on the cheek.

"Thank you again. See you tomorrow."

Glen exhaled, smiling more broadly. "Will do. Good night."

"Good night."

He waited beneath the tree while she made her way down the opposite side of the hill, heading into the brightly lit Town Hall, which was already bustling with townsfolk streaming in.

Then smiled to himself again and descended Tree Hill to his car in the returning rain.

At the primitive campsite

"IF I HAD known this might happen, I would have kept nursing her," Anjolie said, rubbing her eyes. She put her palms against her temples and watched Bram feeding the baby with a bottle he had warmed over the last of the lantern's fuel.

"You had to return to work," her husband said quietly, smiling at the little girl and letting her curl her fist around his finger.

"Some women can do it *and* return to work," Anjolie said, trying to block out the sound of the rain strafing the top of the tent again.

"We can try that with the next one, if you wish."

Anjolie leaned back against the bedroll. "We are almost out of baby formula, Bram. What are we going to do?"

"Rain or no rain, tomorrow we break camp and make our way to Obergrande," Bram said, directing his words to the baby, who was watching him with enormous eyes from behind her bottle. "They will have everything we need there—especially shelter."

"That will be nice. I can't wait to be warm and dry again—and inside."

"The town has a beautiful old hotel, according to the guidebook," Bram said as the baby finished her bottle, sipping air. "We have been frugal so far—we can probably splurge on a night or two there."

His wife sighed wordlessly.

He thought of the second-hand canoe they had bought off a front lawn in Newcomb to the north, now upside down outside the tent to keep it from filling with rain. The man who had sold and delivered it to them looked doubtfully at their set up, but had said nothing, just wished them well.

Bram was beginning to understand the man's expression.

"We'll be all packed to go at first light," he said. "With any luck, the rain will break and we will have an easy ride down the river."

Anjolie, a champion paddler in Holland, nodded and settled down on the sleeping bag, damp with the seepage of the water and mud beneath the tent floor.

Bram set the empty bottle aside and put his daughter on his shoulder.

"Excellent work, *kindje,*" he whispered in her tiny ear, the Dutch word for *baby*. She tucked her head into the crook of his neck and sighed as he rubbed her back. "Tomorrow may be a wet day, but it will be the day you finally arrive at the place our ancestors once lived—and what may well be our new home."

His daughter belched politely, squirmed, and then settled down again.

Rather than putting her in the setup behind them, Bram laid her down next to Anjolie and stretched out on the other side of her, cradling her in between them, remembering what his early camping leaders had taught him.

The largest number of people who die when camping on mountains, and in forests, do so of hypothermia, Heer Von Nostrandt, the scout master, had said. *The second largest are the ones who die from falling trees.*

Bram tried to close his ears to the sound of the gusting wind rustling and cracking the branches outside their tent.

But it roared in his dreams anyway.

Chapter 6

5:55 PM

Obergrande Village

THE OBERGRANDE TOWN Hall parking lot was packed with cars, making Lucy glad she had left hers on the street below Tree Hill. The hall itself was ablaze with light, and even more crowded with people than its parking lot was with cars.

The mood inside the hall was tense and brawly, with many people standing in pairs or small groups, arguing already. A larger number were standing in the hallways, looking grim, or seated already in the rows of chairs inside the largest room in the hall that served as a gathering place for board meetings on the third Thursday of each month, and town court every Wednesday evening.

Lucy had been to almost every Town Board meeting for the last two-and-a-half years, starting immediately upon coming to Obergrande. This was the first time, however, she had noticed more than one uniformed security officer in attendance—she counted five before she even made it out of the main entrance.

Their presence made her suddenly nervous.

She passed Mr. Credman, her elderly next-door neighbor, who was pointing his finger in the face of a man who looked as if he were on the Town Council, judging by the badge he wore and the look of annoyance on his red, wrinkled face.

A group of three women had similarly cornered the Obergrande village major, Ray Tibedeau, who was listening patiently to their concerns, voiced rather loudly, just as another group had surrounded Bob Lundford, the Obergrande town supervisor, who was not looking as patient. His face was set in a stern mask but was as red as that of the man who was being yelled at by Mr. Credman.

Tibedeau was in charge of the central village that lay in the center of East Obergrande, the part of town directly west of the river, where the sawmill and furniture factories stood, along with the elementary school, the library, and most of the middle-income housing in the town that backed up to the lake, and West Obergrande, the wealthier end of the town where expensive houses, historic estates and elegant camps were sheltered in the woods, accessible mostly by private roads.

Lundford was responsible for the whole of the town, including the village.

Neither of the men were looking happy at the moment.

"All right, enough of this hallway blather," said Lundford. "Take your seats, folks. This is a government building, not a boxing arena. The monthly meeting can't start until you are sitting quietly in your seats and we are ready to open business."

The people who were standing in the hallway mostly complied, grumbling and still arguing loudly.

It was clear as soon as everyone was inside the courtroom that there would not be enough chairs for the regular citizens of the town that had come for the meeting. Lucy found a place to stand along the wall, surrounded by a number of parents of her students, who nodded pleasantly at her.

She turned her eyes toward the front of the room.

Sitting at the table were people she had recognized from various events at school, especially the Memorial Day parade, the members of the Town Board and the Town Clerk.

At the far left end of the table sat a man she recognized as the town's lawyer, James O'Connor, who said very little at most board meetings, and two military men in uniform.

The older of the two men had closely cropped hair and wore a number of medals and military insignia, particularly pins that looked like small castles, on his chest, and a stern look on his face. The younger man, whose head bore the signs of what appeared to be a fairly recent buzz cut beneath a military beret, was attired in the uniform of the Army National Guard. He maintained a solemn expression, and Lucy found herself looking at his face, wondering why the volunteer soldiers she had seen wearing this uniform always seemed to be handsome but grim.

Then she remembered the sort of things the National Guard had to do, and answered her own question.

"All right, settle down and we'll get started," Bob Lundford said, sitting down at the place directly in the center of the table in front of a microphone. "We have a number of items of official town business to attend to, which I'm sure most of you couldn't care less about, but it has to be done according to the law, so try and contain yourselves for a few minutes longer. There's no point in being abusive to people you've elected to do these jobs which, believe me, do *not* pay enough to put up with nights like this."

Lucy leaned up against the wall in the midst of the packed crowd. Every seat was taken, with an overflow into the exterior hallways.

Behind her on the wall was a banner with Obergrande's symbol, a tree around which a river flowed in a circle in front of a range of high-peaked mountains. Lucy stared at the town flag as the board meeting started, almost missing the Pledge of Allegiance. She turned quickly toward the American flag at the front of the room and caught up with everyone reciting the pledge, probably the last thing they would all agree on that night.

Then she looked back at the town symbol again, remembering the first day she had seen it.

It had been in this very town hall, three years before, when she had come as a new homeowner to register to vote and get the information she needed about town services like garbage removal. *Obergrande?* she had asked Betty Finley, the town clerk, who now was sitting at the head table, taking notes and looking nervous. *What does that name mean?*

Mrs. Finley, a quiet, kind woman who knew many things about the town that no one else did, had looked up from behind her chained glasses and smiled.

It's an English-ized version of the French words for 'big tree,' she had said. *'Arbre Grand.' The town's most important historic landmark.*

Lucy smiled to herself, remembering Glen Daniels telling her the same thing a short while before, when her mood, and that of the town, had still been pleasant.

It no longer was.

The Town Board sorted through a variety of allocations, amendments, contractual decisions and proposals for almost an hour, making an already largely hostile crowd even less pleasant. By the time they finally reached the agenda item the entire town had turned out to argue about, the citizens of Obergrande were in a universally foul mood.

Bob Lundford banged the gavel angrily on the table.

"We will have order, or we will clear the room of the public," he said coldly. "Town Law 3701-D allows for that action if the Board deems the situation in the hall to be hazardous."

"In other words, sit down, shut up, and wait 'til it's your turn to speak," said Smiley Carpenter, a famously grumpy Town Councilor who had obviously gotten his nickname as a joke. "Keep your comments short and do not repeat what people before you have already said. I don't have any desire to be here all night and into tomorrow afternoon."

"First, before any townsperson says *anything,* we have

an opening statement from the Board, and two invited guests who will speak first," said Lundford to a rising chorus of boos and catcalling. He banged his gavel savagely. "Settle down, dammit."

The noise decreased to a low, intermittent rumble.

"Now," said Lundford, "as most or all of you now know, we have recently had a school budget vote, which passed, along with the election of School Board members, the results of which have been posted in the newspaper." He banged his gavel again as the noise began to increase, then pointed it at the crowd. "Last warning, folks."

The attendees fell into a stony silence.

"On the ballot with the school budget vote, and the election of board members, were three initiatives. The first initiative, for the purchase of three new school buses, and the second, the annual funding package for the library, passed without incident, as you already know," the town supervisor continued. "The third initiative, the proposal that the town of Obergrande once again consider the project that has been put forward since 1898 by the New York State Public Benefit Corporation, that Obergrande join other municipalities in the Adirondack Park and allow a dam to be built—at no expense to the town—"

An uproar ensued, both sides of the room shouting angrily at each other. Lundford banged his gavel sharply.

"For Pete's sake, *let me finish,*" he growled. "I understand there are some strong feelings on both sides of this issue—"

"There is no issue!" a man from Lucy's side of the room shouted at the town supervisor. "There was a *vote.*

The measure failed overwhelmingly—as it does every time it gets put on the ballot. This discussion is *over*."

"Or at least it should be," a woman at the back on the other side of the room added.

"No cost to the town?" another man yelled from the center of the seats. "You are talking about *drowning* East Obergrande, where, in case you've managed to forget, Lundford, most of us live and work and our children go to school."

The voices around the room exploded again, and Bob Lundford banged the table.

"All right, stop it," he said angrily. "If you won't show some respect to your elected officials, at least show some to the military men here tonight. You are embarrassing yourselves and, frankly, our town with this behavior. These gentlemen have come, one from Saranac Lake, one all the way from Buffalo, to speak tonight. At least have the courtesy to hear them out."

The shouting diminished to a smoldering grumble.

The older man in uniform stood up as the supervisor passed the microphone to him.

"Good evening, folks," he said pleasantly. "I'm Colonel Michael Genovese, Army Corps of Engineers, from the Great Lakes and Ohio River Division of Water Management, Buffalo District. Thank you for having me here this evening."

The noise of the room disappeared, replaced by a respectful, if guarded, silence.

Colonel Genovese picked up a remote control and pointed it at a projector that was aimed at the screen above and behind the Town Board's table.

An image of a bulleted list of items appeared on the screen.

"Water Management is a world-class engineering organization that supports eight of the Corps' ten Civil Works business lines—navigation, flood risk management, hydropower, recreation, storm damage response, emergency response, water supply, and environmental restoration," Colonel Genovese continued, naming the items in the bulleted list. "We embrace seven operating principles, but I think number seven is the most important one."

He clicked the remote control again.

A numbered list appeared, the last item highlighted in bold. Colonel Genovese read the seventh item aloud.

" 'Number 7: Respecting the views of individuals and groups interested in Corps activities, listening to them actively, and learning from their perspective in the search to find innovative win-win solutions to the Nation's problems that also protect and enhance the environment.' "

A small amount of grumbling returned to the room.

"In other words, in spite of the reputation the Corps has gained, and occasionally earned, for having to make hard decisions about dams and reservoirs that impact people's property, we really do try to work with citizens to keep their waterside towns and cities safe."

The room's undercurrent of noise got slightly louder.

Lundford banged the gavel again.

Colonel Genovese waited patiently as the room grew quiet.

"We are not here to tell you what to do with your town's water resources, at least not at this point," he said. "But you should be aware of the changes that have occurred over the past ten years that are beginning to show some threat to the safety of the eastern side of your town."

He turned to the younger man sitting beside him.

"This is Sergeant Alex Crandell Evans, a brilliant young civilian engineer from your area—he was born in Newcomb, just north of here—who serves our nation once a month in the uniform of the Army National Guard, currently stationed in Saranac Lake.

"In addition to those duties, Sergeant Evans, who works for the engineering firm of Speziale, Prince, and Foster in Saratoga, where he lives, spends a good deal of his time at the Water Management offices in Buffalo and New York City, lending his engineering expertise to the Corps. He is, as you can imagine, completely familiar with the Adirondack Park, its dams, reservoirs, and waterways, and is a specialist in the control of the flow of the Hudson River. I asked him here tonight to speak to you because of his connection to and knowledge of this area. Sergeant Evans?"

The young man rose as the Colonel passed the microphone and the remote to him. He cleared his throat and turned to the crowd.

"Good evening," he said. "I'm Sergeant Alex Crandell Evans, but I usually go by 'Ace'—it helps me remember my initials. I grew up in Newcomb, so it's exciting to be here tonight in the Big City of Obergrande."

Some of the attendees chuckled or snorted; even

though Obergrande was a very small city, by comparison to the tiny, dying mining town of Newcomb, it was enormous.

"Like Colonel Genovese, I am not here to make recommendations at this point about what Obergrande should do in regard to the building of a larger, hydroelectric dam—"

"That's good, since we've already decided, *again,* at the ballot box," a gruff voice called from the back of the room where people were standing.

Bob Lundford banged the gavel and glared into the thickening crowd.

Sergeant Evans did not seem bothered by the interruption.

"I think it's important to be clear on what this spring could hold for Obergrande from a water-control perspective," he said seriously, turning to the projector. He hit the button on the remote.

The screen cleared. Then the word SNOWFALL appeared.

"This year the Adirondack region experienced a record snowfall," he said, standing remarkably straight, Lucy noted dryly; a military bearing. "An average of one hundred and ninety-one inches of snow fell this fall and winter, considerably higher than the one hundred three, which is the average. This is already showing signs of being a heavier melt than the soils of the region can absorb. In case anyone missed it on the way in, there is also a higher-than-usual amount of precipitation for spring, which is not helping with that."

As if to punctuate his sentence, a crash of thunder rolled overhead.

"Nice timing on the sound effects," remarked Mayor Tibedeau wryly.

"Thank you, sir," the young sergeant said politely. "We spared no expense for this presentation. There will be an open bar with hors d'oeuvres at the end."

A small part of the crowd snickered again.

"Really?" asked Hannah Adams, a gullible young woman from West Obergrande.

"No, ma'am. Just teasing. Sorry." Sergeant Evans' voice was respectful.

He clicked the remote. The screen now read PRECIPI-TATION.

"In addition to somewhat relentless rain over most of the spring season and particularly in the last few weeks, we are also looking to take a hit from the edge rains of Hurricane Clarence, according to the National Weather Service," he said seriously. "The current small spillway dam, which was built beginning in 1892 and completed in 1907, is expected to be able to hold up to this amount of excess water, as it has for over a century. But, as you know, in the last ten years there have been two floods of the western shore of the river, mostly from swollen or clogged local streams, resulting in damage to the eastern edge of town."

"Some boat docks and the historic row of planters and flower boxes at the water's edge were washed away," said Eleanor Preston, the ninety-two-year-old town historian who, even at her advanced age, was sharp as a tack. "That's hardly cause for concern. We had 'em back up, and the flower boxes planted, in time for Memorial Day."

Sergeant Evans fell abruptly silent.

Lucy smiled. She had a special fondness for Eleanor, who always took the time to come and talk in her delightfully craggy voice to the kindergarten students on special historic holidays, usually bringing a basket of homemade treats with her when she did.

"That may be, ma'am," Sergeant Evans continued respectfully. "But it has been over fifty years since the edge rains of a hurricane have come as far inland as the Adirondack region. We don't know what that might mean for the increase in the Hudson's flow this year."

"If you don't know, why are you here?" a snide voice demanded from the other side of the standing area, near to the front of the room.

"Stop giving them excuses!" a woman's voice called from the left edge of the chairs. "You are lending the government's support to rich people who want to *flood* East Obergrande!"

"You blind *fool*," another woman's voice retorted. "Can't you see you're rearranging the deck chairs on the *Titanic*? You East Obergranders are going to go down with the ship sooner or later. We're trying to *help you*."

"Thanks, but we don't need your help going down with the ship—"

All the hostile conversation was brought to an abrupt halt by the scream of air as a young man in the center of the crowd standing in the back of the room stepped angrily forward and heaved a fist-sized object directly at the young Sergeant's head.

Chapter 7

S HAKING WITH SHOCK, Lucy leapt toward the wall with the other people standing around her, who all fell like dominoes against it and into the town flag.

The Town Board members and the clerk dove beneath the table at the front of the room.

Colonel Genovese put up his arm in front of his head, but otherwise remained seated.

Sergeant Alex Evans' body remained rigidly still, except for his arm, which shot up and plucked the hurled object out of the air just in front of his face.

His solemn expression did not change, but his voice, when he spoke, contained a note of humor.

"I always wanted to do that when Newcomb played Obergrande in varsity baseball," he said to the man who had pitched the object at him. "Never got the chance until now. Thank you, sir."

As security officers pushed through the crowd, the National Guardsman looked down at the object in his hand.

It was an apple.

His expression still did not change as he raised the fruit to his mouth and took a serious bite.

The room, still gasping and recovering, started to fill with laughter.

As the security guards led the man from the room, the soldier continued to consume the fruit, then dropped the core in the trashcan behind the long desk.

"Ooops—" he said as he wiped his hand on a piece of paper on the desk. "There went the evidence. I guess he'll get off with a reprimand—unless it was poisoned. I'm in a world of hurt if it was, I guess. Oh well."

He looked back the crowd, which was laughing freely now.

"Folks, there are many lakes and streams throughout the Adirondack Park that are looking at the likelihood of flooding in the years to come, but the Army Corps of Engineers cannot address every one of them. The reason we are here tonight is because the preservation of Obergrande's lake and streams is singularly important to the watershed, largely due to the parts they play in the flow of the Hudson, which ultimately ends up in New York City. Should there be a devastating flood, it could damage a great deal more of the state than just Obergrande—and we don't want to see that damaged, either."

"You have an interesting definition of Obergrande not being damaged, Sergeant," said Donna Marquarte, one of the Town Board members who was retired from her job at the local bank. Lucy assessed her as being a strong opponent of the dam project. "I have a bed-and-breakfast in the area that is proposed to be 'drowned' by your dam project, and I am looking forward to your explanation of how my property will not be damaged by being submerged under seventy feet of water."

A hoot, cheers, and much applause followed her statement.

"First, with respect, Ms. Marquarte, this proposal did *not* come from the Army Corps of Engineers," the young soldier said patiently. "The New York State Public Benefit Corporation requested our input in the form of drawings and estimates to inform the town should it decide to undertake building a new hydroelectric dam in this location. We provided that information. But there were also other recommendations made—smaller-scale steps that could help offset the potential for flooding that would not require the building of a dam."

He saw the townspeople looking at each other hostilely, and cleared his throat, rushing into the end of his remarks.

"Obviously, those may not meet with the vision of the Benefit Corporation, and therefore might require funding from other sources—including the town itself. But Colonel Genovese and I are not here to sell you on the dam. We are here to tell you that we are in fear for your safety as a town if you do not undertake *some* sort of flood abatement program in the near future."

Lightning flashed outside the hall's windows, and thunder rumbled through again.

Mayor Tibedeau smiled. "Truly, your special effects are remarkable, Sergeant."

"In case you folks haven't noticed, your ground is

totally saturated with moisture and cannot absorb any more," Colonel Genovese said from his seat at the table, under which all the Town Council members had momentarily taken refuge but had now returned, more or less gracefully. "Between the snowmelt, the precipitation, and the potential of a hit from the edge of Hurricane Clarence, we are worried about even more severe shoreline loss than you've had in the other two floods this decade."

"All right, thank you, gentlemen," said Bob Lundford wearily. "I am now going to open a *limited* period of public commentary, but I warn you, folks, if there are any more shenanigans like Buzz Cochrane throwing fruit at our distinguished guests, we will be clearing this hall of everyone except the Board and our advisors in Executive Session." He sighed comically. "Thank the Lord for Town Law 3701-D."

FOR MORE THAN two hours, the citizens of Obergrande ranted at the Town Board and its guests.

Most of the commentary initially came from residents and business owners from the east side of town, people who worked in or ran sawmills and factories that made furniture in the famous and less-famous Adirondack styles. There were also homeowners, sports tourism business owners and shopkeepers whose stores were in the area that had been designated to "drown" should the dam be built and Lake Obergrande expanded. To the best of Lucy's knowledge, three of the five board members agreed with them.

On the other side of the room and sprinkled throughout the rest were people primarily, though not always, from West Obergrande, the wealthier side of town where people who could trace their ancestry back almost four hundred years lived. These were the people who favored the idea of the dam and the expansion of the lake, who spoke passionately about the danger of not undertaking to protect the eastern side of town near the river and lake. One of the town board members, George Durant, was enthusiastically on this side of the issue, with the last one, Phil Schirmer, running hot and cold between the two sides, but leaning with the west.

Fights and hostile word exchanges seemed to break out after every other speaker.

Finally it was Lucy's turn to address the Town Council and the attendees of the meeting. She came to the microphone stand and cleared her throat, feeling the intensity of the anger behind her back.

"I'm Lucy Sullivan. I live in town, I teach kindergarten at Obergrande Elementary, and the first thing I want to say is that you should all be using your inside voices. We are adults, and rather than squabbling like we're on the playground, we should be making reasoned arguments—in a calm tone—instead of screaming at each other. If you folks were kids in my classroom, we'd have a ton of people in Time Out."

A chuckle and some muttering rumbled through the room.

Lucy cleared her throat again. "I do not favor the dam," she continued. "I've only lived here for a few years, but I love my little house in East Obergrande. For many of the kids in my class, this part of town, which contains many of their homes and their school, is the only place they've ever known. How can you take away their security? I think the town should be looking at the alternative suggestions that the Corps spoke of that do not include building a dam and flooding East Obergrande. I've worked very hard fixing up my house, as have many of my neighbors, and you are talking about drowning a lot of dreams, hard work, and investments in time and labor when you suggest drowning half the town. I voted no on this ballot initiative, along with seventy-two percent of the electorate. I think the Town Board should take the hint and do so as well."

Lucy sat down to thunderous applause, and a good deal of harsh grumbling. She was pretty sure old Mr. Credman winked at her.

Professor Isaac Byrnes, a stately gentleman who taught Philosophy and African-American studies at the State University of New York at Albany, and the father of one of her students, came to the microphone next.

He introduced himself by name in a voice that rang pleasantly through the room, reminding Lucy of James Earl Jones.

"My fellow citizens," he said, looking around him at the crowd, "I would like to build on a point that Ms. Sullivan just made."

Upon hearing her name spoken by the sonorous voice, Lucy jumped a little.

"Seventy-two percent of those who pulled a lever in the voting booth did so against the proposition," Professor

Byrnes went on, "but I believe it is important to note that only sixty-one percent of the population of Obergrande resides on the east side of town."

The room fell suddenly silent.

"This would seem to indicate that, at bare minimum, eleven percent of the town's population that lives in West Obergrande *also* voted against the proposition. I, in fact, was one of those voters."

The silence grew heavier.

"In addition, the possibility exists that some people in East Obergrande might have voted *for* the proposition," the professor went on. "While I did not personally choose that option, I could certainly cite some aspects of the plan to be fair ideas, including the removal and renovation of the areas with empty factories and mills, which are, to my mind, not only unsightly but actually hazardous."

"My request of my fellow citizens, therefore, including those esteemed folk sitting before us this evening, would be not to let this discussion become polarized, but rather to look at the plan as objectively as possible, with safety being the primary focus. Thank you."

Professor Byrnes sat down to generous, polite applause, having established peace in the room.

Which lasted long enough for the next speaker, a woman from the West Obergrande Elect, the historical society similar to the Daughters of the American Revolution, to take the floor.

"Esteemed Board members," she began, "when considering the dam and the redesign of the east side, please think of this: as you know, next year Obergrande celebrates its quadri-centennial—its four hundredth birthday. Don't we all want our town to be prettier, as much as it's possible to be for its birthday?"

A near riot commenced, with the shouting so loud that Lucy had to cover her ears.

After almost another hour, Bob Lundford leaned closer to the microphone and addressed the long line of people still waiting to speak.

"One more speaker, folks," he said wearily. "The Board is exhausted, and you are beginning to repeat yourselves." He looked at the young father at the front of the line who had been waiting almost two hours to speak. "Sir? Please ask something that has not already been a question so far tonight."

The dark-haired man turned to the people standing immediately behind him, consulted for a moment, nodded, then turned back to the microphone.

"Sergeant Evans," he said plainly and clearly, "if you were the sole decision-maker, and this was your hometown, which of the solutions to this problem would you choose?"

The young soldier, who had been sitting silently beside his superior officer for most of the evening, blinked.

"That's not within my purview to say, sir."

"I know it's not," the man said, "but I'm asking your opinion. You've made it very clear that the Army Corps of Engineers is not at the moment in charge of the decision, and that you've made a range of suggestions to the town. I'm asking you, er, Ace, if it was *your* decision alone, what would you decide to do in this situation?"

Silence filled the room.

Sergeant Evans turned to his superior officer. Colonel Genovese exhaled, then nodded reluctantly.

Bob Lundford handed the young soldier the microphone.

Sergeant Evans looked around the packed room.

"If it was my hometown, I believe I would opt to build the dam, carefully and conservatively," he began as a rising tide of booing started to swell. "There are some outstanding architects who have very good ideas about how to minimize—"

His words were drowned as deeply in the audience's response as the plan would drown East Obergrande.

Bob Lundford banged the gavel louder than he had all evening.

"That's enough!" he shouted, his voice barely heard over the noise of the crowd.

He turned to the soldiers. "Thank you, gentlemen. Sorry for the rowdiness, and that we didn't arrange for that open bar—goodness knows, everyone at this table could use a drink. As for the rest of you, go home. We've heard all your concerns and suggestions, which we will take into consideration as we move forward in the future. For now, it looks like the 'nays' have it. I imagine that we will not be discussing this plan again any time soon. Goodnight."

His last words had to be shouted to be heard over the grumbling crowd.

Chapter 8

10:45 PM

L UCY MADE HER way numbly out of the hall, pushing carefully between groups of arguing citizens who were stopped in the exit line, many of them still yelling at each other. Her head was throbbing, her stomach was sick, and her eyes were blazing in Irish anger.

It was all she could do to restrain herself from using Glen Daniels' umbrella as a weapon to clear her way through the crowd.

Once to the door, she hurried out into the rain, lifting the umbrella over her head, and ran as quickly as she could around the edge of Tree Hill Park to the spot where she had left her car.

She opened the door, collapsed the umbrella and tossed it onto the passenger seat, then jumped in and closed the door as she slid the keys into the ignition and turned it.

Only to hear a clicking sound.

Lucy muttered curse words that her Irish cousins would be proud of, and turned the ignition again.

The car coughed, then fell into silent clicking once more.

The cursing hadn't helped, so instead she thought of her grandmother Maeve. She took the rosary that hung from the rearview mirror in her hand and uttered the prayers she had heard the old woman say in difficult situations.

The car did not care.

Frustrated and tired, Lucy pounded on the steering wheel, then put her head down on it.

One or two more swear words dribbled out.

A tapping on the driver's side window next to her made her lift her head so fast that she bumped her chin on the wheel.

She swiveled in shock and stared out the window.

A face beneath a military beret was looking back at her beneath tiny waterfalls streaming off the soft edge of the hat.

It seemed to be a handsome face up close, with dark, riveting eyes, fringed with thick lashes, and a mouth that appeared sensuous, though it was hard to tell through the beads of rain on the window.

Lucy pushed the button on the door handle.

The window ignored her just as the engine had.

Annoyed, Lucy took hold of the door handle and opened the door slightly.

"What do you want?" she demanded, trying to avoid the rain that was now whipping into her car in the cold wind.

The dark eyes blinked.

"Do you need help?" Sergeant Evans' voice was flat, absent the humor that had been in it during his presentation.

"I do—but I don't want to drown, so I think I will call AAA, thank you."

Thick brown brows over the deep, dark eyes drew together, and the heavily-lashed lids of the eyes themselves blinked again.

"Sounds like you need a jump. I have cables."

"Again, thank you, but no, thank you." Lucy closed the door again, locking it manually.

The face disappeared from the window, replaced by the back of a dark regulation raincoat with long pleats in it as the soldier turned away. Lucy took the opportunity to fumble in her purse, searching for her AAA card.

Only to jump when the face appeared at her window again, followed by another polite rap.

"What do you want?" she demanded through the window in the closed and locked door.

The voice that responded was muffled by the rain and the door.

"Look, I can get you going and out of here in five minutes if you'll just—"

"I—do—not—trust—you," Lucy said loudly with exaggerated slowness through the car window.

Sergeant Evans pulled his head back in surprise. "Why?"

Lucy unlocked the car door and cracked it open again.

"Because you just gave aid and comfort to the enemy, Sergeant," she said hostilely. "What you and the Army

Corps of Engineers fail to understand is that most of the West Obergrande folk would like to see the working side of town systematically drowned, not because they are worried about our fate in a flood, but because they find our side of town 'unsightly,' all those nasty factories and mills where middle-income people work, all the lower-end housing where we live, where our children go to school, along with theirs from the west side.

"If they drown the school, they can rebuild it in West Obergrande, in their own neighborhood, and make it 'prettier,' as that one stupid woman said tonight that started the biggest fight, I believe. When a large part of our side of town is swallowed by the lake and the Hudson River, their property values will go up—most of them will have lakefront property. The rest of us, of course, would be screwed. And you just gave them valuable ammunition to do it. So, while I appreciate your kind offer, I'm going to have to turn it down, because I know where I stand, and whom I can, and cannot, trust. Thank you sincerely for your service to our nation as a National Guardsman, but you can move along now."

She closed the door, her left side wet with rain, and went back to her search for the roadside-assistance card.

Ace Evans stared, straight-faced, through the window for a moment while she turned her purse upside down angrily and shook the contents into her lap.

Then shrugged, turned again and walked away into the dark.

1:35 AM

IT TOOK THE tow truck more than an hour to reach her.

By then, Lucy was kicking herself for her rash rejection of help from the Army National Guardsman, whom she determined, while waiting endlessly, would have undoubtedly gotten her car started while minding his manners after the chaos of the Town Board meeting.

Instead, she was paying for her bad temper by sitting in the heavy cigar smoke of the tow-truck's cab, coughing every now and then, while the operator jumped her battery in the pouring rain.

She had needed to make her way back inside the town hall to use the pay phone to reach AAA, mentally thanking Glen Daniels for loaning her the umbrella overnight. In spite of the umbrella she had managed to get bone-chillingly soaked, as the rain was now blowing sideways, and had broken the heel off one of her shoes on her way back to the car.

I need anger management classes, she decided while she waited.

Finally, when her car was running again, and the tow truck driver opened the door, she stepped down from the cab tiredly and thanked him, got her card back from him along with the paperwork, and made her way under Glen Daniels' umbrella in the heavier rain.

I'm going to get Glen some baklava as a thank-you present, she mused as she returned to her running car.

She put the umbrella in the front seat once more, touched the rosary, fastened her belt and drove off into the night to her tiny but beloved house in East Obergrande.

AT THE CORNER, the lights of a jeep came on.

It sat quietly as Lucy's car drove around the corner and out of sight.

Then pulled away in the other direction, heading to the local motel for the night, too late to start back to Saratoga until morning, a little over an hour's journey home.

OUT BEHIND THE town hall, where cars had been parked like sardines over the course of the night, a dozen or so remaining people finally left the building, exhausted.

Two of them, however, held back as the rest got into their cars, long enough to exchange a glance.

Then opened their umbrellas and hurried into their own vehicles.

Heading off into the black night, the heavy rain and the obtrusive mist beneath a dark, moonless sky.

Chapter 9

THE NEXT DAY, Friday, 7:03 AM

Obergrande Elementary School

KELLY MORAN CAME into the classroom in a foul mood, shaking the rain from her clothing and dripping it from her coat onto her shoes.

"This is ridiculous," she muttered, fighting with her broken umbrella to close it. "Thank God it's Friday."

Lucy was perched atop a small stepladder, hanging up student self-portraits.

"No kidding," she agreed. "Look at it out there—it looks like a tornado is brewing—except there's no separation of light and dark in the sky, and it's not green."

"No, it's pretty much black all the way down to the ground," Kelly agreed, hanging her dripping coat in the teachers' closet. "And the bloody rain is blowing *sideways*—they give us snow days when the weather's awful in winter. I can't imagine those poor little kids waiting for the bus this morning."

"Maybe we'll get an early dismissal," Lucy said, coming down from her stepladder. "Clarence is passing over Philadelphia almost four hundred miles to the south, and dissipating, but the edge rains are supposed to hit us this morning—that's probably them out there now."

"How was the Town Board meeting last night?"

"Awful." Lucy picked up the ladder, closed it, and took it back to the closet. "A total free-for-all."

"Yeah, I can't believe they're bringing that dam thing up again," Kelly said, laying out the morning's WHAT IS SPECIAL TODAY? cards on each desk. "Where does the Board stand on that? I thought we voted it down."

"We thought we did too, but apparently that wasn't enough for the West Obergrande folks."

"Hmmph," Kelly snorted in annoyance.

"Dan Saunders, Donna Marquarte, and Joni Wolfe are all pretty soundly against it, or at least it seems that way," Lucy said, leafing through her lesson plans.

"Donna and Joni don't surprise me—I expect you got a 'how can you do more harm to the poor people in the community?' bleeding heart speech from Joni?"

Lucy looked up from her desk in surprise.

"Well, yes, but I happen to agree with her," she said.

"So do I, but, unlike Donna, there's something so, I dunno, so hippy-dippy about Joni that it's hard to take her seriously." Kelly dusted off her hands, then went over to the calendar. "I'm a little puzzled about Dan Saunders—doesn't he live in West Obergrande? Aren't there streets with his family name on them?"

"I think so," Lucy said, writing the morning's riddle on the whiteboard in yellow, red, and black for Germany

Day. "But he's a business owner and seems like a very practical, hands-on kinda guy. I frequently see him down on the waterfront, working alongside his employees. He owns a lot of businesses in town, some of which are in East Obergrande. And it's not all that hard to name a street in the Adirondacks if you want to. In Cold Brook, there's one called Hooper-Dooper Avenue."

Kelly laughed. "That must be the one across from Sesame Street."

"That would be *Mr.* Hooper-Dooper Avenue. George Durant is all gung-ho for the dam, for the redesign of the town that the Public Benefit Corporation would pay for," Lucy continued, fixing a spelling mistake in the riddle. "He kept saying 'we can be better than Placid!' over and over again. He got unanimous eye rolling when he said that—as if there is enough money in the world to out-class Lake Placid—no way."

"Sheesh. What about Phil Schirmer?"

"He's his usual flip-flop self—you know how he's always with whomever has spoken to him last?"

"Oh, yeah."

"Well, apparently the pro-dam side got to him last night."

"Great," said Kelly gloomily. "Where do the mayor and the town supervisor stand?"

"Mayor Tibedeau seems to be fairly objective," Lucy said. "He seems pretty distressed at the thought of moving all those houses, relocating all those people from the apartments, but he did point out that there would be money for those things. He remained calm, except for the fruit-throwing."

"*Fruit*-throwing? Seriously?"

"Yep. Bob Lundford was mad from the beginning to the end of the meeting, shouting at people and banging his gavel, but I can't say I have any idea where he stands."

Kelly shook her head, as if to shake off the thoughts of the meeting and the weather. "Wonderful. So, change of subject—how was your date with Glen Daniels last night?"

Lucy blinked in surprise. "How did you know about that?"

Kelly laughed. "Girl, *everyone* knows about that. So dish—is he really as dull as the grapevine says?"

"Not at all," Lucy said defensively. "He's great. We had a nice time."

"Oooooooooohh," said Kelly as the racket of approaching feet and the children attached to them began sounding in the hallway beyond the door. "You'll have to tell me more at the end of the day."

7:52 AM

THE CLASS WAS in a somewhat better mood that morning, despite the rain, Lucy decided.

The language arts lesson of the day was one that included poetry, music, self-awareness, and physical movement that she had come up with the year before. It had been a great success then, but the previous year the day on which she had presented it was so beautifully sunny that she had taken the class outside to do it.

This day could not have been more different.

Nonetheless, she and Kelly had brought all the kids

together in a big circle with their sit-upons, low, thin pillows on which most of their floor activities were done.

As Mrs. Moran turned on the CD player, Lucy ran through the rules again.

"OK, who are the Mondays?"

Four children sat forward, waving red construction-paper circles.

"Tuesdays?"

Three hands waving orange circles shot up.

She continued to quiz the class, making certain each child understood the day of his or her birth, as correlated to the colors of the rainbow and, satisfied that they did, she got down on her knees and sat with her backside on her heels, encouraging all but Kristen Feeny, her wheelchair-bound student for whom Kelly Moran was the primary aide, to do so as well.

"Ready, Kristen?" she asked.

The little girl nodded excitedly.

"All right," Lucy said, pulling a thick tangle of curls out of her eyes, "everyone sing—let's go!"

A chorus of young voices, mostly on key, broke into song along with the disc:

Monday's child is fair of face,
Tuesday's child is full of grace,
Wednesday's child is full of woe,
Thursday's child has far to go,
Friday's child is loving and giving,
Saturday's child works hard for a living,
But the child who is born on the Sabbath Day
Is bonny and blithe and good and gay.

When each child's day of birth was sung, he or she popped up off the floor, jumping high in the air and waving their colored circles, then sat quickly back down. The song went through three choruses, increasing in speed each time, giving the kids three opportunities to jump. Mrs. Moran stood behind Kristen, who happened to be a Friday, and spun her around each time that day was mentioned, causing her to giggle wildly.

When the song was over, they fell with exaggerated silliness back on their sit-upons, Lucy being careful to keep her skirt from riding up unexpectedly.

"Good job," she said, a little out of breath. "All right, I think it's time for morning snack." She wiped the sweat off her brow with the sleeve of her sweater. "Whew! All right, guys, while Mrs. Moran gets the juice and trail mix, I just want to say that what you just sang is a very, very old poem, written long before you were born, and while we're not sure who wrote it, the first time it was ever recorded in a book was in 1838, in England."

"Before *you* was born, too, Miss Sullivan?" asked James LaPointe innocently.

"Uh, yes, yes it was, James. Hard as it may seem to believe, that poem is older than me."

The children nodded in agreement at how hard it was to believe her words.

"England? Is that where princesses come from?" asked Sloane Wallace, a little redhead.

"Sometimes," Lucy said, rising from her sit-upon and herding the kids to the long tables where they normally ate their snacks.

"I wish *I* comed from England, then," said Sloane matter-of-factly. "It would be cool to be a princess. You get to marry Prince Charmin' and live happy ever afta."

"Ick," said Sarah Windsor decidedly. "Not me. I don't want to marry no damn prince. I don't wanna live in Inkland. I wanna live in Obergran' for always."

Lucy's mouth fell open, and she clapped her hand over it to keep from laughing out loud, knowing how shocked Sarah's mother would be to hear the word *damn* coming out of her mouth.

"Let's keep our talk nice, please, Sarah," she said. The little girl blinked, then nodded, looking confused.

"Who is Prince Charmin', Sloane?" asked Kelly Moran humorously.

The little redhead stopped comically in mid-stride, crossed her arms, and put a small finger to her forehead, thinking.

"I dunno," she said finally, great seriousness in her tone. "But I fink it might be Mr. Daniels."

Mrs. Moran choked, dropping several of the trail-mix envelopes, and Lucy stepped hurriedly into the corridor before she burst into laughter.

9:14 AM

SHORTLY AFTER MORNING snack, the afore-mentioned Mr. Daniels appeared in the open door.

"Good morning, Miss Sullivan," he said cheerily, in contrast to the gray rain beating against the window. "May I snag some of your students?"

Lucy blinked, having forgotten. "Oh, of course," she

said, looking around at the children cleaning up their trail mix envelopes and juice cups. "Er—Sarah, Sloane, Corinne, Grace, and—and—"

"Elisa," Mr. Daniels said, smiling at the little girl, dressed, as always, very prettily. The little girl looked confused.

"Elisa," Lucy said to her, "Quieres cantar con el Sr. Daniels?"

The new girl brightened. "Sí, por favor."

Lucy smiled. "Go on," she said, sweeping the girls out the door with her hands. She caught Mr. Daniels' eye and winced suddenly.

"I'm sorry," she said, walking closer to him to speak quietly. "I left your umbrella in the car—I was afraid it would turn inside out in the wind this morning."

"No problem whatsoever," Mr. Daniels said, still smiling. "Keep it until the rain stops, assuming it ever does. Thanks again for last night."

"No, thank *you*," Lucy corrected. "You're the one who was magnanimous enough to share that piece of pie."

Mr. Daniels laughed. "We'll be back in half an hour. See you later. Enjoy your morning."

Lucy watched him walk down the hall with the five little girls dancing excitedly around him, talking animatedly to him. He was a sweet and natural teacher who had chosen kids with five very different personalities, from different sides of town, different social classes, and that impressed her.

Sarah, the first child he had requested, was a delightful young girl in spite of her unintentional swear word, quiet and pleasant, a natural leader. She and Corinne, an eager little person who had a deep love for Sebastian, the class turtle, and a gleaming smile contrasting with dusky skin and a head of curls the color of coffee, could always be counted on to get and keep their friends in line, even at the age of five. Corinne's father was the professor who had spoken after Lucy the night before.

Sloane, the would-be princess, was the only daughter in a famous West Obergrande family, and she was used to being asked to do special or difficult tasks. While she was possessed of an impish nature and a lot of self-confidence, Lucy sensed some insecurity below the surface. She had observed the same thing in Grace, the daughter of the pastor of the Obergrande Community Church, who had a warm smile that wavered a little when she was put on the spot.

And, of course, there was Elisa, whom she had discussed with both Mrs. Cox and Mr. Daniels the previous day.

She lingered in the doorway, watching down the hall as the tall young teacher rounded the corner with five of her students, all six of them laughing as they disappeared from sight.

At the campsite between Newcomb and Obergrande

BRAM AWOKE TO the sounds of crashing, screaming, and his infant daughter wailing.

The rain was pounding hard on the tent top, knifing through the seams and dousing the young family with cold water. The wind beyond the flapping fabric sides was howling, pulling the tent taught on its ropes and the stakes that held it to the ground.

He scrambled from the sleeping bag and pulled his still-damp clothes on, once he had made certain that Anjolie and the baby were unhurt, only terrified.

"Come!" he urged his wife, scooping the baby from the tent floor that was beginning to slide in the mud. He reached out a hand to Anjolie, who was unable to stand in the slipping tent. He pulled her to her feet, then quickly packed the baby into the backpack in which they carried her when hiking.

He ran his shaking fingers over the pocket in the baby carrier, and felt the treasure he had received from Mutti, still behind the zipper where he had secured it.

"We have to abandon the gear, the tent and such," he told his quaking wife. "There's no way to pack it now. Help me flip the canoe, put on your life jacket, and grab what you can."

Anjolie, shaking violently, followed him out of the tent and assisted him in turning the watercraft over, then scrambled back inside, scooping up the critical supplies.

"There, there, *kindje,*" Bram said as he secured the hiccupping baby in her carrier, a life jacket attached around it, into place in the canoe. "Hold on, little one— we will have a bumpy ride for certain, but we will be together, finally heading for our new home."

He tried to keep the terror out of his voice.

A sickening snap and a harsh, screeching noise from behind the tent rent the air.

*　　*　　*

It had long been known in the lore of the Adirondacks, and especially in foothill towns like Obergrande, that mountain ranges can trap thunderstorms, then funnel huge amounts of water into canyons and downstream into the towns and cities built beneath their towering peaks.

The soil of the region had already been saturated that spring when the massive snowfall of the previous winter melted, causing the season commonly known to its residents as Mud to be even more like its name.

It had seemed to the citizens of Obergrande, who were still recuperating from their combative Town Board meeting the night before, that the endless storms of spring had just continued to soak their cursed town throughout that meeting and the rest of the night that followed it.

But they were wrong.

In fact, during the six hours after the meeting concluded at 1 AM, almost fifteen inches of hard rain, trapped between the peaks of the mountains on both sides of the Hudson River, fell on the long-weary area.

A parting gift from the far-away Hurricane Clarence.

A billion metric tons of water.

For the watershed of the central Adirondacks, the trapped storm was the last straw.

At 6:41 AM, just as the thunderstorm was finally dissipating, almost every stream and creek in the region swelled over its banks.

Almost as if the waterways had planned it that way.

At precisely 9:22 AM, swollen by the excessive rains of the spring season, and clogged with massive amounts of debris, the Lake Obergrande dam, which had held that lake and the river in check for more than a hundred years, failed.

And loosed an unrelenting flood of terrifying proportions, sending it rolling down the Hudson, swelling over the river's banks, ripping up roadways and swallowing buildings.

On its way to the little town.

Chapter 10

9:47 AM

Obergrande Elementary School, interior music room

THE FIVE LITTLE girls had learned the music faster than Glen Daniels could have imagined.

He had read them the lyrics, played the melody once through on the piano for them, and then suggested they try it with him.

He was pleasantly surprised to hear them, all on key, in time and singing the right words the first time through.

"Wow," he said as the girls giggled and danced excitedly. "That was wonderful, ladies." He stood up and thumbed through a pile of music spread across the top of the upright piano. "Hang on a second—I think I have some solo lines you can each learn."

All of the girls were hovering near the piano except for Elisa Santiago, the young Latina who was always so nicely dressed. Uncertain of what was happening, she wandered the music room while the teacher searched through the music, nervous at the lack of windows in the back wall.

Had Lucy Sullivan thought about it, she might have remembered that the absence of windows in a room was something that Elisa's parents had warned the administration about, a nervousness rooted in frightening things from the little girl's past, but the kindergarten teacher had been occupied that morning with the other students, and the thought had not occurred to her.

So Mr. Daniels had no idea it was an issue for Elisa.

While he and the other girls were occupied, she wandered toward the only window in the music room, the small glass opening in the door that led back out into the hallway.

Elisa glanced around the room and located a small stepstool sitting under a chair, picked it up and carried it over to the door, putting it down below the window. Then she stood on the stepstool and looked out into the hallway.

And gasped aloud.

She stumbled down off the stool and ran to the teacher, grabbing his suit coat and pointing at the door.

She tried to form words, but none would come.

Mr. Daniels, still intent on his music, didn't seem to notice. As her tugging grew more intense, he looked back at her. "Yes, Elisa?"

Elisa pulled frantically on Mr. Daniels' coat. "Agua. Hay *agua*."

The vocal music teacher shook his head. "No, sweetie, you can have water when we go back to the room in a few minutes. I can't send you to the fountain by yourself."

Elisa shook her head in frustration. "Agua en el pasillo!"

Glen Daniels' brows drew together in confusion. "What are you saying? Elisa, use your English, please."

"Hallway! Water! No debe estar!" She pointed to the window in the doorway.

Mr. Daniels went to the doorway and looked through the small window.

Water, clogged with branches and trash, was coursing down the tiled floor of the hallway.

"Oh my God!" he gasped.

He grabbed the room's telephone on the nearby wall, hitting the zero to reach the office, but there was no dial tone, no response.

He glanced around the classroom, looking for the highest ground, then ran to the piano and pushed it up against the long heater that stood against the far wall, his hands shaking with adrenaline.

"Corinne—come, honey," he urged, putting his hands out to the terrified students, who were looking at each other in alarm. "Elisa—Sloane, come here, girls, Grace and Sarah—hurry!"

Corinne glanced around again, then ran to him, followed by Sarah, who waved to the other three girls as she ran. As soon as they reached Mr. Daniels he scooped them up and put them atop the heater, as high off the floor as he could get them without risking them toppling or falling off. Then he turned back to the other girls.

"Follow me!"

He ran to Elisa and picked her up, nodding to the other girls to follow him. The child was shaking violently, so he put his hand behind her neck comfortingly as he carried her back to the heater ledge. He set her up beside Corinne and Sarah, then hoisted the other two girls beside them and pushed the piano closer to allow for another barrier between them and the water.

Then he smiled as bravely at them as he could, sickened by the terror on their little faces.

"It's OK—don't worry. You girls stay here. Stay together. I'll be right back." He smiled at them again, then ran to the door and opened it.

The water began running into the music room, turning the worn industrial carpeting an even uglier shade of gray. Glen Daniels struggled to pull the door shut, and disappeared from their view.

He ran down the interior hallway, banging on doors, pulling every fire alarm he could find, shouting all the way.

As the emergency bells began sounding throughout the school.

AT OBERGRANDE FIRE Stations #1 and #2, the alarms rang ferociously, shattering the morning peace.

And atop each fire hall, the blue light began to spin, sending its beams out into the gray haze that hung in the air.

No one was in Station #1 to hear the call of the county dispatcher, but in Obergrande #2, the fire hall in East Obergrande, the assistant chief, Andy Klein, and Paul Moody, a veteran firefighter who would be taking the position of Captain of Fire Police when the terms for officers changed in July, were both on site, washing the floor and setting up for the annual family portrait fundraiser scheduled for the next day, Saturday.

Both men froze, mops in hand, at the metallic-sounding voice of the dispatcher announcing the site of the alarm.

Obergrande Elementary School, the small brick building close to the river's edge on the east side of town.

Both mops dropped to the floor in an instant.

The men dashed to the wall where their gear hung.

"Dear Lord, the school's on fire?" Moody stammered, dragging his turnout gear off the wall as Klein raised a hand, listening.

Multiple calls were coming in.

"It—it sounds like a flood," the assistant chief said, struggling to pull on his rubberized pants, then pulling the suspenders up to his shoulders.

Outside the hall, they could hear the screeching of cars pulling up.

COLONEL GENOVESE AND Sergeant Evans were just finishing checking out of the Lakeview Motel, west of Tree Hill but still within the area considered to be East Obergrande. They had eaten breakfast at the diner across the street, and were dropping off their keys when the fire alarms began sounding in the office and throughout the building they were leaving.

"What's going on?" Colonel Genovese asked the desk clerk, who looked around, puzzled, and rose from her chair, staring at her desktop computer.

"I've no idea," she said nervously. "There's nothing on the screen—but in a lot of towns and villages in the

Adirondacks, hotels and motels where a large number of guests can be staying are wired into the police and fire scanner from the Fire Stations, because wild fires roar through here occasionally. Almost all the old historic hotels in the Park have burned."

Ace Evans rushed to the door and looked out, scanning the mountains and the areas to the west.

"No smoke," he noted.

Then he looked at the parking lot and the street leading up to it.

Water was coursing from the north in substantial torrents southward.

"Colonel!" he shouted. "Call the outpost!"

Colonel Genovese hurried to the door behind him.

And quietly loosed an expletive under his breath.

"Your phone working?" he asked the desk clerk, who snatched up the receiver, listened, then nodded, her eyes beginning to glaze in panic as the bells from the carillon of Our Mother of Sorrows began to ring wildly.

As the Colonel took the phone and called in the report of the rising water, Ace hurried out into the parking lot, the fire alarms of both Obergrande companies now wailing through the town and echoing off the mountains.

The flood waters had increased dramatically even in the few seconds it had been since he had seen the initial spillage in the street. Ace rushed to his car, which was parked outside the motel office, opened his trunk and pulled his hard helmet and other emergency gear from the back. He left his uniform in the car, deeming his off-duty clothing—an Army Corps of Engineers T-shirt, jeans and boots—to be appropriate enough attire to deploy.

Colonel Genovese was out the door a moment later, the expression on his face grim but calm.

"The hurricane seems to have tipped the scales into just what we were talking about last night," he said as Ace handed him one of a pair of two-way radios, raising his voice to be heard over the screaming sirens and the clanging church bells. "Radar and satellite reports indicate the Lake Obergrande dam may have just failed. Saranac is deploying, not sure who else—I'm heading to Fire Station #1 in West Obergrande, you're to go see what you can do to help Station #2 around the corner until the guard units begin arriving. It looks like Albany will be sending recon and rescue helicopters just in case."

Ace nodded silently and returned the Colonel's salute as the harsh honking of fire trucks began to roar a short distance away.

From the mountain roads and streets overlooking the town, cars and trucks with blue flashing lights, the vehicles of volunteer firefighters, were streaming down toward Fire Station #2.

Ace hurried into his car and joined them.

Chapter 11

9:49 AM

Windsor Gardens

DAVE WINDSOR HAD been at the garden center for almost four hours already when the sirens went off across Obergrande.

He was in the process of shoveling his highly-acclaimed mulch, a secret blend of shredded woods and thick grasses, off of the truck that had brought it back from the shredder and into its standard place of honor, a towering pile at the edge of the alpine garden, when the shriek filled his ears, first from his own station, then joined a few seconds later by #1, followed by the bells of the Catholic church and emergency sirens all across the town.

He dropped the shovel onto the mulch pile and ran for his pickup.

Walt Bentley, the driver of the truck and a fellow firefighter, climbed down from the dump truck's cab and followed him.

Dave leaned over and opened the door from the inside

for Walt, who slid in remarkably quickly for a man his age. Then he slapped his blue light on and gunned the engine.

And spun out of the gravel parking lot of Windsor Gardens, leaving his store unlocked and his register unguarded.

Without a second thought.

9:52 AM

Cavenaugh Street, southwest of Tree Hill

SUE WINDSOR WAS dozing on the couch in the living room when the sirens went off.

She sat up hazily, listening to the babies awaken at the harsh sounds.

And, a moment later, join in the wailing with the alarms.

She rose shakily and made her way to the front door, just in time to jump back as a knock thundered on it.

"Sue!" a muted voice, male and terrified, shouted from the other side. "Sue! Open up!"

Before she could even get to the door, it burst open.

Her neighbor, Lenny Verillo, a retired mill worker, stumbled into the foyer.

"Sue—get the girls—we've gotta evacuate—*now*—come on—"

"What—what's going on?" Sue mumbled as she turned toward the playpen where the baby girls were now sobbing.

"Flood," Mr. Verillo puffed as he made his way to the playpen and snatched one of the babies, Blythe, who let loose with an earsplitting wail. "Get the other one—come on!"

Sue snapped out of her daze, seized her daughter Bonnie, and followed Lenny Verillo out onto the front porch.

And stopped in horror.

The streets around the center of Obergrande were filling with water, rivers of rolling rapids that grew stronger by the moment.

Lenny was already on his way across the lawn where he had parked his all-wheel-drive vehicle.

"We—we have to use my car," Sue protested, following him halfway but waving at her driveway. "They need to be in car seats—"

"*Sue,*" Lenny said commandingly, "your car will never get up the hill! Come *now*." He opened the back door and waved urgently at her.

Sue Windsor ran blindly for his car, clutching the baby as tightly as she could. She scrambled into the back seat and pulled the door closed behind her.

Lenny handed her Blythe, and Sue pulled both girls into her lap, all of them lurching from side to side as the SUV pulled out of the grass, leaving deep ruts and showers of mud behind it.

As they skidded up the street, she glanced over her shoulder to see showers of sparks erupting in the distance behind them, over near the center of town, as electrical lines ignited. Sue's head felt as if the electricity was blasting through her brain as a terrifying thought occurred to her.

"Sweet Lord, Lenny," she whispered as her neighbor negotiated the slanted streets leading up to the western sections of the village terraced into the hillside that

overlooked the lake. "The school—oh—oh—Lenny—
Sarah's in the school."

Lenny's jaw was gritted, thinking of his granddaughter.

"I know," he said. "Abby too. And five hundred other
kids."

9:54 AM

DAVE WINDSOR PULLED into the parking lot of Obergrande Fire Station #2 through water up to the wheel wells
of his tires. His truck was barely in PARK as he vaulted
from it and ran into the station, Walt Bentley only a few
steps behind him.

One of the four fire engines was already staffed with a
team of a dozen volunteers and ready to depart, a second
loading up as he came into the building. He glanced
quickly at the blackboard, where Andy Klein had written
the specifics of the call from the county dispatcher for any
members who arrived after the engines had left.

"Engines Two and Four ready to go, One and Three
starting to load, four teams, roughly a dozen a piece,"
Klein said, pulling on his coat. "Thank goodness for the
law in New York that requires direct alarm wiring from
schools—as close as they are to the river, they're probably
halfway under water by now."

Windsor swallowed, his hands going numb.

Klein blinked. "Sorry, chief," he said. "I—I forgot—"

"S'ok," said Dave, shaking off the thought. "We'll get
'em all out."

"You wanna go with Two? It's leaving now. We're

taking the school, being closer—Company #1 is dealing with a logjam and abatement."

Dave shook his head, heading for the equipment rack. "Send 'em. I'm not gonna hold anybody up. Send Four as well—I'll catch One with Walt. How many departments responding?"

"About eight so far, from what I can tell. The dispatch has been constant and chaotic. I expect we'll see a dozen or more, maybe twenty before this is done. See you out there, chief."

"Godspeed," Dave Windsor said, pulling on his pants.

"Got a visitor," Klein said, nodding toward the door as he headed for the first engine.

Dave looked around.

A young man he had never seen before was coming through the door, wearing a T-shirt with a castle emblem on it, the letters A.C.E. emblazoned above it. He was somewhat shorter than Dave, probably in the neighborhood of six feet, with broad, muscled shoulders and the fluid movement of a trained soldier.

Dave pulled up his suspenders and sat down on the bench, dragging his boots out from under it. Walt Bentley was already suiting up next to him.

"You here to help out?"

The man stopped. "Yes, sir—Sergeant Alex Evans, 3rd Battalion, 105th Infantry, Army National Guard, Saranac Lake. Happened to be in town—what can I do to help?"

Dave was lacing his boots. "You got any water rescue training?"

"Yessir. River Rescue cert, Swift Water Technician,

advanced, Naval Rescue Swimmer—"

"Well, I'm convinced," said Walt Bentley. He put on his helmet and headed for the trucks.

The fire chief snagged his helmet, goggles, gloves, and self-contained breathing apparatus, and nodded at the wall of gear.

"Grab the turnout gear in locker 17—that guy's retired."

Ace nodded and went to the wall.

"Army National Guard—isn't ACE the engineering corps?" Dave asked as he started toward the engine.

"Yessir. I consult with them." Ace already was adjusting his suspenders.

"Well, then, you should ride with me. I'm Dave Windsor—bring your gear—I'll help you suit up in the rig."

Ace grabbed what remained of the turnout gear, and followed him.

Chapter 12

10:01 AM

Obergrande Elementary School

MORNING SNACK WAS put away and Lucy's class was divided in half again, her students studying different kinds of rocks while Kelly's group practiced writing their letters. It was almost time to switch.

Dominic, ever the sky-watcher, stood up, stretched his arms above his head, revealing his little belly, and looked out the window.

And gasped.

"Miss Sullivan?" he stammered.

Lucy was collecting the rock samples from the other kids in the group. "Dominic, help us pick up, please."

"Miss Sullivan," the little boy insisted, "there's a *lot* of water on the playground."

"Don't worry about it," Lucy said, taking the igneous rock specimens out of the box to keep them from breaking. "We can still go outside at recess unless Mrs. Cox makes an announcement."

A violent pounding in the hall, followed by the scream of fire alarms, tore through the air.

Lucy looked up in shock, then out the window.

A small stream, widening by the moment, was rushing past the windows between the playground and the school building.

As if in answer to the internal alarms, from every side of the town beyond the windows, sirens and honking horns took up the call.

The principal's voice came over the loudspeaker, crackling and intermittent.

"Everyone stay calm, please. Faculty members are to initiate fire drill procedures but remain in your classrooms with the doors closed until fire department personnel come for you. Classrooms on the eastern corridor will be evacuated first. Make sure your emergency windows are unlatched. Repeat, everyone, please remain calm."

Lucy swallowed hard. Her classroom was in the western corridor, near the northern door that led out onto the playground and to the sports fields of the high school beyond.

Farther away from the river.

If that stream is all the way over here, I can only imagine what the eastern side of the building is seeing, she thought anxiously.

The students dashed to the windows as fire trucks and rescue vehicles began arriving on the track at the high school, five hundred or so feet away. The circling lights seemed to entrance the students, shaking as they were from fear.

Lucy clapped her hands, but the noise was lost in the thundering alarms.

"Everyone line up like it's a fire drill," she said as calmly as she could. Her voice wobbled a little, but still sounded rational. "Over here, please. Now."

She exchanged a glance with Kelly Moran, who was already bringing Kristen in her wheelchair forward. The assistant teacher's large, dark eyes were wide with barely-controlled panic; Lucy could see that she was unsure how to rescue her student in the event that the hallways were flooded.

She looked out the glass window in the classroom door.

Trickling water was already running down the western corridor.

Lucy went to her desk as the children lined up behind Mrs. Moran and pulled her purse from the bottom drawer. She grabbed her wallet, a slender cloth one, and slipped it, without thinking, into her bra, then looked up to see all thirteen students staring at her.

She cleared her throat. "Line up in pairs, please. Find a buddy. Hold hands."

Loud sounds were coming in from the hallway, the noise of boots and children's voices rising and falling over the wailing sirens and Mrs. Cox's regular assurances over the loudspeaker. Lucy wasn't certain, but it seemed to her that the principal's voice was becoming thinner and more frantic with each announcement.

Or perhaps it was just the crackling of the PA, which was starting to show signs of failing.

Her students were beginning to make noise about needing to use the bathroom, even though they had all visited the restroom after snack. *Oh great,* Lucy thought. She could not possibly let them out of line, but knew the prospect of having an accident was particularly upsetting to children who had only become reliably toilet-trained in the last two or so years.

She loosed the hands of her "buddies" and grabbed a plastic bucket of crayons. She dumped the crayons onto her desk and held up the bucket.

"Who needs to go?" she asked. "You can use this."

The children looked at each other in horror, then stared at her, aghast.

"Is there anyone who can't wait?"

Thirteen heads shook quickly from side to side.

"All right. Well, if anyone needs to go before we get outside, you can use this and we will all close our eyes."

Just then the door opened with a screech, and an ankle-high rush of water poured in through the doorway.

Three first responders in fire helmets came rapidly into the room, scanning the situation as they did, two of them pushing the door shut behind them with great effort.

The one in the lead was someone Lucy thought she recognized.

Ace Evans conferred with the other two firefighters, then held up what looked like a cord belt and a hook, several of which he had slung over both his shoulders, as did the other rescuers, one of whom was carrying a wide coil of rope, which he put down on Lucy's desk.

"Hey guys—my name's Ace. We're here to take you

out. Can you all raise your arms over your heads like this?"

He held up his own, straight, with his hands pointed toward the ceiling.

The children obeyed.

"Excellent." He handed the rest of his belts to the other firefighters and walked over to Kristen, who was trembling in her wheel chair. "You're first, miss. We're going to be partners, ok?" The little girl nodded, looking terrified. He slipped the adjustable cord, called a gut belt, around her waist, and attached a carabineer to it, then slid it through the D-ring on his own belt.

"Keep your hands up until you've got your belt," he said as the two firemen began attaching the gut belts to each of the other kids. "Then you can put 'em down." He turned to the two women.

"Can you put on your own?"

Both women nodded uncertainly.

"Good." He smiled slightly at Lucy. "You're going to have to trust me today, ma'am. Sorry about that."

Lucy just swallowed as she took the webbed belt he handed her and put it around her waist, cinching it tight.

It only took a few moments for everyone to be belted up, after which the man with the large coil of rope took it off the desk and clipped his rescue belt to the reinforced loop at the end of it, tightening the carabineer.

"So here's how this works," Ace said in a voice that was commanding, while at the same time calming, to the children. "We are all getting tied together, as you can see." He leaned down to the trembling child in the wheelchair. "What's your name?"

"Kristen." Her voice was a ragged whisper.

"Kristen and I are the leaders. Everybody else is going to follow the leaders in a single-file line. We're going up the hall that way—" he pointed north toward the exit door. "Then we'll turn left and go right out the door and across to the football field."

"What about the water?" Dominic asked, his voice quavering.

"We're going to walk right through it—there's a line of firefighters standing across the stream, and each of them is going to pass you along to the next one, like you were a football," said Ace as the other two responders checked each of the carabineers, twisting the locking mechanism on each one. "No worries—we've gotcha. Right, gentlemen?"

The two firefighters smiled slightly for the first time since they had entered the room and nodded.

Ace looked at Kelly Moran, then at Lucy. "Let's put her in the center," he said to the first responders, indicating Kelly, "and Miss Sullivan at the end of the line." Then he turned to the kids.

"You ready?"

He got a minimal response.

Ace cleared his throat.

"I said 'are you ready?' " he growled, but his eyes twinkled. "The answer is 'yes, sir!' "

"Yes, sir!" the children shouted back, energized.

"All *right*," Ace said cheerfully. "Let's blow this popsicle stand."

He signaled to one of the first responders, who took up his position at the door, then he bent down to Kristen.

"Ready, Miss Kristen?" The little girl nodded. Ace scooped her carefully up in his arms and signaled for the door to be opened.

Another swell of water, this time almost up to the children's thighs, swept through the door, stinging cold, causing a number of them to scream.

Ace turned back. "No worries, polar bears. We gotcha. And you guys are North Country born and raised—this is nothing for you. Come on."

He started out the door, the children being pushed along by the two firefighters, anchored in the center and at the end by the teachers, who were trembling as violently as the kids were.

This can't be happening, Lucy thought as she struggled to remain upright in the river that was now coursing through the western corridor. The water was slightly lower than it had been when it rushed through the doorway, but still the children were fighting to remain standing in the chilly current.

"Repeat after me," Ace called in between blasts of the fire alarm. "Hup, twop, three-p, *four,* hup, twop, three-p, *four*—"

The students began chanting the cadence, following Ace around the corner to the side door of the school.

They were so engrossed in the chant that they didn't notice the sizzle of the overhead corridor lights as the last of the power in the building blinked out.

Lucy looked back through the windows as the line of kids began to turn the corner and saw similar lines of roped children and staff with other firefighters leading them, making their ways to the bucket-brigade-type lines of rescuers in the rushing river that was spilling now down the sides of the building. Every now and then some sort of trash—tree branches, garbage cans, or other junk swept up in the flood—would impact one of the people in the rescue line, causing a hiccup in the process, but for the most part the passage seemed to be working well.

A growing cluster of kids and teachers was gathering on the football field, out of the way of the flood.

Just as she made it past the exterior door, she looked around for her missing students, the five girls Mr. Daniels had "snagged" earlier in the morning.

And did not see them.

A knot tied itself in her throat.

The baker's dozen of kids from her class were now being passed along the rescue line, Ace and Kristen at the lead. The National Guardsman was sturdy enough to make his own wake as he passed through the floodwaters, leading the rope line of kids, but each person in the bucket brigade of eight firemen put a steadying hand on him anyway, just to be sure.

Every few moments, as the current grew swifter, one or another of them would grab a kindergartner who had tripped or fallen and pull that child up, steadying him or her, before encouraging them onward. It was an agonizingly slow process, especially for Lucy, at the end of the line and looking anxiously around for Glen Daniels, who she was certain would have evacuated with her students.

She saw both of the other kindergarten teachers, huddled with their classes, writing names down on clipboards provided by the fire department, counting and hugging each child as blankets were wrapped around them by rescuers at the scene. The sirens were still wailing, the fire trucks honking and the lights spinning, making the gray world seem like a waking nightmare.

The student line was almost across the rushing torrent.

A bullhorn broke through the noise.

"Evacuate!" the voice, that of a middle-aged fireman, roared across the football field. "All faculty and volunteers, get these kids west to the far side of Tree Hill Park. A new swell is approaching upriver from the dam—repeat, get the kids to the far side of Tree Hill Park!"

Pandemonium and a considerable part of Hell broke loose.

The students and teachers in the water tried to rush forward, causing the roped line to collapse. The bucket brigade reached quickly into the blasting current and dragged the little people up to a stand again, then passed them as quickly across the newborn river as they could.

Beyond the line of students ahead of her, Lucy could see adults, mostly teachers and first responders, but some that she recognized as parents, grabbing children by the hands and urging them forward, in a blind run to the higher ground of Tree Hill.

Except for a scattered number of parents she recognized.

The first to catch her eye was Corinne's father, Professor Isaac Byrnes, standing beside his wife, Dr. Patricia Byrnes, staring at the school, and at her, fear in their eyes visible even as far away as they were standing, surrounded by their four boys. Not far from them was Reverend Fuller, the pastor of the Obergrande Community Church and his wife, holding their son's hand, also searching the oncoming line of children, looking desperately, she imagined, for Grace.

Oh God, she thought, *they didn't get out yet.*

Panicked, she pawed at the carabineer, trying to free herself from the rope without success until she figured out that it was just a metal nut she needed loosen.

She unclipped the carabineer and turned in the water to the firefighter at the end of the line.

"I have to go back," she stammered, handing the child to him.

Then Lucy took off, splashing back through the rising water to the school.

The startled firefighter shouted for Ace.

She cast her eyes around, as best as she could, looking for a passable way back across the rising water, but still did not see a single one of the five girls that had gone with Glen Daniels an hour or so before.

As the evacuation order was repeated over the bull-horn, the Sergeant, who was now out of the floodwaters and pulling kids rapidly out as well, handed Kristen off to other first responders. He unhooked each child as he or she made landfall, then sent them to a secondary line of responders and faculty, including Mrs. Cox, who was at the water's edge, counting every child that crossed.

"Hey! Ma'am! What are you doing?"

Lucy kept going, fighting the current.

"What are you doing?"

"Ace!" she shouted back. "I'm missing five kids!"

The Sergeant heard his name, but not the rest of her call. He pointed at his ear, then made a looping gesture, signaling for her to repeat her message.

"I'm missing five kids!" she shouted again.

The Sergeant's eyebrows drew together as he took a silent count of the line, only two of which had not already been pulled out of the floodwaters.

Then he shook his head, pulled the last two kids out of the water, into the arms of the waiting rescuers on the side of the swollen river.

And made his way angrily into the water, heading after her.

He unclipped his radio as he crossed back toward the school, waving it over his head to keep it out of the water and alert the other firefighters that he was going back in.

"Miss Sullivan!—*Miss Sullivan*—stop—"

Lucy had seized the door, and was dragging back on it with all her strength.

And making little progress.

Her struggle gave him the chance to catch up with her. Ace took his safety strap and clipped it to the end of hers, then exhaled.

"Never letting you go again, ma'am," he said.

"I have to go back in," she growled, pulling with all her weight on the right side of the double door. "There are five of my students still in the school—"

The Sergeant was shaking his head.

"We'll get 'em," he said. "We'll do a sweep once every hall is clear—which they just about are." He reached out for her again.

"You don't understand," Lucy said, still pulling on the door, her teeth chattering from the cold water and fear, dodging. "I had five kids out on a special—to one of the music rooms. I saw their parents—they haven't gotten out. And you don't know where they are—I do. Now *help me open this damned door!*"

Chapter 13

THE NATIONAL GUARDSMAN stared at her a second.

"Let go and stand back, ma'am," he said.

Then he braced his foot against the left door, seized the handle of the right door and pulled, dragging the door open a crack.

The water fought back, swirling and eddying around the opening.

Ace adjusted his position and tugged again, the muscles of his back and neck bulging before Lucy's eyes, even beneath his fire coat.

As the door opened wide enough for her to slip through.

Ace followed her. He stopped as she darted blindly into the water running down the dark hallway, his weight dragging her, without having to touch her, to a stop, because they were tethered together.

"We need a plan of action before you go off half-cocked, Miss Sullivan," he said calmly over the noise of the rising water. "Where is the music room?"

Lucy, standing outside her classroom now, pointed

south down the western corridor. "The east and west corridors are like the legs of an H," she said nervously as she struggled to keep upright. "The interior corridor is the crossbar on the H. That's where the music room is. I think they may be in there."

Ace turned on his flashlight and held it up, casting shadows around the dark halls of the school, then handed it to her. He hit the TALK button on the radio and informed the command of where they were and what they were doing. Then he rested his hand on her shoulder, steadying her.

"All right. You have to stay calm, ma'am. They are going to need us to be confident; they're terrified for sure."

"That makes six of us," Lucy said as Ace started forward again.

"Seven," the National Guardsman said as they hurried down the corridor. "But two of us have to be the adults, since the five little kids can't."

"Are you telling me you're terrified, Sergeant?"

"Completely. I'm always terrified when someone else is in harm's way, especially kids. But I've been trained not to let it get the better of me."

Lucy nodded, grateful.

They hurried around the corner into the horizontal interior corridor, lashed together, Ace's greater size and strength providing some stability for Lucy, who was being tripped up by the cold floodwaters. She flashed the beam around the hallway, looking in the open doors of classrooms for anyone still trapped inside.

"There are four stairs down ahead in the hallway," she

shouted over the increasing noise of the water.

Ace, an architect and engineer, had already made note of the declining slant of the building, but just nodded.

He knew, given that the water into which he was descending was already up to his knees here in the connecting hallway, that the eastern corridor would be vastly deeper.

Certainly chest high, over a child's head.

He shook off the thought and took Lucy's arm as they went down the four steps she had indicated.

Lucy was pointing agitatedly at a door in the middle of the hallway.

"There," she said, her fair face red with exertion. *"There!"*

"Hang tough, ma'am," Sergeant Evans said as they reached the door. "I've got you."

"And you're never gonna let me go. Yeah, I know—I heard you say so when you tied us together."

The National Guardsman smiled slightly.

"I'll get the door," he said. "Be careful of the back-wash—it should be lower in the classroom than in the hallway, so a lot of water is going to head that way when we open the door."

He took hold of the handle. Beyond the door, to his relief, he could hear the sound of sobbing.

Up until that moment he was not certain there would be anyone inside still alive to rescue.

"Remember, we've only got about twenty inches of give between us," he said, bracing his shoulder against the door. "Don't dash in too fast—you could pull us both down."

"Open the door," Lucy growled through gritted teeth.

Ace pushed forcefully against the door. It snapped back, then yielded to his strength, spilling a large amount of water into the room.

Lucy ran past him, her long golden curls hanging in streams behind her.

THE LITTLE GIRLS had actually managed to be rather brave at first. When Mr. Daniels had not returned as promised, they had remained silent, looking at one another and the rising water on the floor, perched as they were on the heater behind the upright piano.

Grace, the pastor's daughter, had retreated as far against the wall as she could, shuddering, but saying nothing. Elisa had followed her, pulling her little legs up to her chest, her enormous eyes wide with fear and glinting in the fading light. Corrine had hung close to Sarah, who sat immediately behind the top of the piano, both of them watching the door intently, while Sloane was making plans and sharing them, to almost no response from the other girls.

"See? It would be better to be princesses," she had said nonchalantly, her voice quavering in spite of her brave words. "When you're a princess, Prince Charmin' comes to rescue you when you need help."

"Or the angels," said Corrine.

"I don' think we want the angels yet," said Sarah. "They bring you to heaven. I don' think we will get back home if they do."

At that moment, the lights in the school had shorted out, sparking and snapping.

Plunging the room into almost total darkness.

All five of the girls screamed.

Then Grace and Elisa began sobbing.

"No me gusta la oscuridad," Elisa wept. "I no like the dark. Tengo miedo."

Sloane moved closer to her, trembling violently, and held up her play wristwatch, a Cinderella one her father had given her for her fifth birthday. She pushed the button on the side, and the pink watch glowed.

"Here, Elisa," she said. "Here's some light. Don't be scared."

Corinne, who was also shaking, took Sarah's hand and interlaced their fingers.

"Look," she said, glancing down at the keyboard of the piano below them, "our fingers look like the piano keys."

Sarah smiled slightly and squeezed her hand, but said nothing.

They remained, clutching each other's hands, Elisa holding on to Sloane's arm near the glowing watch, and Grace backed up as far against the wall as she could be, watching helplessly for aid that did not seem to be coming.

Finally, amid the muted sirens they could hear in the distance, and the sounds of planes and helicopters flying overhead, then disappearing, they all succumbed to despair and cried as if their hearts would break.

Only to hear the sound of the heavy door of the classroom screeching open.

And a familiar voice calling their names.

And what appeared to be an angel, with long golden curls, holding a light in her hand.

"SLOANE! CORINNE! ELISA, Grace, Sarah! It's OK—we're here to get you out."

Lucy had instinctively known that the terrified girls would be at least somewhat reassured by the sound of their own names, so she shouted them the instant she got into the flooding classroom.

A rush of water swept in from the hallway as Ace struggled to brace the heavy door open, the backwash slapping her above the waist for the first time since she had entered the school again.

She spun the flashlight around the dark room and immediately found five little faces, three pale, two dark, all pathetically frightened, hiding behind the piano atop the heater. Lucy did her best to smile encouragingly.

"It's an angel," Sarah said nervously to the others.

"No, it's certainly not," Lucy said wryly. "It's Miss Sullivan, girls. Don't be afraid."

Ace was already speaking into his radio, informing the command center that they had located five kindergartners. He looked questioningly at Lucy, who nodded, then he went on to describe where in the flooded school they were located.

The radio crackled with a message in return.

"Copy that, Sergeant. Be advised the eastern corridor inside the building has flooded at a depth of over five feet, and the western side of the building outside is sustaining flood depth of more than four feet. You won't be able to open the exit door again—get to the closest classroom in the western corridor and prepare to evacuate to chopper via emergency windows."

"Copy," Ace replied. "Will alert when we are at the windows or as necessary." He turned to Lucy as he put the radio away.

"Can you carry two, one on each hip?" he asked. "If the water is high enough, it will help a little. They'll be easier to carry *in* the water, believe it or not. Buoyancy and all that."

"Absolutely," Lucy said, still smiling bravely at the girls.

"All right, then." He passed Lucy by a foot or so, getting closer to the quavering little girls.

"Hello, ladies," he began when Sloane gasped and interrupted him.

"Look!" she said, pointing to the Army Corps of Engineers shirt. "He's wearing a *castle!* It's Prince Charmin'!"

"Well, yes," Ace said humorously. "I was just about to introduce myself like that. Can you show me your guns, ladies?" He lifted his arms in a bicep curl.

Three of the girls managed to imitate him. Ace's eyes wandered over their arms, noting their musculature, then turned to Corinne.

"Do you have brothers, miss?"

Corinne nodded. "Four. All bigger than me."

"Do you wrassle 'em?"

"Sure do." The little girl grinned slightly.

"Do you ever win?"

"Sometimes."

"Good—then you're gonna put your arms around my neck and ride on the back—OK? Can you do that without letting go? Like you're gonna flip me, but just pretend?"

"OK." Corinne exhaled audibly.

"Very good," said Ace gently. "Let me get two more, and then you can climb on. We're all stickin' together. Come're, ladies." He nodded his head at Sloane and Sarah, the two next closest.

The redheaded little girl climbed nervously over the piano and came quickly into his outstretched right arm, which he wrapped around her as he set her against his hip. Then he turned to Sarah, who followed Sloane's example, hanging her legs over the front of the piano and slipping forward to stand on the open keyboard. Ace wrapped her quickly onto his left hip.

"Help her get on," he said quietly to Lucy, nodding at Corinne. She put her arms out and assisted the little girl over the heavy instrument which had formed an impressive barrier between the floodwaters and the children.

Ace backed up, Sarah and Sloane in his arms, their feet dangling in the water, and stood at an incline while Lucy helped Corinne onto his back.

"Can you get the others?" he asked.

"Yes," Lucy said. She looked at Elisa, terrified in the light of the flashlight in her hand. "Come on, Elisa—your turn. Ven conmigo. Don't make me look bad, now. We can do this."

Elisa swallowed hard, then crawled slowly over the piano, shaking like a leaf, and into Lucy's outstretched arm.

Lucy exhaled and kissed Elisa's forehead. "Good job. All right, Grace—come to me."

The child, staring wildly, shook her head.

Lucy cleared her throat. "Grace—come on."

The little girl couldn't move. She reared back against the windowless wall, frozen.

Lucy willed her pounding heart to slow down, and tried to keep her voice steady.

"What's the matter, Grace?" she asked softly, trying to mimic Ace's voice when he had spoken to the children inside and outside of the school during the evacuation. "It's OK—we're getting out of here now."

Grace shook her head violently. "Can't," she croaked.

"Why, Grace?"

Grace looked around her, panic-stricken.

"The faces," she whispered. "I can *see* them. They're watching."

"Faces—what faces?"

Grace lapsed into terrified silence.

Lucy turned to Ace. "You should go," she said softly. "This may take a while, and I'm not leaving her."

"You think *I* would?" Ace retorted. "Keep talking to her. I want to keep this voluntary, but if I have to, I can pry the piano back—it will just make things very difficult. We'll give this another ten seconds, and then it's Plan B."

Lucy handed Sarah the flashlight, then turned back to the trembling Grace.

"Can you see them when your eyes are closed, Grace?"

The little girl just stared at her.

"Let's try this—just close your eyes, Grace. Close your

eyes and forget about them, they're not real—just concentrate on my voice and follow it to me. OK? Close your eyes. Listen to my voice. Please, honey. Just come."

The little girl continued to stare at her, not moving.

"I'm here, Grace," Lucy said. "I'll make sure the faces get stuck in here when we go. Come on—follow my voice. Like when we play The Owl in class—you are always good at that, with your eyes closed—"

Grace swallowed again. Then, slowly, she closed her eyes.

"That's it. Now, step forward. Let's do three steps, then put your hands out—"

Patiently, Lucy talked the trembling five-year-old forward, eyes closed, until she was sitting on top of the piano.

"All right," she said as she maneuvered herself into position, "jump, Grace—I've got you, I promise."

The little girl, her eyes still closed, scooted to the edge of the piano, and dropped off it.

Into Lucy's waiting arm.

Grace leaned her head against the teacher's neck. Lucy kissed the back of the little head gratefully.

Both adults exhaled deeply.

"Name?" Ace inquired, glancing at Sarah in his right arm.

"Sarah," Lucy said.

"OK, Sarah, hold the flashlight so the beam shines in front of us. Can you do that?" Sarah nodded.

Ace started for the door. "All right, ladies—here we go."

Chapter 14

AFTER THEY LEFT the music room, Lucy felt she was sinking deeper and deeper into a nightmare from which she could not awake, no matter how much she tried.

Elisa and Grace, the two girls she was carrying, clung to her in a way that was painful, especially in the cold water. She kept whispering to them in a comforting manner as she and Ace made their way through the dark school, the fire alarms silent now, though they could hear the noise of disaster response beyond the walls.

Ace checked in over the radio as often as he could, having Sloane push the necessary buttons, maintaining contact with what seemed like a large number of first responders tracking their progress.

Almost every time a different one answered, he or she had exclaimed in surprise when finding out that he had gone in with a civilian.

"Not like you had any choice," she said after the fifth time. "Sorry about that."

Ace had merely smiled and continued through the

floodwaters.

They had gone almost halfway down the corridor when the first emergency occurred.

Just as she and Ace had climbed the four steps at the midpoint of the hall, a large rat swam past, shockingly close.

Lucy stopped short, silent, clutching Elisa and Grace to her, both of whose eyes were closed.

But Sloane, watching everything from Ace's right hip, shrieked in horror and wrenched out of his arm, struggling blindly to escape.

And fell into the floodwater, disappearing beneath it, lost in the deep water over the four stairs.

Lucy, who still wasn't certain what to make of the young National Guardsman, found herself grateful for his presence in the moments that followed.

The instant Sloane tore free of his grip, Ace immediately released the strap that bound Lucy to him with his free hand and went closer to the submerged steps. Balancing both Sarah in one arm and Corinne, still clinging to his back, he bent over and swept his arm through the water on the stairs into which Sloane had vanished.

He had needed to submerge Sarah almost up to her waist and Corinne's legs into the cold river running through the hall, terrifying both girls, to search for Sloane, until he finally caught hold of her curly red hair and pulled her up, gasping for air.

Without a word, he had snagged her, one-handed, under her arms and pulled her back onto his hip. Then he looked into her face.

"Y'allright?"

The little girl had broken into hiccupping sobs, coughing pathetically.

"Take some easy breaths, Cinderella," he said gently. "You're OK."

He turned and nodded to Lucy. He came up next to her and attached the carabineer to her belt again.

"You thought you escaped, but, as I said, I'll never let you go," he said with a deadpan expression.

"Ha ha. Come on."

As they approached the corner where the horizontal hallway met the western corridor, Lucy could hear the sound of the water racing, and looked nervously at Sergeant Evans.

"How deep do you think it is?"

"Too deep to get out the way we came in," he answered. "Don't worry, ma'am—the fire department and the Guard have us covered."

"How?" Lucy's voice was harsh with nerves.

"The exit door has too much pressure pushing against it, so we're going back to your classroom and exiting through the emergency windows."

"*What?!* Through the—"

"Shhh," Ace said shortly, his dark eyes flashing. "Get ready to round the corner, ma'am; the current will be a lot faster in a minute."

Lucy had already discovered he was right.

She hiked up the two little girls in her aching arms

higher on her hips, wondering if their legs were as cold and numb as her own.

"Stay behind me, ma'am," Sergeant Evans cautioned as they prepared to turn the corner. "There should be a wake that would be easier for you to walk in."

"I just hope I don't fall back and drag you down," Lucy whispered to him.

"I've got seventy-five pounds and an extra one of the Fearless Fivesome on me," Ace said. "I don't think you can. Hold tight and let's go."

They braced themselves, turned the corner, and were immediately slapped by the rapids that were rushing through what that morning had been a tiled school hallway. Lucy struggled to remain upright, noting that both Elisa and Grace had their eyes clenched shut. The guiding tug of the carabineer-anchored belt, coupled with the wake behind Ace that he had predicted, served to keep her moving, even when her legs felt like they might give out.

Finally they made it to the door of her classroom.

Ace looked at Sarah.

"You're a brave little girl," he said, his dark eyes and expression serious. "If I put you up against the wall near the door, and Miss Sullivan backs up so that you're on her back like Corinne is on me, can you hang on for a couple seconds?"

"I—I think so," Sarah whispered.

"Don't be scared," Ace said, smiling slightly. "It will only take a few seconds. I promise."

"OK," said Sarah.

He looked at Lucy, and she nodded.

Ace turned his left side to the wall, and Lucy backed up in front of Sarah. She pressed back until the little girl was behind her, pinned against the wall, Sarah's small legs draping in front of her, a little arm around her neck.

"Not too hard," Ace said to Sarah, who was still holding the flashlight, which was shaking violently. "You're making Miss Sullivan's face turn white."

"I'm OK," Lucy choked as he unhooked his safety harness from hers again. "Get the door open."

"Hold on, ladies," Ace said as he braced his shoulder against the classroom door, then turned the handle with his now-free left hand. He shoved the door open, then bolted into the room, heading straight for the windows and the tall heater shelf, which was almost submerged in the water.

"Stay still, I'll be right back," he said to Corrine and Sloane as he offloaded them onto the long shelf, tossing an armload of books into the water. "Don't move."

Then he ran back into the hallway and grabbed Sarah and Elisa, leaving Grace tucked in the fetal position in Lucy's arms. Lucy ran into the classroom, and Ace followed her, leaving the door open, knowing it would be impossible to close it now.

Once they had deposited the other three girls on the heater, Ace returned to the radio, and Lucy soothed the children.

"We're almost out," she said as comfortingly as she could, but her voice sounded uncertain.

She was listening to the sound of the rescue helicopter above the roof.

WHILE ACE CONVERSED on the radio with the rescuers outside in words she didn't understand, Lucy stood shivering in water almost up to her waist, surging less than the streaming floodwaters in the hallways, but rising rapidly enough to keep her in barely-controlled panic.

Knowing that she had no more idea of what was happening with the fire department than they did, she turned her attention to calming and comforting the five little girls the best she could.

She was most worried about Sloane, who was exhibiting all the signs of shock, and all five of the girls were cold, making her worry about hypothermia. Lucy gathered them together as close as they could manage and put her arms around all of them.

"Not too much longer," she said, her teeth chattering.

There was far more light in the classroom than there had been in the hallways, but the little girls were too deeply traumatized to be cheered by it. Every cheerful comment she made to try to raise their spirits seemed to fall on deaf ears. They seemed to have lost the ability to do anything but curl up and try to keep warm.

Lucy wondered dully if that might be for the best.

"Copy that," she finally heard Ace say.

He clipped his radio onto his collar again, then put his hands on the shelf on top of the heater and, like a gymnast, lifted himself up until he was standing on it.

"Hold on, ladies," he said as he pushed open the emergency windows that Kelly Moran had unlatched, what seemed like hours before. "We're in the home stretch."

Lucy winced as a number of search lights were suddenly shining through the windows at them, amid the sounds of garbled talking on bull horns from the other side of a rapid river that was running full force now, separating the school from the fire trucks, deeper even than the water in the classroom.

Blinded as she was by the blasting lights shattering the hazy gray of the world outside the school, it took Ace several times to finally get her to look up.

"Miss Sullivan?"

Lucy shook off the looming darkness that was filling her eyes. "Yes?"

The National Guardsman was stripping off his fire coat and helmet, leaving him in his soaking wet Army Corps of Engineers T-shirt, his fire pants and suspenders. He turned and looked at her evenly.

Lucy saw for the first time the oval shape of his face, free from headgear, the short, dark hair matted to his head, deep, dark eyes with long lashes above the sensuous mouth, naturally tanned skin and a slight appearance of what she thought might be Native American blood, and noted hazily, as her head was swimming, that she might be looking at the most beautiful man she had ever seen.

Or perhaps she just thought that because he was standing at the threshold between life and death for them all.

The only one who had a clue what he was doing.

"Here's where it gets complicated," he said.

Chapter 15

"OF COURSE IT does," Lucy said hollowly. "It's been a cakewalk up until now."

Ace glanced out the window.

"In a moment, a rope is going to appear," he said, ignoring her words. "It will have two harnesses on it—a Swiss Seat, a rappelling harness, like for mountain climbing, and a smaller one—a safety harness. There are a bunch of strapping guys on the roof with a winch, who will pull me and each of my passengers up to the roof, then lower me back down for another passenger."

Lucy exhaled steadily but said nothing.

"I'll keep coming up and down until everyone is safely on the roof. Then we'll get hoisted into the helicopter, which you can undoubtedly hear hovering above the school, and get the heck out of here. Does that make sense?"

Lucy just blinked. "Nothing—nothing makes sense," she said, "but I think I understand."

"I'm gonna take Sloane first," Ace continued. "There are medics on the roof, waiting, and she needs attention first." Lucy nodded. "Then Elisa, Grace, Sarah, and finally Corinne, who I judge to be the most fit and whose stamina is likely to last the longest."

"OK."

"Then I'll be back down for you."

"You had better be," she said flatly, "since you un-hooked yourself from me yet again. So much for never letting me go. Hmph."

The National Guardsman smiled his slight smile again. He turned and looked out the window.

As he had said, a rope was dangling outside, two har-nesses attached to it.

While Ace pulled his legs through the harness' loops and fastened it around his waist, Lucy gently separated Sloane out from the shivering pile of little girls clinging to one another.

"Now's your time to play princess, Cinderella," she said softly in the little girl's ear, feeling how cold her skin was. "Prince Charming's about to get you out of here, and all you have to do is hug him tight. Do you think you can do that?"

Sloane said nothing, staring blankly in front of her.

Lucy took her in her arms and kissed her, then brought her over to where Ace was holding a small safety harness. Together they put the little girl into it; Ace clipped her to himself and took her from Lucy.

Then he handed her the radio.

"Simple to use," he said. "Press the button and talk—that's it. Tell the guys on the roof we're ready."

Lucy nodded sharply, her eyes locked on him, gleaming.

"Get up there safely," she said.

Ace smiled a little more broadly. "Yes, ma'am." Then he nodded at her and took the rope in his hand.

Lucy pushed the button on the radio. "He's ready," she said.

"Copy," came a voice in return.

Ace continued to smile at her as the rope went taut, then began to lift him and Sloane out through the emergency window and up the side of the building. His feet came to rest against the edifice, and he walked up the face of it.

Lucy leaned out and watched from below until they disappeared over the edge of the roof.

"Clear," the radio squawked. "Got 'em."

Lucy sighed brokenly, more relieved than she remembered ever feeling.

After a few moments, the radio squawked again.

"Go," the voice said.

She looked up.

Boots were approaching from above.

Lucy stepped back to the huddle of girls and peeled off Elisa, as Ace had instructed, and brought her the two steps over to the window where he was appearing again.

"Clear," she said into the radio as he came back into the room.

"Listen to you," he said, grinning. "You're a pro—you'll be in the department in no time."

"My life's goal," she said sourly as she took the little harness from him and started helping Elisa into it.

The little girl balked suddenly, panicking as if she had just awoken, twisting away and screaming raggedly.

The reaction caught Lucy by surprise. "Elisa—"

"It's just like a swing, honey," Ace said quickly. "Like we're playing on the playground. Come on; I'll make sure you're OK."

Something about his voice, Lucy thought as the little girl's tight face went slack. *So different when he's working than in regular life. He barely talks when he's not running a rescue.*

For what seemed like an agonizingly long time, they worked together with the unseen firefighters on the roof, hauling each child up, until finally he returned for Corinne.

"All right, sweetie," Lucy said as Ace came back through the window. "You ready?"

The little girl, who Lucy was holding in her arms, sat up straight, as if hit by lightning.

She glanced rapidly around the room.

Her eyes coming to rest on the aquarium several feet away on the shelf near the window.

"Sebastian!" she said, her voice raspy. "We—we have to save him!"

"Corinne," Lucy said quietly as the athletic little girl squirmed in her arms, "you have to go with Sergeant Evans now—"

"No!" the little girl screeched. "No—please—!"

Ace's eyebrows drew together. "Sebastian?"

"The turtle," Lucy said, struggling now to keep Corinne from falling into the frigid water. Her arms, weak now from the cold, were throbbing with the effort.

"I'm not going! I'm not going without him—"

"Corinne, *stop*—"

"OK," Ace said, striding through the deep water and putting his arms out. "You've been a good sport, Corinne. Let's get him and get out of here."

Lucy's mouth dropped open. She stood in amazement as the soldier snatched the little girl from her and, in a few long steps, reached the aquarium. He shoved the cover aside, snatched the startled reptile out, and tucked him into the pocket of his fire pants.

Then he carried the child back to the window.

"Now step into the harness," he ordered as he put her on the shelf. The comforting tone was gone, replaced by one that was all business.

Corinne's eyes opened wider, and she quickly obeyed.

"You OK, ma'am?" he asked Lucy as they fastened Corinne's straps. The teacher nodded.

"I will be right back," Ace said as he hooked himself to the little girl and both of them to the rope.

"You had better be," Lucy replied, shaking from the cold and nervousness now. "I will haunt you if you let me go."

"That's incentive to hurry, then," Ace said. "Wouldn't want that. Let 'em know we're ready."

Lucy complied, then felt her stomach drop as the soldier and the last of her students were pulled up the side of the building toward the roof.

She glanced around her drowning classroom, watching the water cover the desks, the bookshelves, the toys and everything that, only this morning, seemed safe and normal. The clock on the wall had stopped exactly at 10:12, probably the time when the electricity had shorted out, she thought. She rubbed her hands briskly up and down her arms, but could barely feel her fingers any more.

"Clear," came the voice over the radio.

She held the radio up in front of her mouth, her eyes still locked on the dead classroom clock.

"Copy that," she said.

After that, for what seemed like forever, Lucy had no idea what time it was. The sky was still gray-black as it had been that morning, so she had no idea whether it was even the same day.

She was still staring blindly at the clock when Ace returned.

"Knock knock."

She spun around as quickly as she could. Her skirt swirled in the floodwaters, and she winced, knowing it had been doing so most of the day.

And, to make matters even more embarrassing, Ace was handing over a harness with leg loops to her.

"Do you need help getting it on?" he asked, watching her take it doubtfully.

"No," Lucy said. She slipped it up over the skirt, anchoring it in place, somewhat uncomfortable but better for her dignity.

"Give me your hand," the soldier said, extending his own. When Lucy did, he hauled her easily out of the water until she was standing beside him on the shelf over the long heater.

Then he clipped their waist harnesses once more.

"Together again," he said jokingly, taking the radio back.

"Good—you're safe from haunting for the moment," she said. "Is the turtle still in your pocket?"

"No, he's most likely in the chopper by now. Come on, ma'am. Put your arms around my waist and hold on."

The world grew dark as Lucy heard him call the fire-fighters on the roof, telling them they were ready. Then he seized the ropes with both his gloved hands. Her sodden hair was wafting around in the wind outside the window, so she tucked her head down against Ace's suspenders and held tight as the winch on the roof above began to turn, pulling the rope up.

As they started the final climb up the edifice of the school.

Chapter 16

LUCY STUMBLED ONTO the roof a few moments later as Ace shoved her up over the top, scraping her knees against the rough pebbling atop it, her hair suddenly spinning in a roaring sound of wind and helicopter blades.

Then looked around at a scene she could never have imagined.

A large rescue helicopter was hovering above the school, ripping torrents of wind around and stirring up clouds of debris in the center of the roof. The last two girls, Corinne and Sarah, were being strapped to a long, flat basket in preparation for being lifted into the chopper.

Even through the currents of air she could see that Corinne was clutching an object that must have been Sebastian.

Ace took her elbow and had her walk beside him, since they were still hooked together, to the two firefighters and a pair of soldiers in military fatigues operating the winch, a much smaller machine than she had expected. They conferred with each other and, over the radio, to the ground below, again in jargon that made no sense to her exhausted brain. Then Ace turned to her once more.

"Come on, ma'am," he said. "We're almost there. Cover your head with your arm."

She walked beside him, stooped over as he was, until they were standing beneath the chopper.

The flat basket was rising now into the belly of the helicopter.

"Do you feel comfortable going up the rope on your own?" Ace asked, watching the crew of the chopper pull the basket aboard.

"Lying down in the basket?"

Ace blinked. "Not unless you're injured, usually," he said. "I think they expect to pull you up in your harness."

He swallowed at the sick look that overcame Lucy's face.

"Or I could go up the rope with you," he said.

"I think I would prefer that."

Ace nodded, disconnected himself from her and stepped away from the area directly below the chopper, speaking into the radio again. He returned a moment later.

"Sorry to ask, ma'am—how much do you weigh?"

"One twenty one, at my last physical," Lucy said. "It's been three months—"

"That's fine," he said. He waited in silence until the rope was dropped down again.

"The helicopter also has a winch," he said as he hooked them together for what she expected was the last time. "It should be a pretty smooth ascent."

"Wonderful. Are they ready? I'd like to get this over with."

Ace checked the cables and the carabineers. "All set. Grab hold."

Lucy put her arms around him again, and Ace radioed their readiness.

The wind tugged at her skirt, anchored by the leg loops of the harness, as they were lifted slowly into the hovering helicopter.

Heavy clouds of fog were hanging over the school. Lucy felt the moisture against her face as she was dragged upward through the mist, a strange sensation in the strangest day she had ever known.

Then, just beneath the opening in the bottom of the chopper, the mist dispersed and she could see the school, the playground, the football field and the river from above.

She gasped so harshly that Ace's grip on her tightened.

The gentle Hudson River, normally a picturesque ribbon of water no more than fifty feet wide, closer to twenty at its lowest point, laughing over visible rocks in the spring and fall, winding its way quietly in summer, was roaring angrily to the east, having swallowed everything between it and the school. And to the west of the school was the overspill, another river, less wide but equally angry, swelling around the bottom of the monkey bars and swingsets of the playground, digging big ruts in the football field beyond.

Where no one remained who had been there when she dashed into the school again.

Ace was being pulled into the helicopter. For a few terrifying moments, Lucy was hanging alone, suspended over the destruction of her workplace.

Her hometown.

A soldier in a helmet and goggles was shouting instructions at her, but she couldn't hear him.

She tried to put her hand to her ear, but when she let go of the rope, she swung from side to side.

Her National Guardsman compatriot was staring down at her from above. Lucy had the uncomfortable realization that he was in the direct line of sight of her breasts, the tops largely exposed by the snapping wind.

As the rope continued to swing, she felt her stomach rush into her mouth and she spat out a foamy stream of liquid.

From within the helicopter's hold, Ace reached out and snagged her rope, pulling her, along with the winch, into the chopper.

As her legs flailed helplessly he seized her backside and upper thigh and dragged her over the edge of the opening. She scrambled as far into the center of the hold as she could, humiliated, as he let go.

Inside the tight quarters of the chopper, two medics were examining the girls, all lying on the floor of the aircraft.

"What about the guys on the roof?" she asked foggily as the helicopter rose into the air and started away from the school.

"They're OK," Ace said, looking out the open door. "They'll wait until you and the kids have been offloaded and put into the ambulances, and then the aircraft will go back for them."

"Ambulances? Why doesn't the helicopter just take us

all to the hospital?"

Ace didn't look at her, but instead continued to watch the ground, calculating the size of the flood.

"There's a lot of demand for the helicopters in town," he said quietly. "A lot of people need rescuing."

"Of course. I'm sorry."

"No need to be." It seemed to Lucy that Ace was thinking about saying something else, but the helicopter was already on the farthest side of the high school fields where soccer was played in the fall, lacrosse in the spring, and preparing to set down in a wide, flat space ringed with survivors, teachers, administrators, and parents, the looks on their faces appearing more and more apprehensive as the aircraft descended.

Lucy blinked at the sheer number of rescue vehicles that were ringing or sitting on the fields, from many different companies in the adjoining towns. Five ambulances were standing ready as the copter set down.

"Don't get out until they tell you," Ace advised. "Those blades are deadly."

Lucy, who was preparing to jump out, stopped.

As a deep whine screamed through the air, indicating the blades were slowing, Ace took hold of her arm again. He pointed into the distance.

"Look," he said.

Waiting anxiously at a distance, accompanied by four soldiers from the National Guard Unit of Saranac Lake, the base where Ace was assigned, was a group of adults standing, singly and in pairs, staring at the opening where Ace and Lucy were now sitting.

Even to Ace, who had never met any of them, it was clear who they were.

The parents of the kids in the chopper.

He leaned closer to her and spoke in her ear.

"You're about to make all those people happier than they've ever been before, ma'am."

One of the helicopter's crew gave Ace the nod. He unhooked himself from Lucy for the last time and jumped out of the chopper, then turned and took her by the waist, assisting her out as well.

Then pulled her out of the way of the five teams of medical personnel and the soldiers assigned to them, rushing forward with five gurneys on wheels, making their way to the choppers, fighting with the muddy grass.

Lucy watched, sick to her stomach, as each of the little girls, already swathed in heavy military blankets, was handed out of the helicopter by its crew to the medics, then stretched out onto the gurneys.

One of the anxious mothers consulted with a nearby soldier and then, as he stepped aside, walked quickly forward, carrying a medical bag. Lucy recognized her as Dr. Patricia Byrnes, Corinne's mother, a well-known and highly respected pediatrician. She breathed a sigh of relief as Dr. Byrnes quickly examined each of the girls, giving instructions to the military medics, and then moved on to another as the children were brought to the ambulances.

"One parent can ride along to the hospital," a soldier with a bullhorn was announcing to the assembled group of parents who were anxiously watching Dr. Byrnes as she made her assessments. "Once that parent has been determined, please step into the ambulance and move all the way to the seat near the front of the vehicle. *One* parent. No exceptions; sorry, folks."

As if her legs had a mind of their own, Lucy found herself making her way to the girls' families who were still waiting for their children to be checked over. She came up to a man in a crisp business suit, slightly balding, whom she recognized at Willis Wallace, Sloane's father. His family was one of the oldest and richest in West Obergrande.

"Mr. Wallace," she said quietly, "I'm Lucy Sullivan, Sloane's teacher."

At first the man did not seem to hear her, staring as intently as he was at the front of the helicopter. Then, as her words registered, he turned abruptly to her.

"Miss Sullivan? Oh, God, thank you—*thank you.* I heard you went back into the school to get them out. Is she all right?"

Lucy swallowed as the other parents, hearing her name, began crowding around her.

"I believe so," she said, her teeth still chattering, still shaking from the water and the exposure. "She was so brave—they were all so—brave—"

A cacophony of voices broke out, each of the parents begging for word on their daughters.

Lucy's head was swimming.

"They—they're all alive, and mostly just scared, I think—Dr. Byrnes will know more," she said, taking Professor Byrnes' trembling hand and squeezing it. "We tried—to keep them out of the water as much as we could—"

Suddenly, the world seemed to be shrinking and turning black.

Ace, who had quietly followed her, caught her as she collapsed on the muddy field, over to the west of Tree Hill Park.

The last thing she remembered was the ring of faces above her, the parents who had been waiting for word of their little girls, staring down at her as everything faded away.

WHILE DR. BYRNES was still examining the girls in the lights of the emergency vehicles, the medic from Ace's unit looked over Lucy.

"She's gonna need fluids," he said to Ace, who had carried her back to the outside of the now-still chopper. "And heat—if there's another ambulance available—"

"There's not," said a senior officer who was directing medical response vehicles around the field, which was being used as a M.A.S.H. unit for the entire town. "We've had twenty-three companies respond, and every one of their transport vehicles is taken."

"I'm fine," Lucy muttered, her eyes still closed. "All I need is a hot shower and a shot of whiskey, Jameson's, if possible. Oh, and to make sure my cat's all right. Other than that, I'm dandy."

She put out her hand. "Somebody help me up, please."

"I think you should stay put for the moment, ma'am—"

Lucy's eyes, a glorious shade of Irish blue, popped

open.

"All right, I'll get up by myself." She started to rise, then felt a large, calloused hand seize hers.

Ace pulled her to a stand, shaking his head.

The children on the gurneys nearby, now more awake, were anxious, looking around desperately for their parents, and beginning to weep. Lucy came over to each of them and smiled as bravely as she could.

"Your parents will be with you in a few minutes," she told them in as reassuring a way as she could muster. "Dr. Byrnes is just trying to make sure you're all OK. I am *so* proud of you guys."

Five nervous pairs of eyes were fixed on her. Even Sloane was awake, staring at her.

"While we wait, let me tell you a quick story," Lucy went on. "It's a story about Obergrande—the tree, and the town, and some brave ladies just like you."

She wrapped her arms around herself, trying to get warm. A moment later, she felt the sensation of heat as a Red Cross volunteer encircled her with a blanket.

"Thanks," she said, turning, but the man was already on to others in need. She looked back at her little students again, a fondness beyond measure swelling in her heart.

"So, a *very* long time ago, hundreds and hundreds of years ago, when Obergrande, the tree and the town, was new, there were only about ten families here. They lived in cabins and had to work very hard, because they were building a settlement from the Adirondack forests.

"One winter, the men of the tiny town went hunting together to gather food for the long winter ahead. While they were gone, another group of men that wanted their land and their things attacked their settlement, with just the women and the children there. This could have been a very bad thing—a lot like the flood in the school today was a very bad thing.

"But the women of the settlement that would one day be our town fought back. They were brave, and strong, and they knew how to take care of themselves. And, most important, they refused to give up, no matter what—a lot like you guys did today."

She lapsed into silence, suddenly feeling weak.

"Did they win?" Sarah asked, her voice shaking.

Lucy smiled raggedly. "They sure did. And when their husbands came home from hunting, they saw their town had been attacked, but it was still standing—and their wives were there, cleaning up the mess from the fight, like nothing had ever happened.

"So the husbands decided to have a celebration and to name the women the Eight Queens of Obergrande, even though it was a silly thing, because you can't have eight queens of anything."

"Right," said Sloane. "Only one at a time." She coughed again.

"The men just wanted the women to know how proud they were of them—just like your parents and I are proud of you today."

"And Prince Charmin'?" Corinne asked.

Lucy glanced around, but did not see Ace. The parents, however, were being led quietly over to where the gurneys were. "Yes—I know he's proud of you, too. So, I think we should name you girls The Five Princesses of Obergrande, like the Eight Queens—" She turned to the approaching parents. "What do you think?"

"Highly appropriate," said Professor Byrnes, smiling down widely at his little girl.

Mr. Wallace was leaning over his little redhead. "Where's Mommy?" Sloane asked her father as he took her hand and kissed it.

"Out of town, remember, honey?"

The little girl looked crestfallen. "Oh, yeah. Gone again."

From across the park, a firefighter was approaching, running, heading for the helicopter. He ran straight to the gurney and, in complete violation of the briefing given to the other parents by the Army medic, bent over Sarah and threw his arms around her, hugging her gently but tightly.

When he released her and pulled up, tears were streaming down his face.

"Sarah," he whispered over and over again. "Sarah. Sarah. Sarah—"

"It's OK, Daddy," the little dirty-blonde girl said solemnly. "I'm fine. There's no need to cry—unless you stuck'ed forks in your eyes. Then I think I would cry too."

Around the assemblage of parents and rescue personnel, a roll of chuckling laughter went up.

The first really happy sound the field had heard that day.

"Mommy and the baobabs will be so happy you're fine, and so proud of you," Dave Windsor said to his daughter, who shrugged.

"Well, now we is princesses, they *should* be proud," she said. "If I'm a princess, does that make Blythe and Bonnie princesses too?"

Dave, who had missed the story, just nodded, overwhelmed with relief.

Hovering anxiously at the edge of the group were Elisa's parents, Mr. and Mrs. Santiago, who looked exhausted, and Grace's mother and father, the Reverend Fuller and his wife, Kathy.

"No sé donde nos alojaremos," Mr. Santiago whispered to his wife. "La casa se ha ido."

Kathy Fuller, overhearing them, smiled and took Mrs. Santiago's elbow.

"Your house is gone?" she asked gently.

The Santiagos exchanged a glance, then nodded.

"I'm so sorry," Mrs. Fuller said.

"Not a problem," Reverend Fuller added. "We have plenty of room at the parsonage of the church. You can stay with us."

Mr. Santiago looked nervous. "We—we are—"

The Fullers waited patiently.

Finally he finished his thought. "We are Catholic."

The Fullers chuckled. "That's all right," Reverend Fuller said. "We speak Catholic."

At that moment Dr. Byrnes finished her exam, then spoke quickly to the Army medics. She came back and signaled for the parents to step away from the gurneys.

"They are in remarkable condition under the circumstances," she said in her beautiful, low-pitched voice, a voice that had a calming effect on the frazzled group of parents. "Sloane has suffered the most by far; she was submerged, it seems, inhaled some water and I'm sure is quite traumatized. The rest of them have some minor hypothermia, which is beginning to be treated as we speak, and, of course, they are all very frightened. I suggest we look into some short-term group therapy immediately. They survived this together; I think it's best we try to facilitate their recovery together."

The other parents nodded.

"Time for transport," said the Army medic who had been managing the triage. "Whichever parent is riding along, please board the ambulance. We'll be leaving in ninety seconds."

Lucy raised her fist in the air.

"Princess Power!" she said.

Each of the little girls responded as well as they could.

"The Fearless Fivesome," Lucy said quietly as the gurneys began to be taken away, remembering what Ace had called them.

Reverend Fuller, whose wife was riding along with Grace, touched her elbow.

"We can never, never thank you enough, Miss Sullivan," he said in his soothing, musical voice that Lucy had heard at parent-teacher meetings. "But we are definitely going to try, when everything is right again."

"Indeed, I'm at a loss for words to express my gratitude," said Professor Byrnes, who was also staying behind. "And, if you told my college students that, they would never believe it's possible for me to be at a loss for words."

Dave Windsor said nothing. He was distracted by the

sight of his wife, exiting Lenny Verillo's SUV, a twin in each arm.

Then he ran at breakneck speed, straight toward her, sweeping the rest of his girls into a wild hug.

"I'm going with Sarah to the hospital," Susan said within his embrace. "Lenny's going to watch the girls with his granddaughter, Abby." She pulled her head up and whispered in his ear. "Lenny's daughter, Abby's mom, is missing."

Dave exhaled deeply, then nodded. His crew was part of the search for her and the other people in her flooded office building that had, until this morning, stood by the river's edge.

"There's a spare playpen at the church," said Reverend Fuller. He turned to Mrs. Santiago, whose husband was already heading toward the ambulance. "I expect we will be opening the church hall to a lot of people in your same situation tonight—can you give me a hand until I see who shows up to help?"

"Of course," said Mrs. Santiago. She was looking at the ambulance with her little girl and husband aboard, pulling away into the dusk.

As the four others did a moment later, one by one.

On their way to the hospital in Emmettsville.

Dave Windsor stood in silence, watching them leave.

Then he took off his glove and turned to Sue. "We won't be able to stay in the house tonight," he said, running his hand over her tangled hair. "That whole area of town is a controlled zone; there's no power or running water, even if the house is still standing. Find a Red Cross worker—you'll know them by the badge, of course—and get directed to putting your name on the list for shelter. Be careful—it's chaos all over town, especially between here and the west end of Tree Hill Park, but that's where a lot of the aid workers are."

Susan nodded and put her hand over his, resting it against her cheek for a long moment.

"We are blessed," she whispered.

"Sure are," Dave said. "I love you. Forever and ever, honey. Give Sarah lots of kisses for me, and have a good ride to the hospital."

Then he kissed his wife and baby daughters, put his helmet back on, and returned to the trenches of Hell.

Chapter 17

A S THE AMBULANCES began to pull away one by one, carrying each of the girls and the parent accompanying her to Medical Emergency Center in Emmettsville to be checked over, Sergeant Evans came over to Lucy Sullivan.

It took him a few moments to find her, because she was wrapped in a Red Cross blanket, her curly long hair hidden from view.

"Miss Sullivan?"

Lucy didn't appear to hear him. Her face was blank, her eyes locked on the emergency vehicles, each one bearing a child she loved away from the nightmare they had all survived.

Together.

Even though the logical part of her brain was not really functioning, the thought that passed through her mind was that somehow this had bonded the girls to each other for life.

And all of them to her as well.

I'm going to worry about them forever now, she thought.

"Ma'am?"

She said nothing.

"Ma'am," Ace said quietly, "who do you have here waiting for you?"

After a few moments, she blinked.

"No one," she said. Her voice was hollow.

"No family in town?" the soldier pressed.

"No family, period." As the flashing lights of the last of ambulances disappeared into the darkness, she sighed and let her head drop. "Lost my mom when I was twelve, my dad four years ago—at least he got to see me graduate from college with my Masters—first one in the family. Then the last one, my grandmother, last year. So, no one. On the bright side—at least there was no one worrying about me the way so many of these folks are worrying. But thanks for asking."

"Let me get you someone from the Red Cross—"

Lucy's head snapped up and she glared at him. "No, thank you. I'm fine."

"OK," said Sergeant Evans.

He turned quickly and disappeared.

Lucy returned to watching the rescue workers—the National Guardsmen in their fatigues, the Red Cross aides with their symbol on their arms and chests, and the firefighters from the Obergrande volunteer companies scrambling like ants, moving with surprising organization through the wreckage that had once been her adopted hometown. She tried to form a coherent thought, to make a determination about where to go next, what to do, but her mind seemed to be filled with the heavy mist through which the helicopter had lifted her.

A moment later, a gentle nudge at her elbow brought her around again.

Ace stood in front of her once more, a cup of steaming coffee in his hand.

"Please drink this, ma'am," he said. "Sorry it isn't Jameson's."

Lucy snorted wryly. *"Ma'am?* What is it with you and 'ma'am'? How old are you, Sergeant?"

"Twenty-seven."

"Well, you're two years older than me. 'Ma'am' seems a little over the top, wouldn't you say?"

The soldier shrugged, but a fragment of a smile touched the corner of his mouth, a mouth that Lucy had first noticed was sensual and pleasant when he was staring in her car window the night before, his upper lip shaped like Cupid's bow.

"Standard operating procedure, ma'—er, Miss Sullivan."

Lucy eyed him humorously, a little bit of light coming back into her eyes. She took a deep swig of the coffee.

"Even 'Miss Sullivan' seems a little formal, given that I know you've seen my boobs from above today at least once, and you had your hand on my butt and up my skirt, or at least on my thigh, when you pulled me into the helicopter, Sergeant," she said jokingly, holding the Styrofoam cup in both hands and trying to keep the blanket from falling off her. "You could probably get away with calling me 'Lucy,' I think."

"Sorry, Miss Sullivan," Ace said solemnly. "I'm on duty."

Lucy nodded. "Ah. I see. Well, I'm glad groping my caboose and my thigh was something you were allowed to do while on duty, but calling me 'Lucy' isn't."

"Yes, ma'am."

She drank the rest of the coffee.

"There's some intake information the Red Cross needs, if you feel up to giving it," the young soldier pressed carefully. "Just information about your residence, your car—"

"Oh crap," Lucy said, desperation rising in her voice, "did the flood get my *car,* too?"

"Was it in the faculty parking lot?"

"Yessss," Lucy said faintly.

Sergeant Evans cleared his throat uncomfortably.

Lucy closed her eyes. "What about my house?"

The soldier reached into his gear and pulled out a folded map of town.

"Where's your house?"

"Second Street," Lucy whispered, her voice almost gone. "River side of the street."

Sergeant Evans opened the map and consulted it in the beam of his flashlight. "Second street is borderline. Maybe yes, maybe no."

"Can we go there?" Lucy asked desperately. "My—oh, no, Sadie—my cat—omigod—"

"It's a controlled zone at the moment," the soldier said uncomfortably. "No admittance, except for rescue workers. I'm sorry, Miss Sullivan."

"Sergeant, *please,*" Lucy begged. "Sadie is my only family. Please."

Ace looked uncomfortable. "Uhmm—"

Lucy did not have to try to look pathetic; her eyes had already filled with tears and her chin was quivering.

Sergeant Evans exhaled in defeat.

"Can you show me a driver's license or some sort of ID that proves you live on Second Street?" he asked, looking around so as not to be overheard.

"I—yes! I took my wallet out of the classroom with me!" Lucy said, her hopes rising. "It's—it's around here somewhere—"

Sergeant Evans cleared his throat again, rumbling deeper this time.

"Was it that *plop* from a falling object as you were being lifted into the helicopter?"

Lucy felt quickly in her bra, finding it empty of anything but what it was meant to hold. She sank to the ground in a flood of tears and a cyclone of curse words.

Ace cleared his throat again. He crouched down in front of her.

"Well, I think I saw your wallet—at least for a moment—so I guess I can take you into the zone. I have to check in with Colonel Genovese, and my commanding officer from my unit—we're deployed for rescue, though I expect they may reassign me to the dam tomorrow. It may be a while before I can get back to you tonight, but, if you want to wait, I'll come back. Without fail."

"Well, I had big plans for a night on the town, but I suppose I can make room on my dance card for you, since you've been so accommodating, Sergeant," Lucy said, a sour note in her voice.

Ace smiled. "I'm honored, ma'am. If you get help or shelter from the Red Cross, or need to go somewhere else, no problem. I will have plenty to do here if you need to leave the dance early."

Lucy looked at him and felt a sudden swell of remorse rise inside her. She had displayed a wide range of emotions that day, many of them ugly, and in response he had been unfailingly pleasant. She cleared her throat.

"No, I'll wait. My dad always told me to dance with the one that brung you, and let him take you home. So, since you brung me, and are probably the only one I know who's willing, and authorized, to take me to my house, I guess I'll just be patient."

The Sergeant's slight smile widened, and he nodded. "All right. Get something to eat and drink, and stay warm as you can," he advised. "I'll grab you another cup of coffee, and I'll be back as soon as I can."

He rose as smoothly as she had seen him do the night before, and melted into the dark.

Chapter 18

7:16 PM

LUCY PULLED THE blanket higher up around her neck and took another sip of her second cup of coffee, lukewarm now. She watched the scenes, some happy, of parents and children being reunited, or sad, parents desperately searching for unaccounted-for kids, most of whom had stayed home that day. As far as she could tell, all of the kids who had been in the building had been successfully rescued.

She glanced at one point to her right and saw a mother huddled with two children on her lap, both boys, it seemed, hugging them tightly and staring blankly off into the coming night.

Lucy squinted in the dark, then allowed the beam of her flashlight to brush across them, as all the emergency lights were routinely doing.

And smiled.

The woman on the ground was Mrs. Burlingame, whom she had threatened with hair pulling to Mrs. Cox the day before, with both her sons, Garrett and Devin.

Safe, and grateful.

She was grateful herself just to be out of the ever-present water in the school building.

Her tired mind wandered back a few hours to the memory of the young Sergeant standing in the window just before he began his series of climbs up and down the outside wall, and shook her head in amazement. The dark eyes were like searchlights, almost looking through her, the mouth that was haunting her thoughts, making her own lips buzz—there was no doubt that Ace Evans was pretty to look at.

She shook her head to drive out the memory of how his body looked as he stood in the window, the strong neck above heavily muscled arms and shoulders, a waist that tapered down into the turnout gear. She had not gotten a clear view of anything below his waist, swallowed as it was in the heavy rubber fire pants and suspenders, but she could only imagine what his legs must look like, legs that had strode without difficulty through deep flood waters, carrying three children on his broad back, or rappelling repeatedly up and down the exterior wall of the school, taking each of the five girls, and her, to safety.

And now he was back in the command of his unit, being deployed elsewhere in the suffering town.

Lucy's brain told her she should feel weak, outclassed, but her mind was too tired to care.

"Lucy?" The voice, craggy and exhausted, came from the air above her. "Lucy Sullivan?"

Lucy looked up.

Eleanor Preston, the ninety-two-year-old town historian, was standing above her, resting both hands on her cane and staring down at her sympathetically.

She started to rise, but Eleanor put up her hand.

"Well, you've had quite the day, I hear. Can I get you anything?" the historian asked. "More coffee? Something to eat?"

Lucy shook her head. "Thanks, Eleanor—I'm all right."

"You're an East-sider, aren't you?"

Lucy nodded. "Second Street."

Eleanor exhaled. "I'll pray for you. Have you found a place to stay?"

She shook her head. "Not yet. Don't know if I need one."

The elderly lady's brows drew together, and she chuckled in her famous rasp.

"Oh, you'll need one, all right," she said, causing Lucy's stomach to cramp. "Whether the flood got your house or not, there's no electricity on that side of town. You'd best be prepared to bug out to higher ground."

Lucy's head came to rest on her knees, suddenly too tired to remain upright.

Just then, several news reporters approached in a jangle of harsh words and voices that were clearly not from Obergrande. They had been traveling back and forth across the fields and the west side of Tree Hill Park all day, documenting and reporting on the flood, trying to stop busy firefighters who waved them away before the reporters could get an interview, or attempting to speak to dazed victims, in one case almost causing a fist fight between a cameraman and a grieving husband.

"Where?" a blond woman in her thirties was saying into her headphones as she walked, a flashlight in her hand and a camera crew right behind her. "What's she look like?"

Lucy's head rose from her knees and she looked up, exchanging a glance with Eleanor.

The reporter looked around, swinging the flashlight, and snapping its beam at Lucy.

"Lucy? Lucy Sullivan?"

Lucy squinted in the light. "Yes?"

"Oh boy," Eleanor muttered under her breath, shaking her head. "Mistake Number One."

"Gwyneth Cumber, Channel Three. You're the first grade teacher—"

"I—I teach kindergarten," Lucy stammered, struggling to get up. She felt suddenly vulnerable on the ground.

"Wonderful. You're the kindergarten teacher who got the four little girls out—?"

"Five," Lucy said, starting to shake. "Five—uh, please, I really don't want—"

Eleanor planted her cane into the ground and took a careful step closer to Lucy.

"Let's get some light here," the reporter said to her camera crew.

A sudden explosion of lights, brighter than the sun at midday, stabbed Lucy's eyes, causing both her and the historian to turn rapidly away, their arms across their faces, Lucy muttering a string of Irish curse words under her breath.

Gwyneth Cumber looked around and muttered a curse word herself.

From other corners of the park and the streets, several other news teams were hurrying over, some in vans, some on foot, running.

"Great—everybody's seen us. Let's roll tape so we can get something exclusive." She stepped as close to Lucy as she could and spoke into her microphone.

"This is Gwyneth Cumber, Channel Three Action News, reporting live from Obergrande, New York, the scene of the worst flooding in New York State on record as counted in fatalities. I'm speaking with Lucy Sullivan, the brave young kindergarten teacher who defied orders of the fire department and ran back into the flooding school to save five of her young students from drowning." She put the microphone in Lucy's face. "Miss Sullivan, why do you think the first responders were willing to leave those students in the flooding school?"

"Wha—what?" Lucy had been shivering from the cold night wind and her sodden clothes; now she was trembling from confusion and shaking with anger. "That's—that's not what happened—"

Voices were approaching rapidly around her, causing her head to spin.

"Miss Sullivan! Miss Sullivan!"

"Where's that handsome firefighter who carried you up the side of the school to safety? Is he around here?"

"Yeah, I got some great footage of that—showed a lot of leg, no ass, unfortunately. Nice gams, by the way, Lucy—"

A crowd was around her now, assaulting her with bright light.

"Lucy! Lucy! Did you hear First Lady Barbara Bush maybe be coming in tomorrow to view the disaster? What do you think of that?"

"Lucy—tell us about your brave escape—"

"Lucy! Lucy—are any of the little girls hurt?"

"Do you think you'll write a book?"

"Who would you like to play you in the movie?"

"What's it feel like to be a hero, Lucy?"

"Did you lose anyone in the flood, Miss Sullivan?"

Gwyneth Cumber, none too pleased at having to share her exclusive, was firing off questions that were too fast for Lucy's foggy brain to process. The reporters' demands had become nothing but noise, sentences piling on top of one another.

Lucy, the focus of live international cable news television coverage and a spotlight of solar-level brightness, burst into tears and wept aloud.

The noise level fell as the shouted questions ceased momentarily.

Resuming a moment later.

"Lucy—Lucy!"

"Miss Sullivan, look over here—"

Eleanor Preston had had enough.

The historian lifted her cane and waved it at the reporters with a stabbing motion.

"Back!" she shouted in her commanding, raspy voice as she swung the cane like a sword. "Back, you brutes! You ruffians—you—you *swine*. Leave her alone! Give her air, for goodness' sake—she's in shock."

The reporters stared in sudden silence.

Then, from the outskirts of the group, a call went up.

"Lucy—do you think there should be a lawsuit—?"

"Bugger off!" Lucy screamed. *"Leave me alone,* dammit!"

She tried to turn, but her stomach rushed into her mouth.

And she vomited in full view of the camera.

Right onto Gwyneth Cumber's shoes.

Splashing her microphone in the process.

The reporters looked at one another. The reporter closest to Lucy recovered first.

"Reporting live from the scene of the disaster, Gwyneth Cumber, Channel Three Action News."

The bright lights were suddenly extinguished, and Lucy, still bent over at the waist, heard the blond reporter as she turned away.

"Well, *that* was gross."

Exhausted and sick as she was, Lucy could not suppress a smile.

SOMETIME LATER, LUCY, sitting alone, wrapped in the Red Cross blanket, felt a warm arm sliding across her back and anchoring itself on her shoulder.

She looked up anxiously, then smiled as tears sprang into her eyes.

"How ya doing?" Kelly Moran asked, holding Lucy close against her chest.

"Oh lord." They were the only words Lucy could

bring herself to utter in the depths of Kelly's embrace.

"You all right?" Lucy asked, wiping the tears away with the Red Cross blanket.

"I'm fine. Rick's with the fire department, so I haven't seen him in a while, but I know—we both know—the other spouse is OK, so we're good. You're a beast, you know that? I couldn't be prouder of my supervising teacher. You are The Woman."

"Now all I want to be is the woman home in bed, but I don't think that's happening," Lucy said morosely.

"Not in your own bed, most likely," said Kelly, sitting down beside her. She looked up into the dark sky split with moving beams of light from television crews and rescue vehicles, almost like an insane dance.

"Can you believe it?" she said, staring above her.

Lucy looked up as well. "What?"

"That tree's arms reach all the way out over here, almost to the edge of the park," Kelly mused, her eyes on the occasionally visible shadows of Obergrande's great limbs. "Like it's protecting us, even all the way over here, even now, after this awful day."

"A truly awful day," Lucy agreed. She closed her eyes.

"Did you hear about Eleanor?" Kelly asked, handing Lucy her fourth cup of coffee that evening.

Lucy took and opened it gratefully. "No—is she OK?"

"OK? She's a new cable news star. After you got out of there, one of the news organizations found out that she is the town historian—as well as being quite the ninety-two-year-old rock star—so they actually *asked* if they could interview her, what a concept." Kelly took a hit off her own cup of coffee. "She's a natural, especially with that wonderful voice. She held court, after dressing down the people who were bothering you, then went on to explain all sorts of interesting history, including previous floods, the historic treaties, the French-and-Indian-War thing about the Queens of the Town, and a few bawdy stories that made both the news reporters and the people sitting around listening laugh. Ooop—here she comes now."

The whirr of a scooter motor approaching caught Lucy's ear. She took another sip of the coffee, then stood, coming over to Eleanor's "chariot," as she called it.

She bent and kissed the lush white curls that looked like pictures of women's hairstyles that she had seen from the 1920s.

"Thank you for sticking up for me, Eleanor," she said.

The elderly historian smiled.

"Oh, that's all right," she said, waving her hand as if to dismiss the thanks. "You get the Save of the Day—you perfectly timed your, er—"

"I try," said Lucy wanly.

Her face brightened after a moment.

"By the way, Eleanor, while we were waiting for the little rescued girls to be cleared by the doctor for transport to the hospital, they were getting nervous and antsy, so I told them the story of the Eight Queens of Obergrande."

"Wonderful!" said the historian. "I don't usually do that until sixth grade—there's some pretty scary details to that story, a little bit of sexual content."

Lucy blinked. "Well, I didn't even know that, so I only told them the more fairy-tale aspects to it. I also told them that, like the Eight Queens, they had been very brave and didn't give up in the face of life-threatening danger, so I suggested we name them the Five Princesses of Obergrande."

"Good idea."

Lucy's brows drew together. "I was just joking."

"I'm not," said Eleanor. "What do you think history *is*, Lucy? It's the records of significant events in the life of a place, like a continent, a country, a state—a beautiful little *town*. The events of this day will most likely be some of the most historically significant *ever*. Probably not a good idea to make a big pageant out of it—there are way too many fatalities already to have a princess parade. But I will write the story of it, if you come by the Historical Society when you're feeling up to it, and you can relate it to me. It will be a first-person account—that's solid history. Blessedly, the Society was spared from the flooding, being on the west side of town. I don't know how I would ever recreate the town records if we hadn't been.

"By the way," she continued, "I put your name on the list for shelter, and I think I may have found someone to take you in. If I recall from the photograph in your room, you have a kitten, don't you?"

"Yes," Lucy said in surprise. "I can't believe you remembered that." Her smiled faded a moment later. "Actually, I'm not sure whether or not she made it. I haven't been back to my house yet, but I'm going to later tonight."

Eleanor shook her head. "That whole area of town's locked down," she said. "But Mildred Caulfield's on her way back from Newcomb. She'll be in rather late, but I spoke to her before she left this afternoon. Her son is driving her—she's way younger than me, but still up there in years. She lives on High Street, number 18, yellow house, up by the Overlook—so her house was out of the way of the flood. She had a cat for almost twenty years, Oscar, who she lost a while back. She's a widow, and is eager to be your hostess for however long you need one."

Lucy bent over and kissed the historian's cheek. "Thank you, Eleanor." She exhaled, feeling her lungs still cramped with anxiety. "You're up so late. Isn't this way past your bedtime?"

Eleanor flapped her hand again, waving away the thought.

"Goodness, no," she said. "I'm usually up 'til at least 1:00 AM. *Bloody Murder* is on the detective channel starting at midnight."

Lucy just shook her head and smiled.

Chapter 19

9:07 PM

At the water's edge

THE CRIES FOR help had stopped a short time after the sun had gone down.

Dave Windsor pulled his fire helmet from his head and rubbed his forehead with the back of his wrist, more exhausted than he had ever been in his life.

And numb. Completely numb.

There had been some successes for his team earlier in the day—the rescue of a sinking motorboat that was spinning helplessly downriver in the blasting floodwaters; the freeing of a pair of women trapped under a dock that had been broken from its stanchions at the river's original edge and flung onto their car; repeated carries of people caught in their flooded homes and businesses to safety.

But the losses were far greater, heartbreaking and awful.

They had been pulling bodies from the water and the mud all day with the help of the Army National Guard, extinguishing propane fires and trying to comfort distraught people searching for lost loved ones.

And Company #1 had lost a beloved member, one of their own, a high school classmate of Dave's, Frank Harrigan, the station officer in West Obergrande. He had been standing in the lee of the raging torrent, assisting an elderly woman trapped in the middle of Heavenly Street, when the crest of a tall wave, full of beams from a collapsed roof, hit the old woman, and swept the two of them away, because Frank apparently had refused to release her hand to save himself.

Dave had had enough.

"Let's take a break," he said to his crew, whose faces showed signs of the same exhaustion, the same numbness in the flashing lights atop police and fire vehicles parked up and down the edge of the flood zone. "There's coffee coming, I hear."

Without a word, the volunteers of Obergrande Fire Company #2 looked around, exhaled, and began laying down their rakes and shovels, utterly spent from the hours of digging hopefully.

But finding nothing alive in the wreckage at the water's edge.

Wearily, Dave sat down on a broken barrel that had, the day before, been part of the landscaping he had undertaken each year to plant around the base of Tree Hill, small, evenly-spaced displays of annuals from the region that bloomed with flowers, vines, and decorative grasses throughout the spring, summer, and fall. Earlier that morning, that display had been more than six city blocks away from the waterfront.

Now, the floodwaters were pooling at the edge of the parking area around the park that had been in the center of town.

The barrels that had survived were half-submerged.

As the Ladies Auxiliary, led by Betty Finley and Emmie Klein, came around, passing out the promised coffee, he tried to focus on the knowledge that Sue and the twins were safe, having been evacuated early on, and that Sarah had been rescued from the flooded school. He tried to recall the feeling of holding his oldest daughter in his arms a few hours before, the relief he had felt knowing she had made it out alive.

But all of the good feelings had been buried forever by a day of other people's tragedies.

Dave had never been so discouraged in his life.

Don Farmer sat down next to him, staring at his steaming coffee.

"I don't think I can do any more of this, chief," he said quietly. "Can't look at one more dead kid. Just—can't. I'm sorry."

Dave let his breath out slowly. "Go if you need to, Don. I understand, believe me."

In the flashing lights, he looked up to see a dozen other faces like Don's staring at him.

"That goes for all of you," he said, taking a sip of his coffee. "Anyone who has to leave, go."

"We don't do that," protested Thad Cochrane. "C'mon, Dave—that's against one of the rules of the constitution—"

" 'Maintain a healthy fear of this job?' I think we all have that rule covered, Cochrane," said Ronnie Halari snidely.

"Actually, I was thinking 'no one leaves 'til the scene is secured,' " Cochrane fired back, "but I know that's never been one you've tested out for, Halari."

Dave rose quickly as the two men turned angrily toward each other and raised his hand.

"Listen," he said sharply.

The crew fell silent, obeying.

At first, there was no sound outside of the noise of the other rescue and law enforcement agencies doing their disaster relief work.

Then, in the distance, a thin noise could be heard over the whine of the wind.

A weak cry, throaty and frail.

Possibly a last gasp.

But unmistakably that of an infant.

An explosion of Styrofoam coffee cups blasted skyward as the firefighters scrambled for their tools and flashlights, suddenly energized.

"SHhhh!" Dave Windsor cautioned. *"Quiet."*

The crew froze.

The noise had stopped.

Dave raised a finger to his lips, new light in his eyes, as the men and women of Obergrande Fire Company #2 inclined their ears into the wind, listening hard, praying silently.

They heard nothing but the gusting clamor of the wind and the roar of the river.

"Come on, little one," Dave whispered. "Come on—tell us where you are."

For an agonizingly long time, the firefighters waited, straining their ears.

Then, finally, somewhere in the darkness they heard what appeared to be the sound of hiccups.

Walt Bentley, the senior member of the team, pointed rapidly upriver.

"There!" he shouted. "It's coming from up there!"

The team scrambled toward the new waterfront, holding their flashlights aloft, scanning the refuse along the shore.

Oh God, oh God please, Dave thought, holding his flashlight high and shining it in the area Bentley had indicated, along with almost a dozen others.

The lights reflected on nothing but endless garbage, pushed up against the edge of the street and floating in the pooling floodwater.

"SHhhhh!" Dave Windsor commanded again.

The firefighters kept their lights trained on the wreckage, falling into anxious silence.

Nothing.

Footsteps running behind him barely registered in his ears until a panting voice spoke next to Dave.

"Chief?" It was a woman's voice, husky and high in pitch.

Dave turned slightly away from the spot, trying to keep his eyes fixed on it.

Lindsay Saboran, one of two women on his team, stood beside him, puffing from the exertion of running so fast in her gear.

She held up a piece of equipment.

Trying to keep from losing the direction of his focus, Dave grabbed it from her and held it up in front of his face.

It was the unit's thermal imaging camera, on loan from Clarkson University.

A new, high-tech camera that sensed, and projected, heat.

His concentration broken, Dave stared at the equipment in irritation.

Then, a moment later, understood her intent.

"Turn off your flashlights!" he shouted to the rest of the team, who were still focusing their beams on the garbage-strewn shore. The firefighters turned in confusion, only to see him switching off his helmet light and sighting the thermal imaging camera.

Looking for heat, even in the smallest amount.

As understanding passed through the crew, lights in their hands and on their helmets snapped off in short order, leaving the rain-swollen streets black, the pretty antique streetlights all dark in the powerless city, save for the distant beams of the television crews and the endless flashing of the police lights.

"Hold still," Dave Windsor directed.

He turned on the camera and made his way closer to the docks, pausing beside his comrades who stood, silent and still in the devouring darkness, holding their breath.

"Where are you, little baby?" he murmured. "Where are you?"

For an agonizingly long time, he scanned the new, clogged waterfront, looking for a heat signature.

He could see nothing.

Then, at the edge of the camera's range, a small flash of heat.

Very dim.

Dave Windsor rotated and pegged the camera on the small flash, then zoomed in quickly.

He saw what might be a tiny limb, in what appeared to be a broken canoe, the rest of the body blocked by heatless refuse.

The little arm twitched, then lay motionless.

He dashed to the mound of lifeless garbage, holding on to the camera tightly, his boots tripping over rubble in the way, righting himself.

And stopping directly above where he'd seen the glimmer of heat.

"Here!" he screamed. *"Here!"*

The men and women of the crew were right behind him, their strength and energy renewed by a blast of hope. Like a machine, they formed a bucket brigade, only rather than applying water to a fire, they were dragging garbage out of water, passing it along and out of the way down the line.

A team of brothers and sisters, their spirits broken over the course of this day of loss and death, reinvigorated and strong.

Beneath him, he could see the heat of the firefighters' faces as they dug frantically, through the lens of the experimental camera which was now crowded with colored readings. He tried to stay focused on where he had seen the tiny arm, giving oral directions to the diggers, until one of them seized something rectangular very close to what he thought was the limb.

And tried to lift it, but it was wedged in mud and sand.

"Help me!" Paul Moody shouted. "Scrape the crap off this thing, it's stuck!"

A knot of bodies in fire gear surged forward, some hands dragging on the rectangle, some pawing at the weeds, mud, and garbage that stuck it to the bottom of the shattered watercraft. Their focus was honed, their training in full use, and within a matter of moments, Moody hauled the metal-and-fabric rectangle out of the canoe and spun it around to face Dave Windsor.

A life jacket surrounded the broken metal frame; the fire chief unsnapped the clasps and threw it on the ground as the crew quickly turned their headlamps and flashlights on, illuminating the scene.

At first he could see nothing beneath it but muddy cloth and webbed straps.

He tore the cloth away carefully, revealing a tiny, dirty face, hair smeared with grime.

Unmoving, seemingly lifeless.

"Nope," Dave Windsor said through gritted teeth. "Nope. Sorry, kid, hope the dream you're dreaming isn't that great, because you're gonna wake up now."

He shouted for the medic, Callie Masino, who slid into place like a runner sliding into home plate, her bag in her hands, which she dropped to the ground.

"Give," she said sternly to the fire chief, plucking the backpack out of his extended hands and laying it quickly on the ground with the help of three of the firefighters around her. She patted the baby's face gently as she spoke to her team members.

"We need to get him or her out of this thing," she said calmly, struggling with the knotted straps for a moment before giving up and snatching her scissors from the medic bag. Two snips and a few helping hands later, the broken backpack was dragged out from beneath the child, who was laid on a blanket another member of the crew had placed on the ground.

As the medic undertook infant CPR, two crew members kneeling beside her, handing her the instruments she asked for from the bag, the rest of the unit stood silently, exhaling the stress from the adrenaline rush they had just experienced, some whispering quiet prayers, others staring without speaking.

All tense.

Betty Finley came hesitantly to the edge of the circle, a tureen of coffee wrapped in dishtowels in her hands.

"Step back, Mrs. Finley," Don Farmer said impatiently, trying not to snarl. "We don't need coffee here now—"

"I thought you might need warm towels," the town clerk whispered raggedly. "The coffee is keeping them hot."

Farmer and Paul Moody exchanged a glance. Farmer took off his fire hat.

"I'm sorry, ma'am," he said quietly. "You're right—it's been—well, it's been—"

Mrs. Finley nodded understandingly, her face white from shock and the lights on their helmets.

Callie was leaning over the infant now, compressing the chest, blowing gently into the nose and mouth.

"Come on," Walt Bentley urged. "Come on, kid. Come on."

Dave Windsor had stepped away, calling for an ambulance on his walkie talkie.

"Get the wet clothes off," Callie instructed when she was back to chest compressions. "They weigh more than the baby does. There's probably ten pounds of water in that diaper."

The two assisting firefighters followed her instructions, gently cutting and removing pieces of the clothing when Callie's hands were out of the way.

"A little girl," Ronnie Halari, one of the two assistants, said quietly. He looked up, his eyes gleaming, and smiled at the other man assisting, Thad Cochrane, who returned the grin, both of them fathers of young daughters who had exchanged cross words a short time before.

Cross words long forgotten in the fellowship of their rescue efforts.

Their smiles faded as the child remained unresponsive.

Just as the medic was bending down for a second round of mouth-to-mouth, the infant flinched, then coughed, foamy water spilling from her mouth. Callie rolled her quickly to her side as she stretched, then spit up.

And let out a furious shriek that split the night and raised the hair on every head gathered around her.

A roar of laughter, followed by gasping cheers and

shouts, hugs and high-fives, ascended into the dark night.

Breaking through the gloom, shattering the pall of death that had descended on the suffering town.

And the men and women who protected it.

At least for a moment.

The exhausted first responders rubbed their eyes, rolled their shoulders or bent at the waist, shaking the despair from their backs.

Celebrating the life they had found in the overwhelming grip of death all around them.

Mrs. Finley pushed her way tentatively forward again and unwrapped the towels from the coffee tureen, holding them out to the medic, who quickly wrapped them around the angry baby.

Who, in turn, stabbed their ears with an even more livid squeal.

"Maaaaamaaaaaa!" the little girl wailed plaintively as the lights of the approaching ambulance lit the area, splashing around, illuminating the drowned town square.

Stripping the smiles from the firefighters' faces.

The word echoed against the walls of the surviving buildings.

Sweeping the joy that had blossomed for a moment into the last winds of the departing hurricane, which carried it into the sky.

Taking it far away from Obergrande.

Chapter 20

10:47 PM

Fire House #2, East Obergrande

LATER THAT NIGHT, after the ambulance had sped away toward the Mountain Medical Emergency Center in Emmettsville, carrying the rescued infant to the emergency room and the care she needed, Dave Windsor sat in the oil lamp-and-candle-lit kitchen of Fire Station #2, a broken backpack and life jacket on the table in front of him.

Lost in thought.

Betty Finley, the town clerk, despite being profoundly shaken, had offered to accompany the infant to the hospital and stay with her until morning, when, with any luck, she would be reunited with her parents. Her husband, Leland, Obergrande's highway superintendent, had agreed to drive his wife to the hospital behind the ambulance so that none of the first responders needed to continue their vigilance into the night.

Dave had known both of them since elementary

school; a half-generation older than he was, Leland had coached his high school football team, and Betty had volunteered in the school library, generous, he thought, for a childless couple who were not, he suspected, childless on purpose.

His mind returned to the baby his unit had found.

He tried not to think too heavily on where her parents might be. There were many people he had seen in passing looking frantically for missing children, and he had every reason to believe that when morning finally came, bringing light and dry air and calm to the Seventh Circle of Hell that Obergrande had been turned into by the flood, her parents would be located, and the family reunited.

Every reason to believe.

Even though, in his heart of hearts, he didn't.

He had saved the backpack, had searched for it and located it while the baby was being loaded into the ambulance. Callie Masino had also volunteered to go with her, and rode along in the rig, holding the squalling infant in her arms while the paramedics checked her over.

While he was searching for the backpack, the dozen members of the crew stood in silence at the back of the ambulance, watching solemnly until the rig pulled out of the area, its lights and siren screaming into the air. They remained in silence, standing there until they could no longer see the flashing lights, could no longer hear the siren's wail echoing off the mountains.

Then, almost as one, they exhaled.

"Hang in there, honey," called Walt Bentley in the direction the ambulance had gone, choking up. "We've got your back, whatever you need. Hang in there!"

"I think when she's back with her parents, we should ask if we can all adopt her, kind of as honorary aunts and uncles," Kevin Moreland suggested. "Make her the official Obergrande Fire Company #2 mascot."

"She broke my damn heart when she called for her mama," Lindsay Saboran said, fighting back tears. "I'm never gonna get that sound out of my head."

"You're the first one in line for aunt-hood, if her parents agree," Paul Moody said to Lindsay, accompanied by a low vocal chorus of agreement. "Never would have found her if you hadn't thought of that thermal camera. It would never have occurred to me—I forgot we were testing it for Clarkson."

"With Callie right on line behind you, Lindsay. She was totally in the zone tonight. That little kid was lucky Masino was on this team," Cochrane said. "No one else here had the cert for infants."

"Any sign of who she belongs to?" Andy Klein, the assistant chief, asked Dave. The chief held up the backpack.

"This is all we have to go on, except for the canoe. Forensics has it now. I'm gonna take this back to the station and go over it with a fine-toothed comb."

He lowered the backpack and took off his fire hat.

"The rest of you, go home, or to the shelter, if your house was in the flood zone. The Red Cross is set up outside the station and on the other side of Tree Hill Park all night. Go there if you need chow or a place to stay. Flood waters usually recede pretty quickly, but the work continues for a long time afterward, so rest up—we're going to be on duty for quite some time. Good work, Fire Company #2. You've earned your bars today, each and every one of you."

He held the backpack aloft in salute.

The crew returned the salute silently, staring with wide eyes at the little carrier that had saved an infant from the raging river.

Dave examined that backpack now. It had no particular insignia identifying its brand, and only one zippered pocket for storage. The life jacket that had been placed around it had doubtless kept the child alive, because the canoe showed signs of traumatic impact of the most devastating nature.

It looked, as far as he was concerned, like a massive tree had run into or fallen on it, either on land or in the river.

The impact had been on the opposite end of the canoe from where the baby had been secured into the watercraft, and had filled half of it with small branches and leaves.

Though not certain, Dave Windsor thought there might have been blood in it as well.

But, he thought idly as he turned the backpack over in the lantern light, he could see literally nothing in the darkness while he was searching for the canoe, because all his attention had been focused through the thermal imaging camera, looking for any source of heat.

The use of which was an idea that had come from Lindsay Saboran, a smart and common-sensical young woman that Dave expected he would serve under as the department's chief someday.

I need to put her personally, and the unit collectively, in for a commendation when this nightmare is over, he thought, running his finger over the backpack's zippered compartment, little more than a pocket.

Inside that compartment, Dave could feel something hard and thin.

Carefully he slid the pull on the zipper across its teeth, trying to keep from breaking it.

And succeeded, after a moment, in doing so.

The pocket was small and shallow, perhaps three inches deep and eight or nine wide.

Dave slipped his finger inside.

Rather than hard metal, what he expected to feel, his finger brushed a soft, velvety material, a bag or pouch of some sort that contained the harder object, with packing foam in the corners of the pocket protecting it.

He slowly slid that container out of the sodden backpack and laid it on the table in the candlelight before him.

The pouch, from what he could see, had a very old and shedding piece of twine sewn through the top, like a drawstring. Dave untied the knot carefully, using his Boy Scout badge-level knot untying ability, then pulled the bag open and allowed the object inside to slide out onto the table.

It gleamed in the light, despite a layer of tarnish that coated it.

A bracelet, formed of hammered silver, old, from the looks of it, with a single dark stone, its color impossible to discern, set in the center of it. The setting was sectioned, with a clasp and a locking piece.

Dave Windsor was a bright man, with more knowledge of horticulture than anyone in Obergrande, and most likely, all of Essex County.

But, other than identifying it as most likely a bracelet of some kind, uncertain as to what part of the body it was expected to be worn on, fairly certain it was made of what appeared to be silver, and set with a dark, translucent stone of some sort, he had no idea what he was looking at.

The way it had been kept in the velvet pouch, and packed carefully with linen around it, Dave could tell it had great meaning to someone.

Someone most likely related to the muddy infant they had dragged from the garbage pile that lined what was serving as the new edge of the river, at least for the moment.

Dave Windsor carefully slid the bracelet back into its bag, wrapped in the linen as it had been. Then he rose from the table and made his way back into the dark office of the fire station.

He tried to snap on the light, then sighed, getting no satisfaction.

He went to the heavy safe, snapped on the light on his helmet, and carefully spun the dial, having to do so twice until the combination fell in line with a click.

Dave opened the door and put the bag inside the safe, far in the back behind the bank envelopes full of cash from Casino Night the prior week. The treasurer had not attended the meeting the previous night and had not made the deposit that week as a result.

That seems like a million lifetimes ago, he thought as he slammed the safe's door closed.

Then he went out into the main room, gathered his coat and boots, suited up and went back out into the aftermath of the storm again.

Chapter 21

11:07 PM

East Obergrande, out of the flood zone, west Tree Hill Park

THE NATIONAL GUARDSMAN finally found Lucy in a sheltered spot on the western side of Tree Hill with her wet Red Cross blanket, her eighth cup of coffee, and his flashlight. He crouched down and looked thoughtfully into her face.

"I'm so sorry, ma'am," he said. "I got back as quick as I could."

Lucy nodded absently. "I'm sure you did, Sergeant. Thanks for coming back."

Ace touched the blanket. "This thing is really wet. We should get you another one."

She shook her head. "There are a lot of people who probably need a first one. I'm fine."

"You still want to go to your house tonight?"

"Yes, please. I am hoping against hope that the cat made it out."

"Will you be all right here for about ten to fifteen

minutes, ma'am?"

Lucy, starting to succumb to exhaustion, nodded numbly.

"My car's at Obergrande Fire House #2, which is just up the street a few blocks—"

"I know where it is," she said flatly. "I take my class there every year for Fire Prevention Day."

"Well, then you know how long it should take me to get there and back with the car." He glanced around. "I've asked a few of the aid workers to keep an eye on you—"

"Thank you, Sergeant, but I'll be fine," Lucy interrupted. "I'll wait here until you get back."

"Right. I'll hurry." He disappeared into the darkness and the quiet chaos that was still milling about in the park and on the soccer fields of the school further to the south all these hours later.

Twelve minutes later he was standing over her again.

He reached down to her and took her hand, helping her to her feet.

"Come along, ma'am," he said, his face as straight as ever. "Let's go rescue the—er, other occupant of your house."

Lucy's face was the saddest he had ever seen.

"Not likely to find her alive, unfortunately," she said softly. "As you've already heard, everyone who's part of my family, everyone I love, has a tendency to die on me."

11:14 PM

At the edge of the Flood Zone

IT ONLY TOOK seven minutes for Ace to get to the

controlled zone, the area from the riverfront halfway up to Tree Hill Park, away from the quaint streets of the resort-like village of Obergrande to the residential area north of the park. The damaged area had already been cordoned off with saw horses and emergency tape, and contained more than eleven city blocks.

Obergrande was a community that gradually rose in a slanted elevation from the lake and riverfront, with the streets along the water rising in a stepped pattern, into the hillier parts of the village and town, until it met the steep hills of High Street and the Overlook, a cliff-like formation from which the town and its lake could be viewed fifty feet above the elevation of the city proper. Until the flood, the area beyond High Street had always been seen as a less desirable part of town, separated as it was from the flat lands.

Today, its height and slant made it seem to be the luckiest area of Obergrande.

Lucy's house was just one street into the zone from the middle of town. She and Ace came to the barriers and stopped.

Throughout the zone, National Guardsmen, first responders and Red Cross staff were searching homes, particularly those closer to the waterfront that were still largely under water.

Ace had brought an electric lantern in addition to his flashlight, the batteries of which he had replaced upon getting out of the car. He followed Lucy to the barriers as she slowly came to a halt, staring at the disaster area.

A National Guardsman, a corporal, was patrolling the

barricades.

"Are we going to be able to get in?" she asked nervously.

"I believe so. Technically I'm still on duty. And I outrank him." His face remained straight. *"Ma'am."*

In spite of her nerves, Lucy chuckled.

Ace waited at an opening until the soldier approached, then saluted.

"Sergeant Alex Evans, 3rd Battalion, 105th Infantry, National Guard, Saranac Lake, requesting entry. This is Miss Lucy Sullivan, who requests entry as well, in my company."

The corporal saluted in return. "Yes, sir. Do you have specific business within the restricted area?"

"Miss Sullivan is a resident of this area, and she wants to make certain that her, er, housemate was evacuated."

"Her housemate had limited mobility, then, sir?"

Lucy had to turn quickly to keep her face from giving her away.

Ace swallowed. "Yes. Difficulty opening doors."

"Yes, sir." The corporal saluted, again. Ace returned the salute, then accompanied Lucy to her house. She leaned close to him when they were out of earshot of the corporal.

"Nice save," she whispered. *"Sir."*

Ace looked down at her and smiled, but just kept walking.

They traveled through the darkened neighborhood, Lucy moving slowly, in shock at the sight of the once-familiar trees, broken and bent, the houses missing shutters and lawns where no grass remained, only puddles of mud. She could not bring herself to look too closely at the lower streets closer to the river, where most of the buildings were still submerged.

Finally she slowed her steps.

"My house is just up ahead," she whispered.

"Would you like my arm?" Ace asked, offering it to her.

Lucy wasn't listening. Instead she was staring ahead in the darkness at two people coming up the street. One was another soldier, dressed in fatigues, walking beside one of her neighbors and colleagues from the school.

Recognizable instantly by the white glowing hair that caught the light from the lantern the soldier was carrying.

"Mrs.—Mrs. Cox?"

The principal heard her name and stopped, then glanced around the street, finally seeing the light from Ace's lantern.

"Who's there?" she called up the street.

"It's Lucy—Lucy Sullivan."

Mrs. Cox, who was carrying what looked like several empty bags with handles, dropped them in front of her and began rapidly making her way up the street.

Lucy broke into a run, slipping through the mud next to the submerged sidewalk.

The two women met in front of Lucy's house, a tiny two-story with a porch and a fenced, postage stamp-sized front yard, throwing their arms around each other.

For a long moment, they held each other in profound silence. Then Deb Cox spoke.

"Lucy, oh Lucy, I can't tell you how glad I am to see you," Deb Cox said as tears streamed down her cheeks, still hugging Lucy tightly. "You brave thing—you, you—you *Amazon warrior*—those five girls—"

"Please, no, Mrs. Cox," Lucy said sincerely, returning the embrace. "I've had more than enough of that, please—I'm just glad everyone got out all right."

Mrs. Cox went stiff in Lucy's arms.

Lucy raised her head and looked up. "What? What is it?"

Deb Cox stared at her, immeasurable pain in her eyes.

"Omigod, Lucy—you—you don't know, do you?"

The blood in Lucy's veins began turning as cold as the water through which she had traveled. "Know what?"

Mrs. Cox glanced at Ace, then returned her gaze to the young teacher.

"Not—not everyone made it out, Lucy."

Her cold blood froze; she could almost hear it crack. *"What?* Who? Who?"

"Carl Spinola at the bus garage," Mrs. Cox said sadly. "He got caught in the path of the flood; he was outside before the alarm went off. Evie Cortwright, the custodian—her shift started just as the flood did. She was coming in from the parking lot. And—"

Her words ground to a halt.

Lucy just stared, waiting.

"Lucy," Mrs. Cox said slowly, carefully, "Glen Daniels didn't get out."

Lucy's face went slack. "Wha—what?"

The petite principal looked up at Ace again, then back

at the shaking young teacher.

"He didn't make it, Lucy. He was the first to see the floodwaters—amazing, given that his room doesn't have a window—and he tried to call the office, but the phones weren't working. We didn't even know that there was a malfunction, or a flood, yet."

Ace put his hand below Lucy's elbow, ready to grip it as she swayed slightly.

"He must have packed those girls up on as high ground as he could find, probably told them to stay put, and ran out into the hall, looking for help," Mrs. Cox continued. "He pulled every fire alarm, banged on doors along the eastern corridor, did everything he could, and tried to head back to his classroom, but—"

The principal choked, then broke down.

"If he hadn't gone out into the corridor, who knows what would have happened? We probably would have lost every room on the lake side of the school, because the eastern corridor flooded so fast, and so deeply. Because of his actions, all the alarms went off at the fire station, so they knew to come immediately—"

She stopped as Lucy turned away, white and shaking.

"I'm sorry," Mrs. Cox whispered. "I'm so sorry, Lucy."

She looked back at the principal. "Did they—is his—body—?"

Mrs. Cox shook her head.

"So they could still find him, right?" Lucy's eyes were starting to gleam with a manic light. "He—he might be—maybe he's unconscious somewhere, hit his head or something—it's dark, maybe he's—"

"Lucy—"

The principal stopped, feeling nausea at the knowledge of the horrifying facts. She thought about sharing them, then looked once again at Ace, who shook his head. She turned back to Lucy.

"I'm sorry, honey," she said. "I—I came to get some of the—school backup documents from my house, for the—for—the obits—but my house—is—there's nothing—left—"

Then she ran out of words and turned away, going back to her soldier escort.

Lucy turned away as well.

She walked unsteadily to the gate that was hanging, one hinge broken, in the fence that encircled her tiny front yard, and walked inside.

Ace followed her.

"Miss Sullivan?" he said softly.

She stopped in her tracks, as if unable to move.

The National Guardsman came to a halt behind her and waited.

Finally she turned around and stared out into the street.

"Was he family—friend—someone you loved?"

Lucy shook her head, the golden ringlets hanging in front of her face.

"No. None of those things."

Ace's brows drew together as his forehead wrinkled.

"No," Lucy continued, talking to the air in front of her as her eyes grew glassy with building tears. "He—he was someone who worked with me for—three years, and until—yesterday, I had never given him the time of day. Instead of—making my—own damned judgments, instead of giving myself the chance—the privilege—to know him, I—I listened to the stupid, vicious gossip of the other teachers about him."

She was starting to shake violently now, and Ace looked around again for someone with dry Red Cross blankets, but couldn't see anyone in the controlled zone with one.

"He wasn't just a nice man, it turns out," Lucy continued, almost babbling now. "He was a hero in the end. Before that, he was kind, and thoughtful, and interesting, and funny, and a *good person*—and I managed to utterly ignore him for *three years*. I managed to *entirely forget* about him until now—it never even occurred to me to ask why those girls were alone. You know why, Sergeant? You know why? Because, unlike him, *I am not a good person.*"

Her legs gave out from under her, and Lucy Sullivan collapsed onto her knees on the muddy ground that had once been her front lawn.

Ace Evans looked around, still hoping to find someone to provide a dry blanket, then crouched down in front of her.

"Well, you're right about that," he said. His tone was hollow and emotionless.

Lucy looked up at him.

"A good person would not have ignored someone sent to help her," the soldier continued. "A good person would have listened when a member of the United States military told her to not to go back into a flooding school, to evacuate, and would have done so, quickly and quietly."

Lucy's already distraught face grew even sadder, as if she had been kicked in the stomach. "You don't need to tell me what a bad person I am, Sergeant. I already know it."

Ace leaned a little closer, still in his crouch.

"With due respect, ma'am," he said seriously, "that's crap."

Lucy blinked.

Sergeant Evans paused, as if gathering his thoughts. When he spoke, his dark eyes were gleaming intensely, and he spoke carefully, as if the words were heavy and important.

"You didn't think about him because you were in shock, just like everyone else was, and your brain was in survival mode. But, even then, you knew there were five little girls in a music room, a room with no windows, no other exits, and, at fairly serious risk to yourself, you went back inside to make sure they got out. You could have left that to us, but you chose to take that risk. While the trained rescuer in me doesn't particularly appreciate it, the rest of me recognizes that you are an *extraordinary* person, not just a good one.

"And, if that wasn't enough to prove it, you managed to keep your head about you for the sake of those kids, to not panic when they balked, to talk to them cheerfully, to be strong for them when I'm sure you were terrified yourself. Here's the truth, Miss Sullivan—those girls would have drowned before the firefighters, or the Guard, or the Red Cross got to them if you hadn't gone back."

Ace's eyes gleamed in the dark.

"In the Guard, the term we use for someone like you is *badass,* ma'am." He cleared his throat. "It's a high compliment."

He took a breath, as if the words were getting even heavier.

"This has been no ordinary day—but, because of extraordinary people, like you, it will not be the last day for this broken town. As bad as it seems now, you will rebuild, and life will go on here."

He stood, rising into a crisp military stance.

Lucy stared at him for a long time, no sound but the muffled noise of the other guardsmen standing watch and patrolling the streets in the distance and the gusts of the wind, finally dry. Then she lowered her head and shook it, smiling.

"Those were more words than you've ever said at the same time in your life before, weren't they?"

"Yes, ma'am."

She looked up and met his gaze again. "Anything else you want to say?"

The soldier thought for a moment. "What happened yesterday?"

Lucy's forehead wrinkled.

"You said until yesterday you had never given Mr. Daniels the time of day."

"Oh. Yes."

"So what happened yesterday?"

She exhaled, deeply and raggedly.

"He asked me to dinner and, even though I really

didn't want to go, I sucked it up and went with him. And, guess what?—I had a wonderful time. Dinner was great. Afterwards, he walked with me, in between bouts of rain, to the top of Tree Hill and showed me how to listen to the music of the tree, of the town, of the Adirondacks. Then he gave me—oh, my God." Her voice broke.

Concern colored the soldier's face. "What?"

It took a moment for Lucy to collect herself. "His umbrella. He let me keep his umbrella so I wouldn't get wet walking back to my car after the meeting. He walked back to his own in the rain. I didn't bring it inside this morning—I didn't get to give it back to him."

"He was looking forward to seeing you again to get it back."

Lucy looked even sadder. She said nothing more.

"I'm sorry for your loss," Ace said. He looked in the direction of the flooded side of town. "I imagine you've heard that too many times in your life."

She nodded silently.

"You made his last day a happy one. That has to count for something."

"Is there anything else you want to say?" Lucy's tone was bitter.

Ace exhaled. "Let's go find your cat."

Chapter 22

"I'M GONNA CHECK the basement," Ace said as they approached the little house. He jogged around the side, squatted down in the muddy grass, and peered through the window near the ground, then stood up easily and headed back to where Lucy was standing at the bottom step leading up to the front porch.

"It's full of water," he said regretfully. "Sorry—I doubt anything down there survived, including the furnace."

"Of course it didn't," Lucy said dully, starting up the porch stairs.

"Well, summer's coming," Ace said, following her up the stairs. "Uh—do you have a key?"

Lucy stopped dead in her tracks and hung her head, remembering the loss of her wallet.

Then it popped up again, making her curls bounce.

"Actually, maybe," she said, heading over to the little tree-branch couch and chair on the right side of the porch. She flipped the chair over, felt around in the dark at the bottom of one of the legs.

Ace held up the flashlight for her.

"Got it," she said, pulling the key from the hollow branch that formed the leg. She set the chair back and came to the door, unlocked it, and waited as Ace swung the light inside.

It looked to Lucy like nothing had changed since she had left that morning, but the smell of the house was different, wrong somehow.

"What's the layout downstairs from this doorway?" Ace asked.

"To the right, dining room in the front, kitchen behind. To the left, living room from back to front. Directly across, stairway that turns right halfway up, with a half bath and a closet underneath. Door down to the damned flooded basement at the end of the hall outside the kitchen. Door to backyard kitty-corner to it."

Ace nodded. "I'll go first and check the floor joists. Don't want you to fall through, ma'am." He handed her the lantern.

"Thanks," said Lucy grumpily.

He turned around and looked at her seriously, his eyes so dark they blended in with the air all around them.

"I know we're here to find the cat, but make sure you get everything else that's valuable to you as well," he said. "The aid workers are not guarding valuables primarily, they're still working mostly with people. There's looting already going on—get whatever you would mourn if it was lost."

Lucy blinked, then nodded.

"Sadie?" she called as Ace started into the house. "Sadie?"

THEY WALKED SLOWLY from room to room, beginning at the left front of the house and walking past the central staircase to the back door, which Ace unlocked and looked out, shining the light into the backyard. He closed the door and locked it again.

He had lapsed into heavy silence as they made their way from room to room, which made Lucy increasingly uncomfortable. She continued to call for the cat, a *pssh pssh pssh* sound that echoed through the house, but heard no reply, not even the sound of tiny footfalls. After they had checked the front hall closet, from which Lucy took a number of things, and were scoping out the little bathroom, she had finally had enough.

"Sergeant?"

"Yes, ma'am?"

"You don't talk much, do you?"

"No, ma'am."

Lucy rolled her eyes. "Sergeant, do you have a girl-friend?"

"A girlfriend?"

"Yes—I assume you know what a girlfriend is? Or perhaps a wife?"

"Of course I don't have a girlfriend or a wife."

"Well, *I* don't know. I don't think it's such an odd question. You're nice looking. You have a good job, I assume. Why do you say 'of course I don't' like it's *obvious* that you don't?"

He thought for a moment. "Because it is."

"Why? Don't you like girls?"

The beautifully-lashed dark eyes rolled, but the soldier

said nothing.

Lucy crossed her arms, stubbornly silent.

Ace closed the door of the bathroom and turned to face her. "I said 'of course I don't' because if I had a wife or a girlfriend, I wouldn't have said that I would never let you go," he said finally.

Lucy blinked. "You—you were just joking, weren't you?"

"Yes."

"Harmless flirtation with a double meaning?"

"Yes."

"So why would it matter, even if you had a wife or a girlfriend, if you were just joking?"

"Because I would never disrespect my wife or my girlfriend that way."

"Even if you were just joking? Even if your wife, your girlfriend, and I all *knew* you were joking?"

"Even if."

Lucy shook her head in amazement. "You are one odd fellow, Sergeant."

"Probably true," said Ace. "But that's not what they call it where I come from."

"Newcomb? What do they call it where you come from?"

"Being a gentleman."

"I see." Lucy swallowed. "I guess I haven't met many gentlemen in my life. Actually, I thought they were all dead long ago. I'm sorry if I offended you."

"You didn't."

She threw her hands up in exasperation.

"Why are you so hard to talk to?" she demanded. "You are so charming when you're making a presentation, and so pleasantly commanding when you're in crisis mode—but when everything is finally quiet, you clam up. *Why?*"

"I haven't clammed up. I've answered every question you've asked, and responded to every statement you've made." His dark eyes twinkled. "Ma'am."

A shriek of banshee-like pitch issued forth from Lucy's mouth that would have made her Celtic ancestors proud.

"If you're using this gentleman-miss-ma'am thing to impress women, prospective girlfriends or wives, I can see why it's not working."

Ace chuckled. "It's got nothing to do with impressing anyone, least of all women."

Lucy crossed her arms, still annoyed. "What does it have to do with, then?"

Ace looked at her solemnly. "Respect."

"Oh, I see. Respect."

"Yes."

"And you think calling women 'ma'am' or 'miss' shows them respect?"

Ace shrugged. "Well, it's one thing that does. Actions speak louder than words when it comes to showing respect, however. And it's not just respect for women, though that's certainly an important population. A gentleman endeavors to show respect to and for anyone."

Lucy threw up her hands, then peered around the corner into the dark kitchen. "Well, that's very nice, but I can think of a lot of people who don't deserve to be shown respect."

"So can I," Ace agreed, shining the light over her head into the room. "But it's not about them deserving respect. It's a choice I make to give it, whether or not it's deserved."

Lucy stepped on the sodden floor gingerly. "I have no idea what you're talking about."

Ace swung the light slowly around the kitchen so she could see all of it.

"Do you remember the sort-of innocent lady at the Town Board meeting who thought I was serious about the open bar and hors d'oeuvres at the end?"

Lucy rolled her eyes. "Yes. Some people are too dumb to live."

"I suppose I could have made fun of her, used her gullibility to score a joke," Ace said, pulling the flashlight back. He looked down the hall. "But I chose to apologize and explain I was just joking instead. Maybe not the best approach, but it's what felt right to me."

His words broke through the fog of trauma that had been wrapped around Lucy almost all day. She stopped, shook off the sarcastic attitude and looked at him intently.

"And that guy who threw the apple at me," Ace continued, shining the light the other way down the hall. "I chose to respond to him with humor, rather than making him part of the pavement in the parking lot—which I did consider for a moment, I'll admit."

"Well, no one would have blamed you, certainly. He's always been a tool."

They were moving on toward the dining room at the front right of the house.

"And whether they would have blamed me or not is something I'm really not programmed to care much about," Ace said quietly. "I'm just guided by what I think is right—not what I think is popular, or advantageous. What most people think of me is not important to me, either. I have to live with myself first and foremost, not worry about impressing other people.

"And, in case you didn't notice, I try to show respect to children as well," he said, coming out of the dining room to the staircase again, Lucy a few steps behind him, carrying an armload of items.

"I did notice," she admitted, her body beginning to feel warmer for the first time since the flood began. "It really made the students you marched out first less frightened, and the five girls in the music room want to trust you."

"Well, it feels natural to take and keep the high ground when working with kids," he said, sitting down on the lower stairs. "I think the earlier that kids, especially little girls, can learn to expect to be respected, the better their lives will be when they're adults. Every woman deserves to be respected."

Lucy put the pile of things down on her sofa, traded the damp Red Cross blanket for the blanket her grandmother had quilted, pulled the blanket closer around herself and stopped in front of him.

She said nothing, but the expression in her eyes had changed.

There was something intense in the blue gleam, a warm, fixed look that rested on the young Sergeant, sitting on the stairs with the flashlight in his hand, its beam pointed at the floor.

"Can we go upstairs now?" she asked.

Ace's face and eyes darkened a bit in the reflected light.

It seemed to Lucy like he was looking into her eyes in a manner that allowed him to see things she had hidden from the rest of the world, deep inside herself.

When he spoke, his voice was a little heavier, a little richer than it had been before.

"Lead on, ma'am."

Chapter 23

A S ACE FOLLOWED Lucy up the staircase, for a moment at least he seemed a little looser, a little less restricted.

"This place is cute," he said, looking around as the stairway turned at a right angle halfway between floors. "It's so little, like a dollhouse."

"It's exactly big enough for me and Sadie," Lucy said, holding the lantern up before her. "I did a lot of work remodeling it, so keep a civil tongue in your head, soldier."

"Yes, ma'am."

Lucy stopped in frustration at the top of the stairs and turned around, holding the lantern up in front of him. "*Again* with the 'ma'am.' Would it kill you to call me *Lucy*? You're in my bloody *house*, for Pete's sake."

Ace exhaled and smiled humorously, glancing at his watch. "Sorry, ma'am—er, Miss Sullivan, but I'm on duty."

"Still?"

"Almost always, at least where the Army and the gentleman thing are concerned."

Lucy growled and spun around again, pointing to the left side of the upstairs.

"All right—guest room, left back of house, usually utilized as an office. Front left and right, master bedroom. And, directly at the top of the stairs, full bathroom." She paused for a moment. "Or maybe it's a half bathroom—it doesn't have a bathtub." She turned back to Ace, still standing near the top of the stairs. "Or maybe it's a three-quarter bath, whatever-ya-call-it—"

"Does it have a john?"

"Yes."

"Then I call it a 'bathroom' ." He came the rest of the way up the stairs as Lucy crossed to the bathroom and held up the light, whispering for the cat, but hearing nothing.

"She never goes in here," Lucy said as she led him to the guest room. Ace swung the light around, but saw nothing, and nodded.

Finally they came to her bedroom. The bed was neatly made, and, with the exception of a single pair of shoes tossed recklessly on the floor, the rest of it was completely tidy.

"In spite of several demerits I can see, you'd do pretty well in an Army inspection," Ace said, shining the flashlight around the room.

Lucy had already headed to the closet, had opened it and was pulling clothing from hangers.

"You may as well have a seat, Sergeant," she said briskly. "This is gonna take a while."

"Were your suitcases in the basement?"

Lucy turned and looked at him in shock, then let out

another screech and a string of impressively vile curse words that made Ace laugh in spite of himself.

"Pillowcases often work in place of suitcases in the Army," he offered helpfully.

"That's a good idea. Thank you. Have a seat."

Ace looked around the chairless room. "Where?"

Lucy, now on her knees going through the shoe rack, waved her hand over her head behind her. "On the bed."

Ace looked around again and scratched his head awkwardly.

"It's fine, Sergeant, I'll straighten it when you stand up so that a quarter can be bounced off it again. Have a seat."

Ace exhaled deeply and sat down, his heavy boots in the center of a hand-hooked rug with a tatted lace edge and red roses in the middle.

For an uncomfortable number of minutes, silence took up residence again. In the distance, the carillon of Our Mother of Sorrows, muted all day since it had joined in the alarm call, quietly began tolling the hour of midnight.

Otherwise, nothing but the sound of Lucy's packing disturbed the stillness of the night.

"Do you need help?" Ace asked finally.

Lucy turned to him and smiled, the sarcasm of stress gone. She sat up straight with her knees tucked under herself.

"You know, your mama sure raised you right," she said pleasantly. "She must be pretty proud of you, turning out to be a gentleman and all."

Ace nodded, rocking a little. "Thanks."

"Is she?"

"Is she what?"

"Proud of you?"

"I like to think so."

Lucy sighed. "Like pulling teeth, soldier."

Ace's brows drew together. "What is, ma'am?"

"Number one, getting you to talk," Lucy said, folding the clothing she had chosen as small as she could and then packing it into some spare pillowcases. "Number two, getting you to stop calling me names that make me feel old, though I think that's a lost cause."

Ace took off his borrowed fire helmet and ran his hand over his bristly hair. He cleared his throat and leaned forward, his elbows on his knees, his hands together with the fingers interlaced.

"I'm sorry," he said at last. "Part of it is military culture. Part of it is safety precautions."

Lucy looked up, amused, in the midst of her folding.

"Safety precautions?"

Ace nodded, his eyes gleaming.

"What do you mean?"

He thought for a moment, then spoke. "It may not seem like it, but there—there is—a lot to me," he said slowly. "A lot of—energy—no, that's not a good word for it. Intensity, maybe. A *lot*."

Lucy chuckled. "That's funny. If I were to describe you, I'd say you are one of the most laid-back people I've ever met. I don't know too many guys who could have an apple lobbed at their head when they're an invited guest at a town meeting they drove an hour or more to get to and not beat the absolute crap out of the moron who threw it."

Ace said nothing.

"And the kids all were very comfortable around you. Kids are a good barometer, a good judge of adults, I've found. I think your mom did a fine job raising you into a pretty cool man—oops, sorry. A *gentleman*."

"My mom had a big hand in teaching me to be a gentleman," Ace said in a low voice, one that Lucy didn't remember hearing before. "A great teacher of manners, etiquette, and hygiene." Lucy chuckled. "But the person who really taught me how to be one, made me *want* to be one, was my dad."

"Oh? Well, that makes sense."

"The way he taught me, unlike my mom, who had lessons for everything, was by example," Ace went on. He ran his finger around the edge of the fire helmet. "My dad was a *true* gentleman, soft-spoken and kind hearted, with a pleasant word for everyone he met, always had a positive outlook, even when other people were being ugly. And, above everything else, he adored my mother, treated her like gold—like fine crystal. Never let a day go by without thanking her for marrying him."

Lucy looked up from her packing and smiled.

Then, slowly, the smile faded from her face.

Ace was staring down at the helmet in his hand.

The helmet was shaking.

Lucy slowly moved her knees in front of herself and, abandoning her packing, wrapped her arms around them, keeping her gaze on Ace.

"We had a really great life, my mom, my dad, my sister, and me—a really idyllic childhood, in a really idyllic place—it doesn't get more magical than the Adirondack Park when you're a child."

"No," Lucy whispered. "I can imagine it doesn't."

"He took us hiking—all of us—climbing the High Peaks, camping, canoeing, fishing. When I joined the Army, I could almost have tested out of survival training, if they let you do that, with all the skills my dad taught me. He was just—just so full of life—he had this big, booming laugh that echoed off the mountains. Sometimes I can still hear it, especially when I'm climbing Haystack or Giant. He laughed boisterously when we first summitted those mountains—and I think he left his laugh behind, because I feel it still at the top.

"He died when I—was eleven," Ace continued, still looking at the helmet in his hands. His voice had dropped to little more than a whisper. "I remember wishing on my birthday candles the next year that—that he—" His words faltered and he fell silent.

"That he could magically come back?" Lucy said softly.

Finally Ace looked up. He stared at her intently. Then he nodded slowly.

"I know," she said, willing her voice to be warm and understanding, in spite of the rasp that had crept into it in the floodwaters. "I *still* wish that on my birthday candles."

"I guess neither of us is buying the right kind," Ace said.

Lucy risked a small smile, and was delighted when it was shyly returned.

"I miss them both so much, my parents," she said,

tears creeping into her eyes. "I can't think about it now, though; I have a feeling that if I stop to think about loss today—about Glen, and the custodian, and the guy in the bus garage, and all the other people who are missing in the dark, and now probably Sadie—I'm afraid I'm going to melt down completely."

"I'm sorry," Ace said. "I shouldn't have brought it up."

"No," Lucy said quickly. The word came out stronger and harsher than she meant it to. "That's not what I meant. When I talk about my dad, my mom, it's like, for a moment, they're—well—they're—"

"Like they're alive again, at least a little?"

"Yes," she said, relief breaking over her like a thunderstorm passing. "It's so good to be able to talk about it with someone who understands." She swallowed as a knot rose in her throat. "I haven't had anyone like that to talk to in—well, in years. I obviously can't tell my students. My friends, my colleagues, that are my age, most of them haven't lost their parents yet. No one comes to stay in my guest room anymore since my Gram died. You're the first person I've told, really, in *years.*"

When she looked back up, Ace was watching her, his eyes gleaming.

"Two years after he died, my mom married again," he said, his voice hollow, the warmth from the moment before gone. "I knew, long before she did, what a mistake she was making, because the man she married was *not* a gentleman. By my father's definition, I don't think he could even have been described as a man. He was a worm; he talked to my mother very disrespectfully, mostly when he was lit. But no one cared what I thought—I was thirteen, my sister was eleven. We didn't have a vote. The saddest part is that I think she believed she was doing it for us."

Lucy exhaled, her eyes gleaming as brightly as his were now.

"The first time I saw him hit her, I was fourteen," Ace said. His voice sounded as if he were being strangled. "I went right after the bastard—and he took me apart. He had a hundred pounds on me easily, and had been in the service—I was a gangly kid. He broke this wrist by stomping on it—" Ace held up his left hand—"and told me if I ever so much as breathed on him again he would break every other bone in my body, turn me inside out and leave my organs for the crows."

"Sweet Lord," Lucy whispered.

"All the—rage—I felt, I couldn't show," Ace went on, his eyes dropping again to the helmet. "I had to bide my time, make a plan. I didn't have anyone I could tell, not a coach, not a teacher, because everyone in Newcomb knew him and loved him, because, on the surface, he was a great guy—the guy who always had your back, who could make anything go away for you.

"So my plan was sports. It was the only thing I had that could make me strong without anyone suspecting I was doing it for a specific reason. Newcomb was a little school, so the training wasn't great, but it allowed me access to the weight room and the track—and I spent every spare moment I had making myself as strong, and as agile, and as fast as I could. There was a guy named Lee Duvall that used to teach kickboxing and capoeira, a Brazilian martial art, at the elementary school gym twice a week at night, and I learned everything I could from him. I was especially interested in capoeria, because I knew that my stepfather had never even heard of it, and therefore would be unable to defend against it.

"So I bided my time. I never said a word, sucked up the rude treatment of my mom, the insulting comments about me—I learned to communicate only as little as I needed to in order to keep a low profile. And it worked—he almost forgot that I was there after a while.

"And finally, one day when I was seventeen, captain of the football and track teams, co-captain of basketball, dabbling when I could in baseball in the summer, and, in my senior year, All-American in two sports, it happened again."

Lucy saw the edges of the helmet beginning to crumble and tear in his hands.

Ace closed his eyes.

"He had started to watch my fourteen-year-old sister the year before," he said, his voice barely above a whisper. "He would make snide and inappropriate— ungentlemanly—comments to and about her, would sidle up to her and pat her cheek, then run a finger down her blouse, or drop his napkin when she was clearing the table, just to make her bend over to get it. And, in a perfect storm of awful, everything came together after dinner one night."

"My sister was late coming home—we both did everything we could not to be in the house, but he had been waiting for her, and was angry that she wasn't around. He was being hostile and demeaning to my mother before my sister got there, but once she was home, he turned his anger on her. I had already left the table, not knowing any of this was coming, so by the time I heard the raised voices, I was already upstairs lifting weights. I heard the shouts, the blows, the screams downstairs—and something inside of me snapped."

Ace took a breath and swallowed. He looked up to see Lucy locked in the gleam of his eyes.

The look on her face not one of fear, or worry, or disgust.

But of complete and total understanding.

"Sometimes at night I have glimpses of what happened, in dreams that cause me to sweat and mutter, or so I've been told by guys in my barracks," he went on. "But I don't have a single clear memory of it. I only remember his back was to me as I tore down the stairs. He was kneeling astride my mom, who was on her back, trying to cover her face; his arm was back, getting ready to backhand her again. My sister was cowering in a corner, her nose bleeding—so I went for his kidneys. That's all I remember—the rest is a total blur."

Lucy exhaled, her mouth open slightly.

"Good for you," she said when she could speak again.

"End of the story—he was arrested, I was almost arrested, but there were witnesses, not just in my family but out in the street, where I dragged his sorry ass at one point. Apparently whatever I did to him was sufficient to keep him in a hospital prison ward for three months, and for him not to return to New York State when he got out."

Ace looked down at the helmet in his hands and flinched in surprise at the damage he had done to the edges. He looked back up, and the fire in his eyes dimmed a little, but the intense gleam remained.

"So that's why I endeavor, in all things, to be a gentleman. Because my father's big laugh is inside me, even though no one has ever heard it. My mother, who has an ability to love anyone back from the brink of *anything*—literally, I'm not exaggerating—I think I may have that inside me somewhere, too. I may seem laid-back and low-key to you, but there's an inferno in here. Usually it's on a low, steady burn; I feel genuinely calm and easy most of the time. But things that are important to me—good and bad—are *really* important to me.

"So, if I had a girlfriend, I would never even look at, let alone flirt with, another woman—not even as a joke. If I had a girlfriend, whenever I spoke her name, it would be with as much respect and awe as if I were uttering a prayer. If I had a girlfriend, I might dance in the middle of the street from time to time, when I was feeling happy thinking about her, not giving a rat's ass what the other engineers or soldiers thought about it. If I had a girlfriend, I would walk or run or swim to the end of the Earth to find something she needed, or wanted, or that would just amuse her. If I had a girlfriend, I would learn stupid ballroom dances if she wanted me to, and learn them to a point of being *good* at them. If I had a girlfriend, I would paint her name on forty-six different rocks and carry them up to each of the High Peaks and leave one there, where the sky could always see her name. If I had a girlfriend, the very thought of her would be enough to keep me happy anywhere in the world—in a war zone, in a flood, at the bottom of a canyon, orbiting around the Earth in a tin can—at the brink of impending death—I would be happy, just at the thought of her. If I had a girlfriend, I would wrap my body and my life around her, so that anyone, any*thing* that even *dared* think of harming her would have to come through me first. If I had a girlfriend, I would spend time every day, somewhere, giving thanks for her— probably most of the time at daybreak, and under the stars at night. If I had a girlfriend, I would worship her with my body, never touch her in anything but love, so that she would always be able to feel how beautiful she was. If I had a girlfriend, and she consented to be my wife, I would thank her every day for doing so, where our sons could hear me, so that they might decide to continue the tradition themselves one day. Because she would be *important* to me. Really important."

The room felt a sudden void and cold when his words came to an abrupt end.

Ace's gleaming eyes broke contact with Lucy's, and his gaze returned to the helmet.

He inhaled slowly, then let his breath go, and swallowed.

Then he looked up. In his eyes was a soft glow now, absent the burning intensity that had been there the moment before.

"So, Lucy, if I had a girlfriend, I suspect it would be obvious."

For a long time Lucy didn't move, barely breathing.

Struggling to keep from weeping.

Then she blinked, and her eyebrows drew together.

"*Lucy?* Did—did you just call me 'Lucy'?"

"Yes," Ace said, hiding his smile. "Did you hear the church bells ringing in the distance a few moments ago?"

Lucy nodded, unable to speak.

"It's midnight. I'm finally off duty."

Deep within her, at a place in the core of her body and soul, Lucy felt a deep warmth blossom and begin to spread, running through her like the river of raging water had run through Obergrande, surging through long-established paths that had been limited with levies she had built herself, flooding over the barriers, a river of heat and desire and need, until she felt like she was burning from the inside out.

Leaving her skin tingling, her ears buzzing, her breasts aching.

Her mouth burning, looking at the Cupid's bow lips across from her.

She rose slowly, as steadily as she could, and, their eyes still locked, stepped over her clothing and walked across the room to the bed where he was sitting.

And knelt down in front of him, so that they were on eye level, and looked deeply into the dark pools that had caught her notice from the first time she saw him.

"Sergeant," she said slowly, her voice husky with unspent tears, "request permission to be your girlfriend."

Ace smiled as broadly as she had ever seen him.

"Copy that," he said.

He put the fire helmet on the floor, then reached out with both hands and gently entwined them in her curls, running his calloused fingers down the golden strands, touching and looking at her with what could only be described as awe.

The unspent tears in Lucy's eyes spilled over and slipped down her face, where they hung for a moment at the edge of her jaw, then fell onto his hands.

She closed her eyes and leaned in until she was resting her nose against his.

"I'm getting you all wet," she said quietly as she felt his fingers dampen. "Which is only fair, since that's what you're doing to me."

"We'd both be dry if you hadn't pulled me back into the school—"

Lucy opened her mouth to retort again, only to find the most sumptuous lips she had ever tasted pressed against it, gently at first, then with more insistence as her own lips clung to them.

The fire coursing through her veins exploded.

Lost in swirling passion, she wrapped her arms around his wide neck, pulling him closer as he continued to cradle her face, kissing her progressively more ardently with each passing second.

Until she gasped in pain, winced, and pulled away.

Ace sat up straight, looking around him in shock.

"What? Wha—"

"Ow! *Ow!* OW!"

Lucy looked down at the tatters of the skirt she had chosen to wear with her flat-heeled shoes today, sodden and torn.

And being torn even worse by cat claws running down it.

Just as her thigh was.

Her eyes, weepy with growing desire, popped open in shock.

"Sadie!" she screeched, unable to contain herself. *"Sadie,* omigod!"

As she pulled the bedraggled kitten into her arms up against her chest, hugging her with unbridled joy, Ace inhaled slowly, then exhaled deliberately.

"Note to self," he said aloud, continuing to breathe regularly to try to offset the arousal that had flared intensely and was now turning painful, "cats, especially those belonging to girlfriends, have *the* worst timing in the world."

Chapter 24

GINGERLY ACE STOOD up, stepping away from the purring cat. "I guess that's our signal to go. Do you have everything you came for?"

Lucy rose as well, nuzzling Sadie. "Everything I need for now, I guess. Except maybe a do-over."

"The whole day, starting from this morning? I would vote for that."

She grinned at him. "I don't think you rank high enough to make that happen, Sergeant. But Sadie seems to have interrupted a very promising conversation."

The National Guardsman chuckled. "Is that what you call it? Conversation?"

"When I tell Mildred Caulfield what happened? Absolutely. We were having a nice conversation and suddenly Sadie appeared. That's my story."

"Who is Mildred Caulfield?"

"The very nice lady I'm supposed to spend the night with. She lives up on High Street and doesn't mind cats, according to Eleanor Preston, who made the arrangements. I think Eleanor's got a Rolodex in her brain. She seems to have placed herself in charge of finding accommodations for everyone who's displaced, and no one ever says no to Eleanor."

Ace sighed. "Well, then I guess we'd better get you two there. Cat carrier?"

Lucy winced. "Basement."

"Of course." Ace shrugged. "You can't just carry her in the car. Have you got another pillowcase?"

"You want to put my cat in a pillowcase?"

"Not particularly. She already doesn't like me, and I don't think stuffing her in a pillowcase is likely to make us friends. Do you have a leash?"

"I keep it in the cat carrier."

"Hmm. Then pillowcase it is. I'll take your other stuff out to the car, so we can minimize her discomfort." He hoisted the packed pillowcases. "Maybe you can put the things from downstairs into a garbage bag. Unless you have more sheets?"

Lucy sighed. "Yep. Super-high thread count I bought with my first paycheck. In the dryer. In the basement."

"OK. Back in a minute."

When Ace came back inside, Lucy was in the living room, loading the second of two garbage bags with the non-clothing items she had gathered from her house. "It doesn't seem like much, does it?" she said wistfully.

"There'll be more, Lucy. Tell me about this do-over."

Lucy's fair skin turned rosy in the light from the dimming lantern. "Maybe we could meet back here tomorrow? After you get off duty? Unless you get a kick out of calling me 'ma'am' ."

Ace laughed. "No, ma'am."

She turned away, crestfallen.

"No to the *ma'am*, not no to the idea of seeing you in better circumstances," Ace added quickly. "But what about the cat?" He looked around. "Where *is* the cat?"

"She's locked in the bathroom with her dinner. Getting her into a pillowcase is going to be a two-person job. And tomorrow she can stay with Mildred."

"I'll take this out, and then we'll get Sadie. And tomorrow? It's a date."

Lucy smiled. "Copy that."

Sadie was reluctant to go in the pillowcase, and Ace held it at arm's length as he escorted Lucy to the car, keeping clear of the screeching, squirming bag. "Are you sure you want her on your lap? I can put her in the back."

"No, I think she'll be calmer in my arms, even if she is tied in the pillowcase. Can you help me with the seatbelt?"

Ace handed the bag over doubtfully and fastened it for her as the pillowcase prison squalled and thumped. "Seatbelt. Cat. Anything else?"

"Dinner? I don't think I ate anything today. Just drank a lot of coffee. And I had breakfast, but it was a really long time ago." She looked off into the darkness down by the river. "Another lifetime."

"I have trail mix in the glove compartment," Ace offered. "There's no electricity in town, so I doubt any of the restaurants are open. And it's after one in the morning."

Jokingly Lucy turned to the bag in her arms.

"So, Sadie, what do ya think: on our first date, he grabbed my caboose, stared down my shirt at my boobs, made it into my bedroom, and all I got for dinner is oatmeal. Should we keep him?"

"There are chocolate chips, too," Ace said defensively. "And mini-marshmallows."

Lucy caressed the cat through the pillowcase. "Sadie says I should stop being obnoxious and thank you for saving her—both of us, actually."

"I didn't save either of you. I just followed you into a flooded building and escorted you into another one. And now I'm driving you to somewhere dry, somewhere you can have pleasant dreams. Where exactly?"

"High Street. Number 18. It's yellow."

"Not in the dark it's not."

"Maybe you can see which one it is in the light of all the emergency vehicles?" Lucy said hopefully.

"You get me to High Street and I'll find you the house."

Lucy directed him out of the riverside neighborhood and up the steep hill, away from the flooding and the flashing lights. As they turned onto High Street, one of the houses with the slanted walkways and stone steps carved into the face of the mountain itself had candles burning in the lower windows, and a very dim spotlight aimed at the house number.

"I like this lady already," Ace said, pulling into the driveway. "We think a lot alike."

He escorted Lucy and Sadie to the front door and pushed the button for the doorbell.

Nothing happened.

"Knock," Lucy said. "There's no electricity."

"Right. I must be tired or something—wait—there's exterior light. They must have power up here. The doorbell must just be broken."

The door opened, and Mildred Caulfield, a sweet-faced woman with graying-black hair, welcomed them into the house with a smile.

"Hello, Lucy, and, er—"

"Ace," the National Guardsman said, offering his hand to her, which she shook pleasantly. "I'm just the delivery man, ma'am."

Mildred seemed slightly relieved. "I've got warm soup on the stove, and a pot of tea. What would you like?"

"Soup sounds wonderful, thank you," Lucy said. She could feel exhaustion hovering at the edges of her consciousness, preparing to shut her down. "And a bed. And a place to put my cat, if that's OK."

"It's more than OK," said Mildred. "I love cats, as Eleanor probably told you. He can have Oscar's bed. You're in the room at the top of the stairs. Why don't you take a nice shower and I'll bring your meal upstairs?"

Lucy looked at Ace, who was smiling, staring at the floor. "But I have to help bring my things inside."

"Nonsense. Your young man will do that. Give me the cat, and I'll bring her up as soon as she's seen where we keep the litter box. I have some cat treats in the pantry. I bet she's had a rough day of it, poor kitty."

"Her name is Sadie. Thank you so much. And thank you, Ace."

She came to him, under the sharp gaze of Mrs. Caulfield, and kissed him goodnight. Their kiss deepened, although not as much as either of them would have liked since Lucy was still holding a bag of squirming cat.

"What time are you off duty tomorrow?" she whispered.

"Eight o'clock," Ace whispered back.

"You know where to find me."

Mrs. Caulfield cleared her throat.

Both of them suppressed a snicker.

"All right, I still like her, but I was wrong about she and I thinking alike," Ace whispered humorously.

Mildred cleared her throat again. "Give me the cat, dear, and up you go," she said to Lucy. She turned to Ace. "This is a respectable house. We'll see you tomorrow, I expect, during appropriate hours. You can just leave everything on the porch tonight." She shooed him out and closed the door behind him.

Then she took the pillowcase from Lucy and gestured pointedly toward the stairs.

Lucy headed up, but she could still hear Ace chuckling quietly as he brought the pillowcases to the porch, then got in the car.

She went to the window in her new temporary room in time to see the headlights turn on as the Jeep backed slowly out of the driveway onto the steep street overlooking the swollen lake and broken lower part of town, invisible in the dark.

The car's high beams flashed, looking for all the world like a wink.

Lucy exhaled and watched until it was out of sight.

Wondering if everything she had experienced on this extraordinary day had been a dream.

Chapter 25

THE NEXT DAY, Saturday, as Ace had predicted, he was summoned to the Obergrande dam to assist the Army Corps of Engineers in making plans to unclog and bring the hundred-year-old structure back online.

As he had noted at the Town Board meeting, the assessment he and the other engineers reached was that the simple spillway dam was crumbling in some places, insufficient to handle the flow of the Hudson that had increased enormously over the course of its lifetime.

Something about the reports of the early details of the flood nagged at the back of Ace's mind, something that did not add up entirely to him.

But it was too soon be making decisions, or analyzing hunches yet, he decided, and told the other A.C.E. participants in the discussion. The river was still in flood stage, though it was ebbing. The catastrophic destruction had not even been fully investigated, let alone catalogued.

All of the dead had not even been found.

He had come that Saturday morning into a somber office in West Obergrande, an office that had received the news shortly before his arrival that the death toll was already over 175 and rising, something unheard of in the past. Each new story, each revelation, was more heartsickening than the one before. Ace began keeping a list of buildings that were going to need to be replaced or rebuilt, a list that grew longer by the hour.

And everyone at the table knew that, until the final toll was taken, until the funerals and burials and every other state of mourning had been undertaken, they could only do band-aid engineering, as Colonel Genovese called it.

The streets were still catching fire in places, power lines still falling down, sparking, sinkholes opening in the middle of roads.

The conditions both in and around the flood zone were hazardous.

Ace thought about the new acid that burned in his stomach when contemplating these conditions, a worry he had never experienced in these types of situations before. It actually surprised him how ill the whole realization of the instability of the flood zone made him.

Until he realized what it was.

Someone that he loved lived in this place.

And therefore was threatened by it.

Then, a moment after the realization came to him, a smile followed it.

Because now he had someone that he loved.

LUCY, LIKE THE other citizens of Obergrande, spent the day walking around in a fog for the most part, assisting in rescue efforts where she was qualified to do so, comforting people who had lost loved ones or who were still searching for them.

Each time she ran into someone else who had survived was a joyful reunion, yet relief was not always present, because around every corner there seemed to be someone else she knew who was missing or dead.

She came to the edge of the flood zone in the center of the village and looked to see which of the businesses had survived, and which had not, which were going to need renovation but would recover. She was relieved to see that her favorite street in town, Heavenly Street, was mostly intact, though damaged.

Heavenly Street was so called because seven of the quaint stores along the avenue had the word 'heaven' in the title—Pancake Heaven, Sneaker Heaven, Knitter's Heaven, the travel agency, Heaven on Earth, the candy store, Seventh Heaven, Hardware Heaven, and the liquor store at the end of the street known as Heaven Can Wait, all interspersed between the other shops. All the shops were closed now except for her favorite, Hardware Heaven, the door of which was standing open.

Lucy had managed to remember to pack a sweater and had worn it into town that morning. She had worked up a head of steam on the walk down from High Street, the farthest place of Obergrande to still be part of what was considered the east side. She pulled the sweater more tightly around her, and carefully climbed the wet wooden steps up to Hardware Heaven.

The proprietor of the store, John Grimes, was a long-beloved fixture to the people and especially the children of the town. His store contained virtually any houseware or dry good that was needed, as well as many things no one could ever recall seeing before. And he could always be counted upon to produce a stick of Wrigley's Spearmint Gum if a child wanted one, as long as that child could locate him within the insanely crowded aisles of his store.

Lucy knocked lightly on the glass window in the front door.

A moment later, the tall, slim man appeared, wearing his work apron, carrying a mop. A slight smile came to his face.

"Good morning, Lucy," he said, leaning on the mop. "Glad to see you made it."

"You too," she said sincerely. "That's what I really came to find out."

Mr. Grimes nodded solemnly.

"I had hoped to get to speak to you on the way out of the Town Board meeting the other night," he said, drying up a few small pools of fetid water with the mop. "I thought your commentary was insightful and very well spoken. Thank you."

"Well, thank *you*," she said, feeling awkward. "Was that really just the day before yesterday?"

"It hardly seems possible, doesn't it?" Mr. Grimes twisted the mop handle in his hands. "Odd, don't you think, that the flood took down the very areas of town the Board was discussing drowning?"

Lucy's eyebrows drew together as silence thudded against her eardrums.

"Well, yes," she said after a long moment. "But, as

impressive as they think they are, the Town Board can't command the weather."

"No, no, they can't, can they?" said Mr. Grimes. "There are some who would think this is an act of God, endorsing their plan."

Lucy shuddered, feeling suddenly colder.

"You—you don't think that, do you, Mr. Grimes?"

John Grimes smiled.

"Goodness, no," he said. "But I don't think in this case He is necessarily on our side, either. Stay well, Lucy—look after yourself. I hope you will stay in Obergrande—in the Adirondacks. You're a wonderful teacher, and a wonderful townsperson. Every special place needs special people to live in it. Have a good day—as good of one as is possible to have on a day like today."

He went back to mopping the floor.

Lucy stood in the street for a few moments longer, watching him. She cast a glance up Heavenly Street at the beautiful little shops and restaurants, including Charlie's on the corner, the place Glen Daniels had considered for their first date, all closed and dark now.

Then turned around to make her way back to Tree Hill Park, the eastern half of which had been largely under water the day before.

And was cheered to see that it was drying out.

She looked up at Obergrande, standing tall and upright against the lightening clouds, its enormous trunk straight, the heavy limbs steady, the slender branches waving the spring leaves in patterns in the wind.

The iconic tree under which historic events had occurred.

Where treaties of peace had been signed.

Where lovers met.

Her cheeks grew warm at the thought, her heart beating faster in the knowledge of the one she would meet that night.

We will live through this after all, Obergrande, she thought. *You, and the town you have always protected.*

She closed her eyes, listening for the music of the tree, and heard it singing.

The song of the town, on the other hand, was silent.

Chapter 26

8:23 PM

A CE PARKED HIS car a few streets west of the controlled flood zone and sighed.

The day had been a fairly miserable experience all the way around, the sadness and the horror inescapable. But he had determined to take the chance that Life had finally offered him and make the most of it.

So he got out of his car with the long-stemmed red rose he had managed to find in Newcomb, the last one available at the mini-mart that sold them singly, and hurried down the dark streets, flashlight and flower in hand.

His heart pounding increasingly each step of the way.

He was allowed almost without notice into the zone; the privates and corporals patrolling the place now routinely saluted and allowed him entrance, largely owing to his superior rank.

When he came around the corner of Marshall Avenue, a cross street to Second, he noticed lights flickering in the air on her side of the street, in contrast to the complete darkness everywhere else in the neighborhood.

Puzzled, he came closer.

They were glowing beyond the drapes in the windows of Lucy's tiny house.

Along the curb in front of her house, black garbage bags sat neatly, the only place on the street where any were.

He jogged to the fence, walked through the broken gate, hurried up the steps and knocked on the door.

"Come in," a muffled voice called beyond it. "Ready for your re-do?"

Ace turned the handle, choking back his irritation at finding it unlocked.

Beyond the door a candle was flickering in the hall in front of the staircase. Ace walked up the stairs.

At the top more light appeared, flickering on the wicks of a dozen or so lighted candles lining the hallway to Lucy's bedroom.

He took a few deep breaths to cleanse his mood of worry, then spoke as he approached her door.

"Babe, you've gotta be more careful," he said as passed the bathroom and headed toward the front of the house. "You can't leave the door unlocked like that."

He had reached the doorway.

The master bedroom was full of small spheres of glowing radiance, hovering above the wicks of even more candles, carefully placed in the windows, atop her dresser, and on the bedside tables. It seemed to Ace that he was looking through the doorway into a land from a fairytale, a forest full of magical spirits in the devouring darkness of the now-dead neighborhood.

Standing with her back to him, looking out the window into the night, was a figure in a long, sheer nightgown, the type of which Ace could not possibly have thought to name, though he could see it had a matching robe, equally translucent.

Her long blond hair had been carefully swept up atop her head, with tendrils of soft, light curls cascading down from it at the base of her neck, which was much more willowy and long than he had realized. He could not tell what color the negligee was in the candlelight, but it seemed to glow like a candleflame itself, and it clung to the gentle curves of her body, narrow shoulders that tapered to a slim waist blossoming out to a backside the outline of which made his heart pound and heat rise within every muscle of his own.

" 'Babe,' huh?" Lucy said, still looking out the window, her back to him. "Is that what you intend to replace 'ma'am' with, Sergeant?"

"Only with your permission, ma'—Lucy," Ace answered. He was not surprised at the weakness in his own voice. "I will call you anything you want me to—although a new idea came to me just this afternoon."

She chuckled, still not turning around. "Something other than 'babe'?"

"Yes."

"And what would that be?"

Ace cleared his throat, which had suddenly gone dry. "How do you feel about—'my love'?" he asked quietly.

He saw Lucy's back stiffen, her head raise up.

Slowly she turned around.

For a moment, Ace didn't recognize the woman standing in front of him.

The hair that had caught his attention at the Town Board meeting from the moment she came into the room was gleaming in the candlelight, pulled back from her face for the first time since he had known her. The face revealed by the updo was far more beautiful than he had even remembered in his dreams, high cheekbones and an elegant jaw line that had always been swallowed by her curls. Her lips were smooth and soft in a way that made every part of his body recall what it had felt like to kiss them yesterday.

But the eyes were the element he could not pull his gaze away from.

Lucy's eyes had been what had really captured his interest the night before last, large and long-lashed, taking up a substantial part of her fair, heart-shaped face. They were absolutely transparent, clear as the sky above the atmosphere, full of light and warmth and openness, transmitting any emotion she was experiencing—anger, sadness, vulnerability, joy—all of them were clearly seen the instant they entered her eyes.

He stared at them, utterly entranced, trying to decide what emotion he saw in them now.

They were gleaming, soft, with a hint of tears making them even more gorgeous.

She returned his stare, but with a look that made his knees tremble.

"Does that mean that you love me?" she asked, her

voice trembling as well.

Ace swallowed again in the hope that his voice wouldn't shake.

"Yes. Yes, it does. I realized it when I couldn't stop worrying about you today."

Lucy pursed her lips and nodded. The expression in her eyes changed.

Ace would have guessed that what he was looking at was relief.

"Thank God," she said. "I was afraid I was going to have to be in love alone. Because today I discovered the same thing."

Ace held out the rose to her, stretching his other hand out to her as well.

"Come to me," he whispered. "Come to me, my love."

A smile came over her lips, and into her eyes as she shook her head. She slid the outer robe of her negligee slowly over her alabaster shoulders and let it drop to the ground behind her.

"No, soldier," she said, "you come to me."

Before she could take another breath the rose was in her hands and she was in his, both of them spanning her waist, lifted from the ground and being carried to the bed, trembling with passion.

And something else that felt very much like joy, though she was not certain she had ever experienced it before.

As much as she had contemplated what her eyes had seen in him over the past few days, it was a totally different experience being in his grasp.

The muscles of his arms were stronger than she could have imagined, his shoulders wider, his back broader, his scent more clean and masculine as well. She ran her free hand through his hair and felt a thrill shoot through her, each tiny nerve in her body on fire.

Feeling small, vulnerable in his grasp.

And loving the feeling.

He was kissing the hollow of her throat as he laid her gently down, his hands lifting her arms over her head alongside her ears, which were ringing now in time to the pounding of her heart.

As his sensuous lips continued up from her throat to her neck, one of his calloused hands, a soldier's hand that had seen the steel not just of weapons but of tools, the tools of his profession, flattened against her palm, so big atop her small one. He gently slid his fingers down between hers until they were entwined together.

His mouth was now just outside her ear.

"I told you yesterday that there was a lot to me," he whispered, sliding his other hand behind her waist and drawing her close, pressing his chest to hers. "An intensity when something matters to me—I don't want to frighten you—"

"I want it," she whispered, forestalling his question. "Reach deep inside me. Wear me out. Take me up mountains and to the bottom of the ocean. Give it all to me, Alex."

At the sound of his real name, Ace raised his head and looked into her eyes.

"I want to be important to you," she whispered.

He was on fire now, his skin burning. "Believe me," he said, his voice husky with arousal, "you are. You're the most important thing in my life."

Lucy smiled impishly.

"Prove it," she said. "Give me everything you got."

She pushed him up until his arms were straight on either side of her, took hold of the bottom of his shirt with both hands and slid it up over his chest, off his arms and over his head, then giggled with merriment at the feel of the satin skin over his muscles beneath her flat palms.

Imagining the thrill of how they would feel against her own chest once it was bare.

"I told you," she said, leaning up and kissing his neck and throat in the same places he had on her, "the first night we met, that I didn't trust you."

"Yes, you did," he said, straining to remain in control. "It hurt a lot."

Lucy stopped. "It did?"

"No. I'm only kidding. Please don't stop. I may die if you do. And I'm not kidding about that."

She chuckled, returning her lips to his neck.

"I want to prove something to you, too—that I do trust you," she said between kisses. "Completely. Let me prove it—I promise I will tell you if you frighten me. Otherwise—"

Her negligee was sliding rapidly up her body and off it a moment later.

A REMARKABLY LONG time and satisfaction in at least three positions later, Lucy fell back against the pillows on her simple department store mattress, sated and glowing as if she was in one of the famous mile-high feather beds at the Lake Placid Lodge.

Ace was stretched out atop her, still within her, breathing heavily, his heart pounding against her chest.

"Great re-do," he said between breaths. "So—much—better than last night's attempt. Thank you."

"Copy that," she said, grinning and stretching luxuriously in his arms. "I didn't realize when you said there was a lot to you that you were also speaking anatomically." She chuckled as Ace turned red. "I'm so blessed."

"How do you feel?" he whispered in her ear. "Are you all right?"

Lucy looked up at him. Their lovemaking had been playful, romantic, intense, passionate, sensitive, athletic—funny, even. The red rose, little more than shredded petals now, had been utilized, gently, lovingly, thoughtfully to the point where she had shed blissful tears and he had needed a long time to recover, panting.

It had been amazing beyond her wildest notion of what making love could be, especially between two people who had only met forty-eight hours and a whole lifetime before.

And in an entirely different world from what they inhabited now.

But there was something that remained afterward, something warm and deep and meaningful that she didn't have words for.

She took his face in her hands and brought his lips down to hers, clinging to them as if for life itself. Then she broke away from them and put hers next to his ear.

"I feel *sought*," she said, her voice low and warm. "Like you came looking for me in the flooding school that was my world until you found me—I feel *treasured*."

His hand caressed her face. "You are. You so are."

"Are *you* all right? How do you feel?"

He exhaled so deeply she could feel it where they were still connected.

And kissed her gently.

"I feel home," he said simply.

"You are, too."

"Can I ask one more thing of you?"

Lucy nodded, love shining in her eyes.

"I know I have to get you back to Mrs. Caulfield's by midnight—which isn't long from now," Ace said, humor changing a moment later to something deeper. "But I dreamt last night—and the night before, in fact, when I was still an objectionable, odious giver of comfort to the enemy—of holding you while you slept in my arms."

"Really?" Lucy asked, amazed. "Even after that Board meeting?"

"Especially after that Board meeting. I sat in my car and waited until you got yours started again, you were so fascinating to me. I needed to be sure you got home safely."

"You would have done that for anyone, being a gentleman. Admit it."

Ace sighed. "All right, I admit it. But I think anyone else would have let me jump their battery. And I wouldn't have dreamt of any of them sleeping in my arms—it turns out Colonel Genovese had car trouble that night, too." He shuddered at the thought. "Only you have ever done that to my dreams, my love. So, what do you say? Can we take a nap? Will you let me hold you? Will you sleep in my arms, if only for a little while?"

Lucy giggled. "Well, when you ask *that* nicely, how could anyone say no?"

"I can't reasonably imagine." Ace rolled onto his back, grinning, and held out his gloriously muscled arms. "Come'ere."

Lucy rested her head on his shoulder and put her arm around his waist as he drew her close.

"My alarm clock has no power," she said drowsily. "You better have an internal one, otherwise Mrs. Caulfield is never going to let me see you again."

ON THE WAY back through the dark side of town to the soft lights of High Street, they rode in contented silence.

When they were just past the end of the barricades, Lucy spoke.

"I think my mother likes you."

Ace's brow wrinkled. "Your mother?"

"Yeah. That wedding picture at the foot of my bed? My mom was smiling at you."

"And your dad?"

"He'll come around."

Ace coughed. "I'm not sure I'm comfortable with them watching us."

Lucy sat up straight. "Oh, *dammit!*"

"What?"

"I meant to take the pictures off the wall. I got the stuff from my closets yesterday, but you kind of don't notice pictures on the wall. It's like they're a part of the landscape."

"Or part of the wallpaper," Ace agreed. "Do you want me to go back?"

"Past the guard again? Not tonight. We'll miss curfew." She sighed. "I'm sorry that my living situation means we have to feel like teenagers again."

"Nothing wrong with that," Ace said, taking her hand and kissing it. "You make me feel like a teenager again anyway. I can think of a lot of fun things we might do to make the most of that. And anyway, curfew is something I live with daily when my unit is activated or training. It's no big deal to me."

His smile faded.

"I'm not comfortable with you coming here alone," he said seriously. "I agreed to meet here tonight because I knew I'd be with you, but it's still a dangerous area."

"What danger?" Lucy said, breaking open one of the sleeves of trail mix from his glove compartment. "There are guys with guns on the street."

"There are also live wires on the ground, sparks everywhere, propane tanks exploding, rats, mold—it's not a healthy environment. And besides—"

He stopped.

"What?" Lucy asked.

His words were soft, but they carried great weight.

"I need to know you're safe. I recovered a disturbing number of bodies today and yesterday. I need to know that the next body I find isn't going to be yours."

Lucy nodded in understanding, then leaned over and kissed him. "I thought you found my body likeable," she teased.

"I thought I'd made that pretty obvious."

"That you did."

He pulled into Mildred Caulfield's slanted driveway, put the car in PARK and turned it off.

"Well, then, please keep it out of harm's way. For my sake as well as yours."

Chapter 27

SUNDAY, 9:00 AM

O N THE SECOND day after the flood, those who were not dead, burying dead, searching for the missing, or tending to the wounded gathered silently on the slanted slope of Tree Hill Park, mostly close to the top, to take part in an ecumenical religious service and to see how their friends, neighbors, coworkers, and family members were faring.

So soon after the disaster, with the floodwaters still present, the mood was not a joyful one.

Even though the observance was a somber one, however, it was meaningful to most of those in attendance.

Father Charlie Minor, the pastor of Our Mother of Sorrows Catholic church, had been invited to participate in the more religious aspects of the gathering, along with the Reverend Benjamin Fuller, the pastor of Obergrande Community Church, itself non-denominational. In addition, Rabbi Sheldon Feist had graciously come in from Lake Placid, about twenty miles to the north, the only town in the Adirondacks with an active synagogue.

All three men had stood in silence together, facing one another, heads bowed in prayer, for about fifteen minutes before the ceremony began. As a result, the normal noise and banter that might occur before any type of public event was minimized by the sight of three holy men, their arms across each other's shoulders, praying quietly for the lost.

Rabbi Feist had kept his remarks short, expressing the condolences of his congregation and noting that his Temple would be praying for those impacted by the flood, as well as offering kosher meals for anyone who needed them due to lack of electricity. He stood in silence while Father Minor read a passage from Psalm 69:

> Save me, O God, for the waters have come up to my soul. I have sunk in deep mire, and there is no foothold; I have come into deep waters, and a flood overflows me. I am weary with my crying; my throat is parched; my eyes fail while I wait for my God.

When Father Charlie looked up, he saw tears in the eyes of many of the assembled.

Finally, Pastor Fuller, one of Father Charlie's best friends, stepped forward to speak.

Before he did, the carillon of the Catholic church played a hymn that was familiar to many from the Community Church, but utterly unknown to those who attended mass at Our Mother of Sorrows, causing a bit of confusion. The carillon played for a verse and a chorus, after which a pick-up choir from the Community Church joined in at the end:

> When peace like a river attendeth my way
> When sorrows like sea billows roll
> Whatever my lot, Thou hast taught me to know
> It is well, it is well, with my soul.

Then Pastor Fuller went on to explain that the words of the hymn had been written in 1873 by Horatio Spafford, a successful lawyer who had lost his four daughters when the ship that they and their mother had been traveling on sank in the Atlantic.

"Shortly after the sinking, as Spafford traveled to meet his grieving wife who had alone survived the disaster, he was inspired to write these words as his ship passed near where his daughters had died," Reverend Fuller said gently.

The members of the Community Church in attendance had looked at each other in horror. The hymn was one that they sang regularly, especially for fellowship, but they had no idea about its grisly beginnings, or why the minister had played it now, as they were all grieving for their losses in a water disaster.

"I asked Father Charlie if he could make the Mother of Sorrows carillon play this hymn of comfort, and for a short moment there was a conflict," Reverend Fuller explained. "This hymn is not one used by Catholics, and so the carillon at Mother of Sorrows does not have it programmed. The organist at the Catholic Church, however, offered to play the hymn from the sheet music, so that the members of our church could have it at this ceremony. I believe this should be seen as an example of how we can reach across lines to people of other religions—or no religion at all—in a time of grief this widespread."

He stepped away, leaving Ray Tibedeau, the mayor of Obergrande, standing in for Bob Lundford, the blowhard Town Supervisor who had been injured in the course of the flood.

Ray Tibedeau wiped his eyes with the back of his hand, looked around at the people of the town gathered there and below him on the hill, and spoke in a wavering voice.

"First, I hope you know that I am only speaking at all this morning because Bob Lundford, our Town Supervisor, is unable to do so," he said nervously. "Please, if you are able, keep him and his family in your prayers. I know everyone has a very long list.

"When something of this—magnitude happens, the voice of any one person is insignificant by comparison, unworthy to try to make sense of the nightmare that has just been visited upon this—this—*our*—beautiful little town." He had choked on the first few words, so he took a deep breath and a moment to become calm again. "I don't want to even pretend I know what to say.

"The loss our families, our citizens, have suffered is profound," he went on, "and in the face of profound loss, I think it's wise to say as little as possible, and only what has to be said.

"This place we now gather is the place our ancestors have gathered for four centuries, in times of profound loss, as well as great joy. This epic tree, Obergrande, this national landmark, has seen great victory and terrible defeat, beginnings and endings, and through it all has endured, has stood as an example for our own endurance.

"This tree has witnessed the signing of peace accords between the Native peoples of this land and the French, Dutch, and British settlers who colonized it. It has seen the forging of a new nation one hundred seventy or so years later, and has seen that nation go into World Wars twice, each time its citizens standing beneath this very tree to hear the bells ring, announcing each war's beginning, and its end.

"It has been the place high school seniors come to take a photograph that will grace the halls of the school through the years; it has seen countless marriage proposals, weddings, and bereavements, and still it stands, unbowed by all that life.

"And today, it stands as silent witness to this terrible event, a natural disaster that has taken such an awful toll on the people of the town that shares its name. I can only ask that we all come here, gather when the carillon bells ring, to hear important tidings, to grieve together, to work together, that one day, down the long road, we may gather together to celebrate life once more.

"I wish you peace and consolation. Thank you."

He turned away and had started back toward the clergymen when a voice from the crowd below broke the silence.

"Now, *now* can you people see what waiting all this time has caused? We've been trying to tell you all along that the dam would fail, that the river was growing stronger. You people who have resisted dealing with nature have blood on your hands."

The mayor turned back in shock as a low rumble began.

"No!" Ray Tibedeau shouted. "Please! This is a day of peace, of mourning—"

"All of which could have been avoided if—"

"It was a *natural disaster*, you *idiot*—"

"Liar!"

"You're to blame, with your money and your manipulations—"

The gathering exploded, fueled by the misery of grief and the volatile history, into a fireball of anger.

The clergymen looked at each other in horror, while the mayor held his hands aloft, shouting words of calm that no one heard.

Parents hurried their terrified children away as the elderly attempted to flee the full-blown riot that took place, beneath the very tree that had seen so much life.

The Army National Guard, deployed to help rescue and rebuild, were quickly dispatched to Tree Hill Park, this time to put an end to the stupidity of violence taking place there.

Lucy, who had been standing about halfway down the hill, had been ushered away by Ace at the first moment that a shout went up, and so was several streets away before the actual donnybrook began.

As he hurried her along the streets toward the dry end of town, his hand clutching hers, she turned back to see the people of the town she loved dissolve before her very eyes into madness.

Chapter 28

8:17 PM

High Street

A CE HAD BEEN called in for duty moments after he had delivered Lucy back to Mildred's house on High Street, and had been deployed all day.

Shutting the riot down had actually taken less time that it might have, due the overwhelming exhaustion and despair that was gripping most of the populace. Ace was trying, not particularly successfully, to find the mood and outlook he had possessed for a very long time, the sort of calm, casual acceptance that stupid things happened, and that people could not always be counted on to be reasonable, or rational, or even sane. He had seen this before, time and again, and had learned to have a passive, respectful attitude about sorting it out.

Only now there was a woman he loved in the thick of it, in harm's way.

And it infuriated him.

The gentlemanly calm he had described to Lucy the

night his own personal dam had failed, releasing the flood of words that had brought them together, was more or less gone. He had gone from the short-spoken, mono-syllabic, three-words-or-less-per-sentence Ace of the past to Alex Evans again, a man who had a woman he cared for more than anything else in his life.

And anything that put that woman in jeopardy was a problem.

Words from the past came back to haunt him. He had painful memories of the night in the emergency room after the evening he had described to Lucy, the first time he had intervened in the violence his stepfather had committed against his mother. His wrist had wrung with agony until it was set by the good-natured ER doctor in Albany, but even more painful was the expression on his mother's face the whole time she was watching him being treated.

When the doctor had left to go about his rounds, promising to return with the X-rays shortly, his mother had risen from the chair in the corner in which she had been encamped and had come to the table on which he lay in the little treatment area curtained off by drapes of fabric.

She stood above him, tears in her eyes.

Alex, I'm so sorry.

Why? he could hear the fourteen-year-old voice in his memory ask her. *Why do you need him? Why can't we be rid of him? He's* mean *to you, mom.*

His mother's words still turned his stomach.

I know you don't understand this, honey, but I'm doing it for you.

His mother was still alive, still in his life.

Ace made a mental note as he was physically separating two arguing men in the street on the wet side of Tree Hill Park to talk to her soon and ask her why.

He had been more physically rough than he needed be with both of the men, pushing one off the other so aggressively that they had stopped arguing and stared at him in shock.

"You got a wife? A family?" he had demanded of the one he considered the aggressor.

The man had nodded sullenly.

"You're a lucky man," Ace had said harshly. "Get home to her, to them; stop being a jackass."

The last remnants of the conflict in Tree Hill Park had been resolved by noon, and by eight o'clock that night he was finally off duty again. He hurried to sign out and drove as fast as he could, his spirits rising at the thought of being back in the arms of the woman he could not stop thinking about.

He parked in the driveway at 18 High Street and climbed up the steep, rocky staircase to the door, avoiding the broken doorbell, and knocked twice.

Mrs. Caulfield opened the door. "Yes?"

"Good evening, Mrs. Caulfield. I've come to pick up Lucy."

"Lucy?"

Ace had blinked. "Miss Sullivan?"

Mildred Caulfield was confused. "I know who you mean, Sergeant. But I thought she was with you already."

"No, ma'am. Could she be upstairs, asleep?"

Mrs. Caulfield shook her head. "I'll check, but I'm certain I heard her go out earlier. Sadie can't open the door on her own."

Hearing her name, the kitten came down the stairs and rubbed up against Mrs. Caulfield's legs.

Ace bent down to stroke the soft fur while Mrs. Caulfield climbed the stairs. Sadie began purring, but then started and ran under the nearest armchair when Mrs. Caulfield called down the stairs.

"She's not here."

"Where could she have gone?" he asked.

"She's under the chair. Can't you see her tail sticking out? They all do that, you know."

"Lucy," Ace said, trying to remain calm. "Do you have any idea where Lucy is?"

Mrs. Caulfield thought. "She did say something about wedding pictures. She was admiring the picture of my husband and me, and said something about her parents."

Ace nodded, but his stomach was turning over. "She must have gone back to her house to get the picture from her bedroom."

Mrs. Caulfield raised an eyebrow. "Her bedroom?"

"Uhm, yes. I facilitated the removal of her personal effects from her home the day of the flood, ma'am. All those bags and pillowcases you had me leave on the front porch?"

"I see. Very well, go find her. And give me a call if you can. So far, the phone still works. Lucy has the number."

"Yes, ma'am." Ace turned away and started across the porch toward the stairs when he came to an abrupt halt.

Out in the darkness of the flood zone, sparks were flying.

Tiny little fires, some in the air, most likely on power lines, others lower down, were cropping up, turning the utter blackness intermittently orange and yellow.

"Mrs. Caulfield?" he said, his voice shaking.

"Yes?"

"If your phone still works, please use it to call 911."

ACE DROVE LIKE a maniac down the steep hill and through the abandoned streets to the edge of the cordoned-off area and threw the car into PARK. He ran to the barricade and saluted the guardsman.

"I'm Sergeant Alex Evans, private. I think you may have a series of fires, electric or otherwise, sparking in the zone. I saw them from High Street. I'm also looking for a civilian, Miss Lucy Sullivan."

The young guard nodded, looking concerned. "The teacher who saved all those kids? Yes, sir. She requested permission to access her home a few hours ago."

"And you *let her?*"

"A badass like her? Yes, sir. She's been in and out of the zone with you, sir. I assumed she had clearance."

"Has she come out again?"

"No, sir, not past me."

Ace ducked under the rope, noting that the water had receded. The height of the flood was clearly marked on each house in the discoloration left behind. The closer to the lake the house had stood, the higher the water, with some homes still completely submerged in the new, wider lake.

In the distance he heard the sound of the fire siren ramping up.

He took off in a dead run as he could begin to see the sparks in the zone now.

As Ace rounded the corner at Marshall Avenue, he could see the flicker of candlelight in the second story window of Lucy's house again.

Looking past her house, he could see fire. Not the small, smoky bonfires that had been lit throughout the day by people burning flood-soaked debris, but flames, shooting into the darkened sky.

One of the dark houses in the already hurting area of East Obergrande was on fire.

Ace doubled his speed.

The closer he got to Lucy's house, the closer the fire appeared to be, until he rounded the corner and skidded to a stop.

An entire block of little houses was aflame.

Ace knew that East Obergrande had propane tanks outside almost every home.

Including Lucy's.

The conflagration that was about to erupt would be an inferno.

He broke into a run, screaming her name.

Moments later he was pulling open the door of Lucy's cottage, and sprinting up the stairs.

He met her in the doorway of her bedroom, wrapping her parents' wedding portrait in a towel.

"I thought you were picking me up at Mildred's, but

this is even better," she said, confused, as he strode toward her. "You can help me carry the pictures—"

He seized her arm. "We gotta go!"

"But I'm not—"

"Fire! We have to go!"

Shock was setting in. "Let me get my other pictures—"

He dragged her toward the stairs. "Lucy, the only thing I care about in this house is you," he said as they ran down them. "Everything else is just stuff."

"But—"

"Your whole neighborhood is on fire," Ace said as they reached the turn in the staircase. "You, and everyone else, has a propane tank. They're gonna blow, and we don't want to be here when they do."

They raced out the door, Ace holding the portrait under his arm like an over-sized football, Lucy holding a flashlight in her other hand, clear, within seconds, of the house.

When they got outside, it was eerily light. The flickering flames cast shadows against the clouds in the sky.

"No," Lucy was screaming, choking. "Dammit, *no!* Not again. *Not again!*"

"Hang tight, Badass," Ace called behind him. "Come on!"

They ran down the street, the smell of smoke acrid in the air.

The corporal was running toward them.

"There are no other civilians in the area, sir. We've been given orders to evacuate. The fire department is on the way."

The sirens were screaming through the air, growing louder.

Ace stopped and let go of Lucy's arm. "Do you need a ride to somewhere, Corporal?"

"No, sir. I'm to meet the fire trucks."

"All right, get clear of the houses."

When they reached his car, Ace tucked Lucy rapidly inside it with her portrait and looked back. The fire was growing now, spreading throughout the entirety of the zone.

There was a deafening boom, and Ace was nearly knocked over by a wash of air.

Followed by more and more explosions.

Lucy was staring, glassy eyed, at the building inferno as he got into the car.

"I forgot to blow out the candles in my bedroom," she said dully.

Ace recognized the signs of the shock into which she was sinking, so he kept his voice gentle.

"I don't think it's going to be an issue, honey," he said as he peeled out of the zone and drove like mad for High Street.

Chapter 29

The village of Obergrande

T HE NEXT DAY, those who were still mobile gathered at the base of the hill in Tree Hill Park, in shock and covered with black soot.

The fire that had erupted from the power lines had been thorough in its devastation, burning the streets in the eastern neighborhoods that had survived the flood, making it seem as if an asteroid had hit the Earth there.

Amid the ruins of the arts and mercantile district, the pretty streets Lucy had admired from atop Tree Hill Park only a few days before with Glen Daniels, stood a rising black structure, reminiscent of the infrastructure of a high-rise building after a skyscraper fire. From a distance it resembled a work of modern art, a single column leading up to large, dark vertical and horizontal lines, otherwise bare.

Immense.

Most people who came into the town in years to come

had to squint very hard, or be possessed of excellent eyesight, or be informed by a townsperson, that the immense structure had actually once been a tree.

A historic and beautiful tree, a Northern Red Oak.

Blackened, but not broken, no longer alive.

But not really dead either.

In a way, some people would say in later weeks, it was actually a blessing that the fire came when it did, roaring through streets and buildings that had already been abandoned. The death toll from the massive blaze was minimal, the same people with heart disease or breathing difficulties that always die in fires.

A lot of silly tongues spoke of acts of God, wondering what Obergrande had done to make Him mad. People whispered words like *terrorism* or *incompetence*, blaming the reason for the blaze on the flood, or shoddy building standards, or the dust in the sawmills.

Largely because they did not have any reason to know that it was nothing like that at all.

But on that day, in the shadow of the mystic Adirondack Mountains, the Hudson River, though having receded somewhat, was still rushing south over its banks to bigger, more important places than this tiny little town, a town that was once an outpost of early settlers, long before America was born, people who staked out territory and made treaties among themselves and those who had lived here first, a town of loggers and miners, furniture craftsmen and silversmiths, and later artists and hoteliers and people who just wanted to live in one of the most beautiful places in America.

While the rest of the citizens were wandering around, lost and vacant with shock, one person stood apart, musing about all that had happened, a tragedy that was part Act of God, part bad luck.

And partly intentional.

Obergrande, that person thought sympathetically. *Truly, you are suffering so damned unfairly.*

But you will be rebuilt, and one day, you will be vastly better than you were before.

Like birth, rebirth was painful, but worth it.

AT NOON, THREE of the same four men that had attempted to comfort the town the day before summitted Tree Hill again.

Every one of them wide-eyed with shock, trembling, but maintaining a respectful attitude.

Rabbi Feist had returned to Lake Placid the evening before, prior to the fire breaking out, and the Obergranders who had invited him initially to come and speak did not have the heart to try to contact him again.

Pastor Fuller and Father Minor climbed Tree Hill together with the mayor, trying to breathe in the low-hanging smoke that was everywhere in the town. It had even moved west, against the currents of the wind, until it came through the window screens of West Obergrande, causing the residents to slam their windows shut and breathe through wet tea towels.

Ray Tibedeau's eyes were hollow, but his jaw was set. He stood with the two pastors and stared solemnly down at the townsfolk who had come to the park again, looking for comfort, or meaning, or answers, or aid—whatever they were looking for, there was little to none to be had.

Mayor Tibedeau began speaking exactly at noon, cued by his wristwatch, because the carillon of Our Mother of Sorrows was silent.

He did not have any particularly inspirational words; he had only spoken the day before, as he had nervously admitted, because the real leader of the town, Bob Lundford, was recovering from his flood injuries. The mayor limited his comments to the aid plans that had been put together by the Red Cross, the food and water deliveries and other items of information that needed to be shared.

Then he looked out over the blackened town square again for the second time in that place in twenty-four hours.

"I believe we will return, bigger and better from this," he said gravely. "I also believe it will be the hardest comeback I will have ever seen in my lifetime. Good luck, everyone."

The pastors offered prayers, but had nothing else to say.

Chapter 30

THREE MONTHS LATER, August

Ginny's Sleep-Easy, Danville, southern Virginia

JEREMY WAS DOZING on-and-off in front of the TV in the bedroom area of the unit he and Sam were renting by the month in the one-floor motel at the edge of town.

In spite of having moved into a somewhat more comfortable place in life, Jeremy still had trouble sleeping, so any opportunity to doze was a blessing.

Sam was out at the moment, picking up groceries for the weekend. She had landed a part-time job as a cashier and waitress at the diner nearby, and was a lot easier to deal with, now that she wasn't trapped inside, twitching like a nervous cat, waiting for him to get home every day. She also had some money of her own, which helped make life even better.

Her absence provided a little down-time, time when he could let go of the invisible net of anxiety and regret that he was still entangled in, even after all this time.

Jeremy was growing to love the town of Danville. It

had beautiful hills, reminiscent of the tree-covered splendor of the Adirondacks, with the added glory of six different speedways and raceways, places for him to let go of his worries in the scream of NASCAR engines and motorcycle rallies.

He had found work with a road-crew, a non-union job that didn't pay him half as well as the lazy guys with the highway flags, but still a damn sight better than he had been making in New York, all under the table, of course. Now there was food in the kitchen cabinets and the fridge, cold beer and nachos on Friday nights, like this one.

And Sam seemed happy, which was a plus. The sex had never been better.

Best of all, the reports about the flooding and fire that took out a serious piece of Obergrande, New York, had ceased being featured on the national news for the most part.

The first night they had checked into the motel months ago was the day after the flood. Even as he dozed now, Jeremy still remembered his first sight of the disaster, which had appeared, coincidentally, on the TV screen the moment he snapped it on. He had frantically grabbed the remote and tried to change the channel, but had to flip through five others to get to one on which the news report was not playing.

Then, feeling guilty, he turned back to the first news station and watched the whole thing, Sam sitting on the bed beside him, both of their faces reflecting the pale light and colored graphics on the TV.

Both of them sick to their stomachs.

In the back of his mind, exhausted from the long motorcycle ride and the fumes, Jeremy was convinced then that he could hear the devil laughing at his distress.

That same devil laughed in his dreams still.

He was mostly asleep, his head jerking back and forth nervously, when the door opened and Sam came in, carrying two brown paper bags.

"You OK, babe?" she called from the tiny hallway in their unit.

"Hmmmpf? Yeah." He swung his feet over the edge of the bed and quickly rose to a stand, shaking off the nightmares. "Yeah."

He could hear her puttering about in the one-butt kitchen area, unpacking bags, opening and closing the three cabinets over and around the small sink and the efficiency stove. Jeremy rubbed his head, trying to dispel the bad thoughts, and wandered out into the front part of the unit.

Sam was buzzing around, as he had heard, humming an unfamiliar tune. On the kitchenette's table were two extra-large cupcakes, one with a grotesque amount of brown frosting, one with the same amount of white.

Each with a candle in it.

"What's this?" he asked, his brow furrowing deeply.

Sam smiled, her luxurious dark hair pulled up in a high ponytail. She came over to the table, snapped the wheel of a lighter and put the flame to the wicks of the two candles.

"Happy anniversary, Germ," she said, her face reflecting the glow of the tiny fires. "It was two years ago today that you snuck me out of that bachelor party after I finished the groom's lap dance and drove me away on your motorcycle—in nothing but a feathered thong, I might add."

"That guy was a putz," Jeremy said, walking closer to her and taking hold of the empty belt loops on her jeans. "I didn't like seein' his hands on you, especially since he was gettin' married the next day. An' I gave you my jacket, so you weren't topless for long."

She took hold of one of his hands, freed it from the belt loop, brought it to her lips and kissed it. "Well, for two years exactly, this has been one of only two hands on me."

He turned her hand over and returned the favor.

"I'm surprised you were able to walk out of there," Sam said, chuckling. "You were so drunk I thought you told me your name was 'Germ' when I asked who the hell you thought you were."

"It was a bachelor party—duh."

"Come over here and help me blow the candles out," she said, pulling him to the cupcakes. "Make a wish."

She was surprised when he followed her willingly, closed his eyes and blew when she did. Under normal circumstances, she would have expected him to get grumpy and refuse to do something so dumb.

But he had changed since Obergrande.

At least tonight, she thought it was in a good way.

Maybe he felt he needed a wish.

"Which one do you want?" she asked, pulling out a chair from the table.

Jeremy shrugged. "Whatever."

"Be a sport. Pick a cupcake."

He sighed. "Fine. Chocolate."

"Great." She snatched the vanilla one, then led him to the chair and pushed him down in it.

"What are you *doin'?"* he asked, whining a little.

"You can be a putz, too, ya know, Germ. Shut up."

Sam set the cupcake on the table's edge, then seized the top of Jeremy's jeans and unsnapped them.

Slowly, like the lap dancer she once was, she slithered to the floor between his knees, dragging his zipper down with her.

Then slid up his calves until she was leaning her chest on his thighs. She put her arms around him.

"Arch your back," she said huskily.

Jeremy closed his eyes and followed her directions as she pulled his jeans down to his ankles.

He could hear her inhale, as she often did at moments like these, as if she was impressed.

That little inhalation of breath always did wonders for what she was watching and breathing about, making it, and him, more eager.

"Open your mouth," she whispered. "Your eyes, too, if you want."

Puzzled, Jeremy opened his eyes.

Sam was close to his face, her own eyes shining. "You wanna pull my hair down?" she asked, taking his hand.

"Yeah," Jeremy said, his voice wavering.

"Do it," Sam commanded, guiding his hand toward the ponytail. "But then put your hands on the sides of the seat. No touching 'til it's your turn."

Trembling, Jeremy reached over and wound his fingers through the scrunchie that held her pretty hair back from her pretty face. He slid it down the thick ponytail and dropped it beside the chair, inhaling a little himself as her hair cascaded around her shoulders and chest, which was still clad in the camisole she had worn under her waitress uniform.

Sam shook her head slowly from side to side, loosing her hair even more, making Jeremy's groin feel like it was on fire. She closed her eyes and ran her hand erotically through her hair, making the fire rise higher.

Then, still smiling, she turned to the cupcake on the table's edge, and, with her index finger, scooped a lane of the frosting off it.

With her other hand, she took a small dollop onto her finger, and stuck it suggestively into her mouth.

Her smile grew wider.

"Mmmmmmm," she said. It was more of a groan than anything else.

Jeremy swallowed hard, trying to remain still.

"Wanna taste?" she asked in mock innocence, holding out another dollop of the frosting near his mouth.

"Yeah," Jeremy muttered. He was having trouble concentrating.

Sam looked displeased.

"Try again, Germ," she said, a rough edge in her voice that she knew he liked. "Say 'yes, please,' or I'll go back to making nachos."

"Yes, please," he whispered. His throat was getting

tighter as he strained to stay in the chair, his hands gripping the sides of the seat.

"Open up," Sam directed, holding the fingerful of frosting near his mouth. "Lick it off."

Jeremy obeyed.

Slowly, carefully, she slid the tip of her finger just past his lips, then allowed him to wrap his tongue around it. He inhaled as he did, sucking the frosting off it, making her blink as her own face grew warmer.

"I thought I picked chocolate," he said.

"You did," Sam said smugly. "You'll get it when it's your turn to be in charge of the chair."

"Ahhhhh," Jeremy said. It was the only sound he could make now, because Sam had quickly returned to the cupcake, scooped more of the frosting off it, and began painting him with it, opening his shirt and swirling a little on his pecs, which she inhaled immediately, then went back to the area she had laid bare a few moments before.

Jeremy closed his eyes again and gritted his teeth as she took her time, applying the frosting liberally to everything that was exposed.

By the time she set to removing it, he was almost out of control already.

"You can arch your back again whenever you want," she said, pulling her hair that had fallen into her face out of the way before she set about her sensuous task.

She took her time, bringing him to the brink repeatedly, encouraged by the wordless sounds coming from his throat, only to back off playfully again. The sounds grew more desperate as she teased him, until finally she sat back and looked up at him, hovering at the knife's edge, his eyes squinted shut.

"What's the magic word, Germ?" she said jokingly.

"Please!" he whispered. "Please—*please*—"

"All right," she said. "Happy anniversary."

She turned her attention back to the task at hand, applying her talents and the warmth of her mouth as liberally as she had applied the frosting.

Lovingly as well.

Jeremy was panting now. He had just enough time to take one last deep breath before the ceiling exploded above him in rapidly-changing colors, and the chair below him caught fire, his entire body wracked with tremors that shot from him like a gigantic, whole-body sneeze. The reaction was so violent that Sam had just enough time to grab his knees as she fell back, rump first, on the floor behind her.

"Sorry, baby," he murmured as she pulled her hair out of her face, laughing. "That was—that—*wow*—amazing—ahhh—"

Sam stood up and brushed off her jeans.

"S'ok," she said, wrestling for a moment with her hair. "That's what you get when your boyfriend's hung like a horse. Fortunately, there are other things you get, too."

"You'll be gettin' it as soon as I can breathe again, believe me," Jeremy mumbled.

"You just sit there until you feel up to it," Sam said, heading for the kitchen.

Jeremy followed her suggestion, inhaling lightly to calm his racing heart, feeling the blood slowly leaving his burning face as his pulse simmered down. He could hear

Sam banging around in the kitchenette behind him, but he was afraid to open his eyes yet.

The hum of the microwave vibrated off his temples, but still Jeremy sat, his head back, chin pointed at the ceiling, as the hottest parts of his body cooled in the breeze from the motel's extremely loud air conditioner and the occasional opening of the fridge behind him.

Finally his nose caught a whiff of something appealing, and his ears were stabbed by the sound of a plate rattling as it was placed on the table in front of him.

Followed by a light *thud,* a hiss, and the slight screeching of the table legs.

Jeremy opened his eyes.

Sitting before him was a plate of steaming hot nachos.

Next to a steaming hot girl.

And a just-opened bottle of beer, cold from the fridge.

"Damn, I am the luckiest guy in the world," Jeremy said, finally able to breathe.

"You're sure right about that," Sam said humorously. "You have a decision to make."

"An' what's that?"

"Well," she said, moving the nachos aside, though still within reach, and scooting herself in front of him, "you have to decide what you wanna eat first."

Jeremy's sense of humor was returning.

"Well, the nachos are likely to get cold," he said, winking at her.

"They're not the only thing that can." Sam's voice was light, indicating that she was joking.

Jeremy knew better than to risk it. He pulled his chair

closer to the table and seized the waistband of her jeans, just as she had done to him, and pulled them apart at the snap.

Then sat back in his chair, puzzled.

A green rectangular piece of paper was sticking up at her waistband.

"Wha—what the hell is that?"

"Your third and last anniversary present," Sam said, her voice warm and loving now. "Number one was the cupcake, number two was, well, what the cupcake helped with, and now this is number three." Her face gleamed with excitement. "Open it, Germ."

Jeremy was still staring at the paper, confused. He looked up at her again, and was touched by the expression on her face, a face that could look as innocent as a four-year-old's when she was planning something nice for someone.

And something more.

Jeremy was pretty sure he was looking at love.

"I didn't get you anything," he said, embarrassed, as he picked up the beer and took a swig.

"Figured you wouldn't. You never remember dates."

Jeremy swallowed the beer, but said nothing.

There were a few he was bound to remember now.

"But, I do have somethin' for you," he said hurriedly, his mouth moving faster than his occasionally-stalled brain could think.

"Oh? An' what's that?"

"A—a proposition," he said, his thoughts still lagging behind his words.

"A proposition? For what?"

"To make an honest woman outta you." Jeremy's words screeched to a halt, having gone a few miles farther down the road than he had intended.

Sam exhaled, then smiled slightly. "I think the word you wanted was 'proposal,' not proposition," she said, her hands now grasping the rim of the tabletop on either side of her legs. "You proposition me almost every morning before you leave, usually with dirty suggestions on a post-it under the peanut butter jar." Her face grew serious. "And, for the record, Germ, I've always been an honest woman. *Always*. I just didn't wait for marriage to have sex. I thought that was somethin' you liked about me, but whether you do or not, it's somethin' I like about me. And only I get to make me an honest woman or not—not you. Ever."

Jeremy, his brain finally caught up, just smiled.

"We can talk about your—your proposition later," Sam said, her humor returning. "Open your card."

"It's a card?" Jeremy put the beer down and pulled the green rectangle carefully out of her waistband, realizing how stupid his comment had been.

"Open it," Sam urged, getting excited again. "I hope you like it."

Jeremy opened the envelope, sliding his finger under the seal to keep from damaging what was inside it. He pulled out a paper brochure, printed in color on glossy paper.

Lake Rawlings, Rawlings, Virginia, it read.

He scanned the text, his hands beginning to shake.

"It's a scuba diving place, about two hours from here," Sam said excitedly, turning the brochure over in his hand and pointing to the pertinent parts. "The water's real clear, and they have all kinds of stuff to see underneath it—like a plane, cars, school buses, sunken boats an' stuff like that—and the equipment rental wasn't that bad. There's cabins and tent camping—and—"

She paused, looking proud.

"And we're going next weekend! I already got the time off. It's all paid for."

Jeremy, who had been staring at the brochure, raised his head.

His eyes wild and panicked.

The look of pride, and the smile, were stripped from Sam's face like water running off the edge of it. She tried to explain, tripping over the words.

"I—I felt bad it was so—so—expensive in the Adirondacks that—that you—you didn't—get to—go diving—there—"

Jeremy lurched back in his chair, stood up, shaking violently, and lunged for the bathroom.

Slamming the door behind him.

Sam blinked in astonishment as sounds of retching came from behind the door.

"What the hell?" she murmured. They were the only words she could form that survived the shock that had taken her over.

After what seemed like a very long time, she heard the toilet flush and the water in the sink being turned on. Then, everything went silent.

The bathroom door swung open violently.

"Germ—" Sam said, stunned by the speed at which everything in the little motel unit seemed to be happening.

Jeremy said nothing, completely avoiding her. He strode to the closet near the door, pulled his motorcycle jacket and helmet from the bar and shelf, and ran to the door.

He tugged on it, forgetting Sam had locked it behind her.

Then violently turned the deadbolt, rushed out and slammed it behind him.

In the distance, Sam could hear the sound of his bike revving up.

She rose from the table on which she was still sitting, and walked to the window, pulling the low-quality, heavy-motel-fabric curtain back.

In time to see the bike streak around the corner.

Wondering what had just happened.

She was too shocked to cry.

At least for the first hour that he was gone.

JUST BEFORE DAWN, Jeremy returned to the hotel unit.

He opened the door to see Sam's meager possessions packed and sitting at the door.

The owner of the possessions was curled up on the couch, asleep, wadded-up tissues on the floor in front of it.

Jeremy cursed himself silently.

He went over to the couch and crouched down next to her.

"Sam, baby, I love you," he whispered into the hair

that lay along her ear. "I'm so sorry. Please don't leave."

She opened her blood-shot eyes slowly and stared at him.

Their gaze stung his, and he lowered his head for a moment.

Then he lifted it again and looked into her eyes once more.

When he spoke, his voice sounded like he had swallowed ground glass.

But his eyes looked as if he had seen the end of the world.

"I have somethin' I have to tell you," he said.

AFTER SHE HAD heard what Jeremy had to say, Sam left anyway.

As quickly as she could.

Chapter 31

LUCY SULLIVAN KNOCKED on Pastor Fuller's office door, an armload of books and supplies balancing in her hands.

As she waited for a response, she glanced around the narthex, the foyer of the church, and smiled.

Just as she had expected, the door was opened by a small girl, working on six years old, with long chestnut-brown hair.

Who grinned widely upon seeing her.

"Hello, Miss Sullivan," Grace said.

"Well, hello, Grace," Lucy responded. "Is your daddy around?"

"He is," called Pastor Fuller from deeper within the office. "Be right out, Lucy."

Lucy exhaled and tried to maintain the balance of her supplies.

Pastor Fuller appeared at the door, his face wreathed in

a smile that quickly faded.

"Oh, I'm so sorry," he said, rushing to her aid and offloading some of her burden. "I didn't realize you were bringing your supplies already."

"I like to start early," Lucy admitted, following him down into the church's classroom wing.

"Can you keep an eye on the office, honey?" Pastor Fuller asked Grace, who was following them.

The little girl's eyes lit up. "Can I answer the phone?"

"Hmmm. What do you say when you do?"

" 'Obergrande Community Church, how may I direct your call?' "

"Good," said Pastor Fuller as Lucy hid a smile. "Go for it."

"So how did your meeting go?" he asked as Grace hurried back to the office. He opened the door to a mid-size classroom with many toys and a long, low table. "Did the principal honor your request?"

"Yes," Lucy said. "I'm getting to keep my same kindergarten students for first grade next year. It was deemed a 'measure of stability.' "

"That's *great*. Grace will be so excited."

"Anything to provide healing for the Fearless Fivesome," Lucy said. "They seem to be doing well. How's Grace liking summer?"

"Loving it. We've been spending a lot of time in Schroon Lake."

At the words, Lucy's smile faded. She thought back to the night of the Town Board meeting, three months prior, the night of her dinner date with Glen Daniels.

Why aren't you attending the hearing? I thought everyone in town was itching to be there tonight.

Maybe, but I don't live in town. I come over from Schroon Lake.

"That's a lovely place." She inhaled, preparing herself. "Have you noticed any, well, anxiety?"

Ben Fuller turned around in surprise.

"Well, there's the occasional nightmare from the flood, but the girls' therapist has said that it's normal."

Lucy pursed her lips as she tended to do when she was thinking of how to say something tactfully.

"I think I noticed a little bit of uncertainty *before* the flood," she said carefully. "For Grace, I think it might be biological—maybe inherited."

Pastor Fuller's brows drew together.

"Really? That's strange—I've never noticed it. And neither Kathy nor I have any problems with that."

Lucy, who had seen Kathy Fuller in a few social situations, thought otherwise, but merely nodded.

"Since the girls are still seeing a therapist regularly about the flood, you might want to just mention it to him—or her."

"Her," Pastor Fuller said. "Thank you; I'll keep it in mind."

Lucy just nodded and began unpacking her materials, inwardly disappointed.

It was the brush-off most parents gave her when they didn't want to see what she was talking about.

"Thank you again for letting us borrow your classroom space," she said, setting the books on the shelf. "I do hope the new school is open and ready for business next year, so you can have your religious ed space back. It was great to have it this year, to finish out the school year for those kids."

"It's not a bother at all," said Pastor Fuller. "We're glad to be able to help out. Isn't that what neighbors are for?"

Lucy smiled. "Absolutely."

Grace appeared at the door.

"Someone on the phone for you, Daddy," she said importantly. "He has a special offer on magazines for you—hurry!"

Lucy laughed as the minister rolled his eyes and followed his daughter out the door.

Murray Street

DAVE WINDSOR RANG the doorbell, a package in hand.

As he waited, he cast a glance around the neighborhood.

Leland and Betty Finley had found a nice home in an area of the remains of East Obergrande distant from Tree Hill Park. He admired the landscaping and the pristine driveway leading up to the little Cape Cod home with Adirondack styling, the cedar shakes and pitched roof, typical for the area.

He and Sue had decided otherwise, had chosen to rent a townhouse nearer to the garden center, three bedrooms, bath and a half, that was just big enough for the family. Sarah had her own room which she had decorated herself, with a little help from mom, and Blythe and Bonnie were still sleeping in the same crib, refusing to be separated.

For the moment, all was well.

The door opened, and Betty Finley appeared, a baby in her arms. She smiled broadly.

"Well, hi, Dave! What brings you by?"

"Got something for ya," Dave said. "I won't keep you."

Betty pushed the screen door open. "Come on in."

He followed her into the kitchen, which was in the center of the house, a variation on the style he thought was nice, having been in many houses in the course of his fire training and experience.

"Rosemary lemonade?" Betty asked, heading for the fridge. "I'm having some."

"Sounds delicious. Sure."

As she filled the glasses he admired the way she was managing, a forty-or-so-year-old woman who had never had children taking care of a one-year-old. The little girl seemed content, a pretty infant with beautiful auburn hair and deep dimples who rarely cried.

And rarely smiled.

The official mascot of Obergrande Fire Company #2.

"How's she doing?" he asked as Betty set a tumbler with a long sprig of rosemary in it down on the table in front of him.

"Beautifully," Betty said proudly. "She's a good girl. A lovely child."

Dave took a sip of the lemonade and nodded. "That's delicious," he said.

He reached into his jacket pocket and took out a velveteen bag.

"I thought you should have this, for MaryBeth," he said, cringing, as he always did, at the name they had given the little girl. For many weeks after the flood, in the hospital and after her release, she had been known just as MB, for Missing Baby. The Finleys, who had volunteered as her foster family, had given her the name, but it always bothered him, as it evoked the night of her rescue.

Something that still gave him nightmares, proud as the department was of it.

He pulled the frayed drawstring open, carefully removed the contents of the package, and held it up.

A tarnished silver bracelet, primitive in manufacture, with a translucent red stone set in it.

Betty Finley blinked. "What's that?"

"Something I discovered in the backpack she was found in," Dave said, turning the bracelet so the stone caught the light dimly. "It doesn't seem like they're going to find her parents, alive, at least, so I thought you should have this for her."

Betty Finley's face turned red.

"It's only been three months, Dave," she said, her voice barely above a whisper. "You never know—"

"No, you don't, and if they ever do find 'em, you're just as capable of returning it to them when you return her as I would be," Dave said, placing the bracelet on top of the bag and pushing it in front of Betty. "But I think the odds of that are pretty unlikely, Betty, so I'm turning this over to you now. It's a simple thing, not worth much by the looks of it, though I'm no expert, certainly. But apparently it was important, or at least meaningful to whoever had her before you, so I thought she might want it someday, when she's old enough to understand."

Betty nodded, not looking up from the table.

"Besides, you're an officer of the town, bonded and all," Dave said, finishing up his lemonade. "Far more appropriate for you to have it than me, anyway. I was putting some stuff in the safe where I stuck it the night we found her, and came across it. Thought you should have it, and now you do."

He stood up from the table and rubbed the little girl's head, letting his fingers slip through the beautiful, baby-fine hair.

"She's a pretty thing," he said. "A very pretty little thing."

"Thank you," Betty said awkwardly.

"Well, I'll show myself out," Dave said, pushing in the chair. "Best to Leland."

"Thank you—best to Sue."

"Thank you as well. Goodbye."

He made his way to the door, feeling the eyes of both foster mother and baby on his back all the way out.

Obergrande Community Church parking lot

WHEN LUCY LEFT the church about an hour later, there was someone sitting on the hood of her car in the parking lot.

Someone handsome and important enough to her for

her to drop her canvas book bag and purse and run to him, laughing out loud, her long curly hair billowing in the wind behind her.

"Hi!" she called excitedly as she approached. "I've missed you *so* much—how did you get back here so quickly?"

Ace remained sitting atop the vehicle, grinning broadly, both his hands behind his back. He was attired in what he referred to as "civvies," the military expression for civilian clothing, a pair of khaki pants, a white shirt and navy blue jacket.

"Pick a hand," he said as Lucy leaned in and kissed him, leaving her lips a good long while on his, reveling in their lusciousness.

"Lwfft," she said, continuing the kiss.

Ace brought his left hand around from behind his back and presented her with the single red rose. Then he slid the empty hand around her back, anchoring it to her waist and drew her closer, pulling her between his legs and kissing her even more deeply.

"You're going to make my knees give out," Lucy warned him when their lips parted. She lifted the rose to her nose and smelled it. "Thank you."

"I'm not sure it's gentlemanly to be making out in a church parking lot anyway," Ace said. "I'd rather take you back to the hotel and do things I would need to come to church to repent for."

"Ah, the Catholic in both of us—Fun on Friday, confession on Saturday."

"Well, then we're at the wrong church. Isn't this

Protestant?"

"Yes. I'm just teaching here again, starting next month, and checking up on Grace. So what's in the other hand?" Lucy asked mischievously.

Ace's smiled dimmed. He pulled out a standard-issue canvas bag from behind him.

"They've finally confirmed, cataloged, and released the contents of your car."

"All these months later? They found my car?"

"They had a giant pile of them, stacked up like, I dunno, giant metal picnic tables leaning against one another," Ace said, holding it out to her. "There wasn't much in it—anything paper, like your road maps, dissolved or was unsavable anyway. On the positive side, you kept an impressively neat vehicle, something pretty rare for a kindergarten teacher. High marks on the military inspection scale."

"I'm a first grade teacher now," Lucy said. She took the bag and opened it.

Then put her fist to her mouth.

Ace took her by the waist, encircling it with his hands, and caressed her there as she continued to stare into the bag.

Then reached in, her hands shaking, and took out her grandmother Maeve's rosary.

Connemara marble from the mountains of Ireland, green, the beads that had once been cubes, but had been worn into a slightly oval shape by the many loving caresses of Maeve's devotion, and her own mother's thereafter.

And her own touchstone caresses.

The Celtic cross at the end was dimmer than she remembered it, but then she realized it was silver, and likely to be tarnished.

Ace's rough hand caressed her cheek gently where the tears were falling.

"I remember this hanging from the rearview mirror the night your car wouldn't start," he said quietly, kissing her neck as her head bent under the weight of the emotion.

Lucy nodded, unable to speak.

"It gets worse, my love," Ace said, pulling her even closer and moving his hands to the small of her back, encircling her in his arms. "Hang on to me."

"Why?" Lucy said, sniffling from within the depths of his jacket lapel. "I didn't keep anything else in my car but the maps, a little cup of change, and a troll doll."

"Yeah, that's in there," Ace said, continuing to kiss her neck. "Ugly. Really ugly."

"Her name's Persimmon, and don't insult my troll doll."

He kissed her ear. "OK."

Lucy finally swallowed, looked up and moved back enough to reach into the bag again.

She started to tremble.

"Oh, God," she whispered.

Her hands shook as she pulled out the compact black umbrella.

Ace's strong arms drew her close again and held her tightly.

There, in the parking lot of the Obergrande Community Church, she laid her head on his shoulder, her arms around his neck, the red rose trembling in her hand, and cried.

"I forgot about him again," she wept.

Ace just ran his hand up to the back of her head and squeezed her gently.

LATER THAT EVENING, just as the sun was beginning to set, Lucy and Ace walked hand in hand to the place where the old dam stood, now no longer active.

It was nothing more than a right angle of sheer walls reaching about fifteen feet down to the water below.

But it was also a beautiful, out-of-the-way place to sit and watch the sunset over the lake, which the couple settled down to do.

Lucy carrying a bouquet of wildflowers they had gathered together in the grasslands of the Overlook.

They sat in comfortable silence, his arm around her, watching the sun bathe the clouds in glorious shades of pink and gold, the sky turning a beautiful spectrum of blue from the aquamarine at the horizon to a dark cobalt above them, where stars were beginning to appear.

Finally, when the sun had finished its dive and had disappeared beyond the end of the world, Ace turned and kissed her forehead.

"You ready?"

Lucy exhaled, then nodded.

She held her hand with the flowers over the water.

Then slowly let them go.

The wind caught the grassier, lighter ones, wafting them gently down to the lake below.

"Goodnight, Glen," she said softly. "I hope you're listening to an even more beautiful kind of music now."

Then, with Ace's help, she rose, brushed off her trousers, and slipped into her lover's embrace.

As the sky turned dark, they turned and walked together, still hand in hand, back to the town, now no longer east or west.

Just Obergrande.

Chapter 32

Danville, Virginia

LOUIE, THE MANAGER of the Mountaintop Café, nodded to Sam, who had just started refilling all the salt and pepper shakers from the morning rush.

"Table Eleven," he said, looking up from the newspaper behind the counter.

Sam exhaled and grabbed an ice water, then headed toward the booth where a man sat with his back to her, his hair rumpled above a similarly rumpled shirt.

Great, she thought, *a singleton.* A low-paying table, almost not worth the interruption.

She placed the water down in front of the customer along with a menu, then pulled out her pad.

"Coffee?"

The man looked up, his face sallow, the bags under his eyes dark.

"Yes, please—cream, no sugar."

Sam exhaled again, this time angrily.

"You can't take a hint, can ya, Germ?" she said tersely. "I'm not sure how much more clear I could have been."

"I heard ya," Jeremy said, wiping his nose with the back of his sleeve. "It's worth beggin' if you'd reconsider."

Sam looked back over her shoulder. Louie was deeply engrossed in the comics.

"Why the hell *should* I?" she whispered fiercely as she bent close enough for him to hear.

"You prolly shouldn't," he agreed. "But I'm prayin' ya do, because I love you and I can't live without you."

Sam stood straight up.

She walked rapidly away from his table, back to the kitchen window.

And returned a moment later with coffee with cream, no sugar.

She set it on the table in front of him.

"Thanks," Jeremy said, lifting the cup to his lips. "Are you about finished with your shift?"

"Do you want anything else?"

"Nope—just to talk to you."

Sam exhaled deeply for a third time in the last few minutes. Her head was starting to feel light.

"My tables were all clean before you sat down," she said, trying to sound petulant but failing. "Once the salt and peppers are done, and you're gone, I'm done."

"Go fill 'em while I drink this swill down. Then we can get outta here."

"Who says—"

"Sam," Jeremy said, holding his cup away from his mouth, "I love you." He put the cup down on the wet placemat, then pulled a box out of his shirt pocket. "In all my life, you are the only good thing that's ever happened to me." He looked up at her, and his eyes were gleaming, though he looked exhausted. "You've got every right and reason to kick my sorry butt to the curb; I've never deserved you, God knows. And if you tell me to hose off, you're prolly makin' a smart decision. But before I go drive off a mountaintop, which is all I feel like doin' right now, I need to beg you one last time to give me another chance."

He put the box down on the table across from him and nodded to the seat with his head.

Her eyes wide, Sam sat down across from him, ignoring the sharp glance from Louie.

She seized the small box and opened it.

The morning light coming through the blinds at the window made the small, central diamond sparkle as though it was set in one of the crowns in the tower of London like she had shown him once in *National Geographic*.

On either side of it were two small, clear pink stones.

"Rose zircon?" she asked as her voice clogged up with tears.

Jeremy nodded, his eyes locked on hers. "October, right?"

"Yeah." Sam looked back up at him. "You remembered my birthstone."

Jeremy ran his hand awkwardly over the hair at the back of his neck.

"You want me to get down on one knee?" he asked, his voice ragged.

Sam sat back against the upholstery, oblivious to Louie, who was getting off his stool.

"Yeah, I do," she said, staring at the ring, then at Jeremy, then at the ring again. "An' I want you to put it on me."

"I'll do that once I've said one last thing to you," Jeremy said, looking hard at her. "You know I come with baggage—terrible baggage that'll never get lost. I don't know if it will come back to haunt me in the future, and that could be a problem for you. I told you my secret because it wouldn't be fair to marry you without being honest about it. I *totally* understand if you don't want to deal with it—or me."

Sam's eyes filled with tears. She started to smile, then saw Louie's round stomach waddling over to their table.

"Buzz off, Louie," she said in a threatening voice.

The manager froze in his tracks, then spun around and sauntered back to his newspaper and stool.

Sam's eyes returned to Jeremy.

"Is there anything—*anything*—that you haven't told me?"

Jeremy shook his head solemnly.

"You sure? Nothing?"

He thought for a long moment, then bowed his head. "OK, one thing."

The smile fell away from Sam's face. "What?"

Jeremy lifted his head and looked her in the eyes.

"Your nachos could use some Tabasco," he said flatly.

Sam blinked. "That's it?"

Jeremy nodded. "Otherwise, you're perfect. And you know every secret I have now. The question is, are you willing to marry me in spite of everything you know about me?"

"I'll let you know if you get down on one knee."

Jeremy rose from the booth just as two older women and a man were making their way into the restaurant. He put up his hand, then got down on one knee.

" 'Scuse me a minute, folks," he said to the startled group, who stopped just past the doorway. He turned to Sam. "You are the best thing that has ever happened to me, Samantha Phyllis Melnicki. I don't deserve you, but I'll try real hard to be worthy of your love if you'll marry me. So, uh, like, will you?"

She nodded, then smiled.

Jeremy took the little ring from the pasteboard box and slid it onto her finger. It took a moment to get past the knuckle, but once it did the fit was good.

He looked at her hand.

"Cool," he said. "C'mon, let's get out of here."

The three people at the door applauded politely.

"I can't," Sam said regretfully. "I'm the only waitress on—and Louie's useless—so drink your coffee and I'll wrangle you up some toast and bacon while I wait on these folks. Then we'll go home and never come back here."

"Works for me," Jeremy said, returning to his seat. "Wheat toast, if ya got it."

He stared down into his coffee cup, hoping he had done the right thing.

Sam, grabbing water and menus for the three new customers, was hoping the same.

Chapter 33

ELEVEN MONTHS LATER, June

L UCY WAS BUSY applying her lipstick when the door of her room in the Obergrande Hotel burst open suddenly.

Kelly Moran, who was helping her with her hair, carefully winding pearls through her upswept curls, dropped the rattail comb and cursed quietly.

Which was good, because the open door was admitting five little girls, all of whom were dressed in white flower girl dresses, crowns of white daisies, tiny lilies-of-the-valley, and white violets in their hair.

"Oh, my goodness!" Lucy laughed as they crowded around her in her satin dressing gown, hugging her and dancing in place. "Look at you! What beautiful princesses!"

"You're getting married in your *bathrobe*?" Corinne demanded, a look of disapproval on her pretty face.

"No, no, I have a princess dress too," Lucy said.

"Well, that's good, 'cause a bathrobe would be *embarrassing*," Sloane decreed like a style maven.

"Miss Sullivan, will you be our teacher again next

year?" asked Elisa, backing up and plopping herself in Lucy's lap.

Lucy kissed the top of her head of beautiful, almost-black hair.

"No, honey," she said, checking her makeup in the mirror again and discovering she had dotted her teeth with lipstick. "I'm moving away with Prince Charming."

"*What?* Why?" Grace asked, her bottom lip suddenly quivering.

"He's finished with the dam project," Lucy explained.

"Miss Sullivan," said Sarah, "let's keep our talk nice, please."

Lucy laughed out loud. "You remember that from last year?"

"Yes," Sarah said, looking at her crown of daisies in the mirror and straightening it. "It's about the only thing I do remember."

Lucy took note, but didn't say anything in response.

"Anyway, he spent the last year fixing the dam, build-ing the new one, and helping design the buildings and houses that got lost in the flood or the fire, like the school and Pancake Heaven. He has other jobs to do for the Army, and we need to go where his work is," she contin-ued, touching up her eye shadow with her pinky.

"Where will you live?" asked Elisa.

"In a castle," Sloane retorted. "Duh."

"I'm sure it will be a castle to us," Lucy said, pulling one of Sloane's curls straight and tucking it into her crown. "OK, time to get into the dress."

As the little girls danced in excitement, Kelly and Lucy

went to the closet, a rustic Adirondack rough-hewn mahogany room with, in contrast, satin-covered hangers, and pulled out the dress.

While the flower girls oooohed and ahhhhhed and worked themselves into a frenzy, Kelly helped her into it, a classic style, sleeveless with a dropped waist that accentuated her slim figure and the curves Ace was so fond of. It was made of blush satin, and picked up all the pink tones in her otherwise-alabaster skin. The skirt was wide and simple with a sweep train.

The result received high ratings from all six judges.

"All right," Lucy said once she was turned out properly, "let's head for the limo."

"Where's your bouquet?" Sloane demanded as they each picked up their basket of flower petals. "You can't be a bride without a bouquet. It's *embarrassing*."

"Well, actually, Sloane, I *don't* have a bouquet," Lucy said. "But I do have a flower."

She picked up the long-stemmed red rose, around which was wrapped her grandmother's rosary.

"Let's go."

AT THE TOP of Tree Hill Park, at the approach of dusk, stood three men beneath what had once been a grand Northern Red Oak, now a smooth, black form, without leaf or twig, but massive and beautiful nonetheless. The stains of fire had been washed gently away by the rain that had fallen since the night it had died. A long, horizontal arm stretched out as it always had when it was covered in leaves, a place where children climbed still.

Father Charlie looked down the hill to where the torches had all been set up to light the way of what would shortly be the new married couple.

"Here she comes," he said to the young man who stood, attired in the dress uniform of the United States Army, a smile on his face that competed with the stars for brightness.

Ace glanced around at the people standing a little farther down the hill, still encircling the tree. His best man, Jordan Nguyen, his longtime friend and bunkmate in the Guard, was grinning almost as widely as he was, happy to have been asked, and thrilled to be there. His mother and sister had traveled in from Colorado and were beaming at him. Mrs. Cox and the other teachers had formed a group, whispering excitedly.

As the bells of the carillon at Our Mother of Sorrows began to play the hymn of vespers, evening time, a procession of gorgeous little girls in white dresses and floral crowns began to ascend the hill, wiggling excitedly but staying mostly in step and time. Behind them, Kelly Moran followed, her dress a deep rose-red.

"It's going to be a blessed life for you both from now on," said Father Charlie, watching the bride begin to ascend the hill on the arm of Mr. Grimes. "The two of you have gone through more heartache in your time together than most people suffer in a lifetime."

"Exactly," Ace said, jockeying to get a better view. "All the bad is behind us now. What could be worse that what we've already vanquished?"

Then his power of speech was taken away from him by

the sight of his bride.

Later, he would admit that he remembered little of the ceremony other than the sight of the beautiful woman standing next to him, pledging their love as so many other lovers had done in the past.

"We wrote our own vows, so it's not like I didn't know what I was agreeing to," he told her on their wedding night, soaking in the two-person tub in their honeymoon suite. "But the picture of you in my memory, standing beneath the tree, will be the last thing I see before my eyes when I die."

Lucy had just smiled, leaned forward in the soapy water, and kissed him.

But for now, when their ceremony was complete, their union pledged, and they were finally husband and wife, a few dramatic whispers had issued forth from the peanut gallery.

"Miss Sullivan?" Lucy recognized Sloane's voice, followed by Corinne's, correcting her.

"She's Mrs. Evans now. Didn't you listen?"

"Mrs. Evans? Mrs. Evans?"

As the assembly of guests chuckled, Lucy had turned around and smiled down at her students, the children she had walked through water to save.

"Yes, ladies?"

"Since you just married Prince Charming, are you gonna live happy ever after now?"

Lucy laughed. "Yes. Yes, I am. Very happily ever after."

Father Charlie and Mr. Grimes had shepherded the guests down the hill, leaving the couple alone beneath the tree in the last rays of the setting sun.

Ace let his hand come to rest on his new wife's cheek.

"I have one more thing I would like to do beneath Obergrande, before we head off to the reception," he said, his eyes gleaming.

Lucy inhaled. "All right. What?"

"I'd like to start a tradition." He got down on one knee and placed his hands on her hips.

Lucy stared at him. "What are you doing?"

"Shhhh," Ace said. "Just listen—'Mrs. Evans, I want to thank you for marrying me. It's the greatest honor I will ever have bestowed on me.' "

The new Mrs. Evans laughed. "This is the tradition, passed on to a new generation?"

"Yes."

"And those are the exact words your father said to your mother?"

"Yes."

"Do you always have to kneel?"

"No, just tonight."

She looked at him in amusement. "Why tonight?"

Ace leaned forward and kissed her abdomen.

"I wanted our boys to hear it from the very beginning—even if we don't start on them any time soon."

Tears welled in Lucy's eyes. She pulled Ace to a stand and put her arms around his neck, then rested her nose against his.

"Copy that," she whispered.

~ **End** ~

About the Author

Polly Becks is a professional writer and has taught Spanish at the high school level for more than 25 years. She attended the State University of New York, where she met and fell in love with her husband of over 30 years.

She has a love/hate relationship with cats.

For more information, go to www.pollybecks.com and www.facebook.com/PollyBecks.

LINKS TO

Other books in the

EXTRAORDINARY DAYS series

The first four books of this spectacular new series are being released each month from January 5, 2015, to April 1, 2015. Get yours now!

Book 1: No Ordinary Day

The free download of the book that started it all.

Available Now!

Each book in the *Extraordinary Days* series makes a direct cash donation to a different charity or non-profit organization. Your free download of *No Ordinary Day* benefits **The American Red Cross.**

The Extraordinary Days series
[set in present day]

Book 2: MONDAY'S CHILD: Fair of Face

Where has supermodel Briony, the one-named wonder of the fashion world, disappeared to? That's what style magazine maven Katherine Bruce desperately wants to know—and she's manipulated Pulitzer Prize-winning investigative journalist and war correspondent Erik Bryson into chasing that story down. A serious writer, he's resentful about being stuck with the fluffy task—and utterly unprepared for what he discovers.

Preorder/Purchase NOW at:

www.pollybecks.com/coming-soon/mondays-child-fair-of-face

Available: Monday, February 2, 2015

Your purchase of *Monday's Child: Fair of Face* benefits **The American Cancer Society**.

[See next section for a free sample of MONDAY'S CHILD: Fair of Face]

Book 3: TUESDAY'S CHILD: Full of Grace

Grace Fuller, the youth pastor in her father's church, is guarding several painful secrets that threaten her future. Will she find a happily-ever-after with Steve, the confident, handsome assistant pastor with whom she's vying for her dream job, or will the mysterious bad-boy biker who has just come to town, darkly guarding his own painful past, steal her from her chosen path?

Preorder/Purchase NOW at:
www.pollybecks.com/coming-soon/tuesdays-child-full-of-grace
Available: Tuesday, March 3, 2015

Your purchase of *TUESDAY'S CHILD: Full of Grace* benefits **Tuesday's Children**, a non-profit organization founded to promote long-term healing in all those directly impacted by the events of September 11, 2001.

Book 4: WEDNESDAY'S CHILD: Full of Woe

Life in the fast lane has never been an easy place for twitchy high-society event planner Sloane Wallace, a woman born to privilege and pristine family lineage. But when a freak snowstorm and auto mishap leaves her stranded in the freezing mountains in her designer heels, a burly mountain man, unimpressed with her pedigree, shows up in time to save her couture-covered backside—and completely mess up her world.

Preorder/Purchase at:
www.pollybecks.com/coming-soon/wednesdays-child-full-of-woe/
Available: Wednesday, April 1, 2015

Your purchase of *Wednesday's Child: Full of Woe* benefits **Wednesday's Child: Dave Thomas Foundation for Adoption**, Finding Forever Families for Children in Foster Care

PREVIEW

Monday's Child: *Fair of Face*

Publication Date: Monday, February 2, 2015

Fair of Face

Polly Becks

Book 2 in the EXTRAORDINARY DAYS series

Your purchase of this e-book provides a direct cash donation to
THE AMERICAN CANCER SOCIETY
for cancer research and programs for those affected, those at risk,
and those who may one day be affected

For more information about The American Cancer Society, go to:
www.cancer.org

Chapter 1

DAY 1

Madison Avenue, New York City

THE STREET TRAFFIC was whining behind him, making Erik Bryson's head hurt just slightly less than the sight in front of him did.

He was staring up at the Sesqui-Centurion building, a ten-story Arts-and-Crafts-style monstrosity, home of the offices of *In-2-It* magazine, the third most influential fashion periodical in the world.

Erik was looking at his personal vision of hell.

Bryson, a stringer for the *New York Times*, had been convinced when he got the text from his boss earlier that morning ordering him to come here that the message had been misdirected. Surely a man whose entire adult life had been spent doing investigative journalism in war zones and the twin cesspools of corporate corruption and international politics could not possibly have business here, the frou-frou capital of the world.

And yet here he was, being greeted by a beautiful

Latina in a trim red suit who ushered him into the building of his nightmares.

"You know, I believe *you* invited *me* here," Bryson protested at the security screening facility, where a uniformed African-American guard was silently holding out a hand, demanding to check his camera case and cell phone.

"Not me, sir," said the guard as Bryson grudgingly handed his equipment over. "That would be Ms. Bruce, and you can take it up with her when you get upstairs. I'm just doing my job."

"I hear ya," Bryson muttered. "So am I."

Another young woman, this one a winsome blonde in a stylish black suit, looked up from her desk across from the security table.

"Excuse me," she said, rising and making her way across the lobby, "but are you Erik Bryson?"

Erik turned away from the security guard. "Who's asking?"

The woman blushed. "My name's Zoe. I'm a big fan of your work."

One of Bryson's eyebrows rose suspiciously. "Really?"

She nodded. "*Postcards from Zabul*, series one through three," she said. "Brilliant stuff. The photos are utterly haunting."

Erik's second eyebrow joined the first at his hairline.

"Oh—sorry, I'm a journalism student," she hurried to add.

"I see. Well, thanks. Glad you liked the series."

A grumbling cough came from behind him. The security guard was holding his camera case and phone out to him, looking unimpressed. Erik quickly took them back and nodded goodbye to Zoe as the woman in the red suit escorted him past the security checkpoint into a lobby where the *In-2-It* name was boldly emblazoned on an ebony wall, the only thing in the place that wasn't off-white. He followed her to the elevators and sighed miserably as she punched the button for the penthouse. The car arrived silently, and they stepped inside.

"Why am I here?" he asked the young woman, who stared straight ahead at the elevator door as it closed in front of them.

"Why are any of us here?" she answered, not turning her head. "Ms. Bruce wants you to be here. So you are."

The door opened onto a lobby so full of spectacularly arched windows that Erik had to shade his eyes. Those eyes were intensely Norwegian blue, the color of glacial ice, staring out from beneath a crown of soft black curls that needed a trim. The sun blazing through the glass stung them. He mumbled an inaudible curse and followed the red suit out into the sunny penthouse lobby.

He was ushered almost immediately into the corner office.

There, sitting behind a surprisingly simple wooden desk in an opulent chair was a middle-aged woman of elegant bearing, her coal-black hair tied back in a chignon at her neck. Bryson, had he been asked, would not have had a clue what the word *chignon* meant.

But he did recognize Katherine Bruce, the world-famous fashion publishing magnate, without hesitation.

"Sit," she commanded as he approached her desk.

"I'm sorry," Erik mumbled. "I believe there has been a mistake—"

"You're Erik Bryson, by way of the *Times*?"

"Yes."

"Then there's no mistake. Sit."

Awkwardly, Erik sat down on the severe, high-backed swivel chair in front of the simple desk. "Next, are you going to tell me to roll over?"

The woman smiled slightly. "Wrong command. I want you to fetch."

"Excuse me?"

Katherine Bruce picked up a crisp sheet of photographic paper and dropped it on his side of the desk in front of him.

"Briony. I want you to bring me Briony."

For the first time since he had entered the Sesqui-Centurion, Erik did not need a fashion-speak dictionary.

The face in the color photo staring back at him was one he had known since high school, when he secretly kept a folded magazine cover with a close-up of it under his bed.

The international supermodel Briony, the one-named goddess of magazine covers.

The face of the enormously successful fragrance Doce Cherio, and of its similarly successful high-end cosmetic line.

And the body that most of the top designers in the fashion world used to display their designs.

For a long moment Bryson stared at the face in the

photo: the smoldering gray eyes on either side of a thin, smooth nose, the sensuous mouth with a top lip shaped like a long bow, the rest of it curling into a famously crooked smile that seemed at once humorous and sad, as if hiding a secret. Luminous skin that covered perfect cheekbones, glowing with light. Erik shook his head and looked at the publisher once more.

"Why do you want *me* to fetch her? Can't you send a limousine for her? I drive a crummy old Corolla that gets parked on the street in Brooklyn."

"No, I can't—we don't know where she is."

"Can't you just call Doce Cheiro and *ask* where she is?"

Katherine Bruce shook her head. "They just launched a contest to find the new face of Doce Cheiro."

Erik took a deep breath, then exhaled. "What happened to the old one?"

"No one knows. Briony has disappeared."

"Have you contacted her management?"

"Daily."

"What do they say?"

"That she's retired, and they have no other comment."

Erik exhaled again, this time with a little more annoyance.

"Well, that's your answer, then," he said testily. "She's retired. End of story. Thanks for a fun morning. I'll be going now." He began to rise.

"Sit," said Katherine Bruce again in a voice that sounded like it came from a military commander. "That is most certainly *not* the end of the story."

Erik was struggling to keep from exploding. "What in the world do you want from me? I'm an investigative journalist—my specialties are political corruption and war zones. I cannot imagine something I'm less qualified to cover—and less interested in—than high fashion."

"That doesn't matter. I pulled some strings at the *Times*, asking for their best investigative reporter who was on stringer status. They recommended you."

"That's very nice, but—"

"*Sit.*"

Reluctantly Bryson sat down again, glowering, feeling four years old and hating it.

"For a relatively famous young hot-shot journalist, you have an appalling lack of curiosity," Katherine Bruce said. "I want Briony back, but I'm not getting anywhere with the search. There's got to be a story here, and whatever it is, I want it first."

"I think you got the story," said Erik. "Headline: *Supermodel Retires.* Ta da. End of story." He looked out the arched window. "I can't believe I'm still here."

"The rumor mill is rife with other suggestions. Maybe she's pregnant. Maybe she is hidden away with a married man, carrying on a sordid affair. She was spotted a while back in the company of an eastern European prince—"

"Maybe she's pregnant with a married eastern European prince's octuplets?" Bryson suggested snidely. "Can't you just make up something more interesting than that? Isn't that what you scandal sheets do anyway? The sheep you write for can't tell the difference anyway."

Katherine Bruce drew herself up taller, and her face

took on a hard expression.

"We don't write for the sheep, Mr. Bryson," she said seriously. "We write for the shepherds. *In-2-It* is a serious fashion magazine."

"Isn't that an oxymoron?"

"No. We are not the tabloid you pick up in the beauty salon. We are the magazine for the buyers, the producers, not the consumer. That's not to say consumers don't pick us up and get a secret thrill that they're learning insider information—and frankly, that's a large percentage of our circulation. We are the innovators, the leaders. We tell the fashion industry—especially the buyers and the stores—what's hot. And Briony is hot. I want the story before the private dicks hired by the other fashion rags get it."

"Private *dicks*?" Bryson said, trying to keep from laughing. "Where do you think you are, Ms. Bruce, in a 1930s Raymond Chandler movie? Those were made long before we were born." His captivating eyes took on an evil gleam. "Well, at least before *I* was born." He struggled to keep from laughing at the ugly look that came over the elegant woman's face. "Come into the 21st century, Ms. Bruce. Why don't *you* just hire a private investigator?"

"Those bastards would sell me out to the highest bidder once they locate her," Katherine Bruce said bitterly. "And they have no respect for the integrity of the story. There is undoubtedly a story here, and I want that story, unembellished. You can find the story, Mr. Bryson."

"Why me? Why in the world did you hire *me* for this nonsense? This is a waste of my time *and* yours. A private eye—"

"The *Times* hired you," Katherine Bruce corrected. "You aren't a private eye, you're an investigative *reporter*; you can ferret out the truth *and* understand the value of the story."

The fashion maven sighed wearily, looking suddenly older.

"You and I, Mr. Bryson, we are both in the same profession, we want to sell magazines, or newspapers, or whatever's left of the print world—even if that world is about to go solely digital. A shame—great photography and the beauty it captures will be lost with the death of the last fashion magazine, the last coffee table book. Whether it's beautiful women and men in beautiful clothes, or African vistas, high-end clothing or endangered animals, we, Erik, we are the last protectors of a dying art form. When you and I are gone, everything we have worked for will vanish into digital glare full of typos and harsh fonts. You have kids?"

"Not that I know of."

The publisher opened her mouth to continue, then lapsed into silence. Erik exhaled.

"Sorry for being a smartass. The correct answer would be no."

"Well, your children, assuming you have some one day, may never even know what a magazine was, let alone a newspaper."

Erik Bryson rose again slowly, hoping if he took his time she wouldn't notice.

"I admire your commitment to the art of the printed word, Ms. Bruce, to your shepherds and your sheep. But I know absolutely nothing about the fashion world—*nothing*. Even if I wanted to help you—and even in the very smallest of ways, I don't think I do—I am unqualified to do so. I am a war correspondent. The runways that are part of my world have planes full of bullet holes landing on them. I'm very sorry for you if Briony has decided to get out of the fashion world and have a normal life, but I can't say I blame her for that. Thank you for a most entertaining conversation, but I think I will take my leave now. Good luck with your story."

He turned and started toward the door.

The ice in the words that came next almost froze the pleats in the back of his shirt.

"So, Mr. War Correspondent, you don't cover damsels in distress? Because no one knows if Briony disappeared on purpose or not—or even if she is still alive."

Chapter 2

B RYSON STOPPED IN his tracks. He turned slowly and shifted his camera case to the other side, then rolled his shoulders, loosening the heavy muscles that had suddenly cramped at her words, to see the magazine publisher watching him cagily.

"Meaning what?"

Katherine Bruce's face lost its cat-and-mouse expression, and she shrugged silently.

"Are you suggesting foul play was involved?" Erik pressed.

"Well, I certainly hope not. But if there's not a sexy answer to the question 'what made Briony disappear?' I hope there is a juicy scandal or a murder mystery involved."

"So if the story's not sexy, you hope she's disgracing herself, or dead?"

Katherine Bruce said nothing, just stared at him unblinkingly.

Against his will Erik Bryson blinked, then shook his head.

"I've spoken with some cold people in my day, Ms. Bruce," he said, his eyes boring into hers. "War lords, corporate raiders, *politicians*—but you can hold your ice with any one of them."

"Thank you," said Katherine Bruce stoically. "You may think the fashion industry is a fluffy joke, Mr. Bryson, but I can assure you, it is a deadly serious business. There is more than half a trillion dollars involved in the farthest reaches of all the economies that it touches. Briony by herself represents companies with a net annual income in the tens of billions of dollars. This is no place for lightweights; those who underestimate the seriousness of fashion do so at their own peril. There are a number of sad examples of people in the fashion industry being kidnapped or killed. The longer Briony remains unable to be found—"

Erik Bryson exhaled.

"I'm listening," he said.

"I'll give you one magazine cycle, about six weeks, to find Briony and, more importantly, find out why she dropped out of sight."

"Did you ever consider that you already *know* the story? Maybe Briony just got sick of the life and decided to retire? What if the story's no more interesting than that?"

"Then that's the story we'll tell. You may not think much of the fashion world, Mr. Bryson, but while it is a cutthroat place, it's a reputable one—for the most part. The public hasn't truly figured out that she's gone, but when they do—the blowback may threaten both the industry and her life, depending on what has happened to her. Neither of us would want that, would we?"

Erik Bryson stared at her in silence.

Katherine Bruce leaned back in her chair.

"Six weeks, at three times your hourly, plus expenses, no matter what happens. Bring me Briony, and you can have editorial oversight of the breaking story. Two questions that need to be answered in that story, and only two—where is she, and why did she drop out of sight? But if after six weeks you come up with nothing, I'll hire a detective and kiss off the chance to tell the story without sensationalism. If there's a skeleton in her closet, a sinful tryst, a scandal or some other character-destroying story, I will not hesitate to tell it—I'll need to pay for your time, and that of the private detective, somehow."

Erik Bryson looked at her for a long moment, then came back to his chair and took out his tablet with a sigh. "Tell me everything you know about her. Every stupid little detail. I will try to keep my eyes from rolling back in my head."

The magazine maven leaned back in her ridiculously expensive chair.

"When she first showed up she was just a kid, and *really* rough—had never even put on a pair of high heels, had no sense of fashion or understanding of the industry. But the best of them usually don't—those things can be easily learned. What Briony was born with, you can't teach. Perfect biometrics, my *lord*—I've never seen a better face for makeup or perfume lines. Her management auctioned her, and Doce Cheiro set a new record price for her exclusive cosmetics work.

"Her hair is amazing; in daylight it's a fabulous shade of dirty blond, but in the right illumination it can look silver, or gold, or white, or even a gorgeous shade of ash, without dyeing it. It also holds color beautifully. The camera loves her, but light loves her even more—and that girl knows her light. Totally a natural. She can do print or film, runway, swimsuit, bridal, negligee, body paint, fine art, street-punk, high fashion, ready-to-wear—she's a dream. But she's missing in action—has been for more than a year. We need her back—'we' meaning the entire fashion industry."

"Anything you can tell me about her that won't make me gag—er, that isn't about her work?"

"She is a reader, a voracious one," Katherine Bruce said after a moment's thought. "The first day she came to this office she was fresh off the plane from wherever the hell she came from, a school backpack full of doorstop-thick history books and a copy of *Paddington Bear*."

Erik's brow wrinkled. "Paddington Bear? The kid's book?"

"Yes."

"How old was she?"

"Sixteen—just barely. She seemed intelligent and pleasant, though she didn't say a word. Her manager, Brian Hanoway, is a total pain in the ass; he has both a business and a law degree, and *the* A-list of names for every type of industry—writers, models, actors, athletes, musicians, you name it—the people who are so famous that they can buck the major agencies and who need a shark like Hanoway to keep the problems that come with mega-celebrity at bay. It's a small, select office; he hasn't had a new employee in decades."

"How do you know that?"

Katherine Bruce looked surprised. "We always try to pay off someone on a manager's staff," she said, looking as if what she was saying was obvious. "The easiest and best way to get inside data. But no one at Hanoway Ltd. is ever biting. The bastard pays them too well."

"Truly, you are turning my stomach," said Erik, not looking up from his tablet. "What else can you tell me?"

"Not much. We were given exactly zero information about her, other than her measurements. I have no idea what her last name is, if she even has one. Her management built a brick wall around her. That putz Hanoway laid the law down clearly, as he did each time she has entered into a major contract with anyone—*leave the kid alone*. 'She will work full-out for you on shoot, but her personal life is off limits,' he said. 'If you can't abide by the terms, we're done talking.' Hmmpf. That jerk had an office in the Times Square area on the 27th floor *before* he signed her; I can't even imagine what his setup is now."

"Still in Times Square," Erik Bryson said, reading the tablet.

"She always had an extra day or two put into her contract when she was working in foreign locales so that she could visit their historic sites. The clients weren't expected to book or pay for those days—her management handled the details, as they always do. But she wanted to take the time to see the history of the places she visited. I can't remember any other model that ever wanted to see anything abroad but the nightlife. It was a colossal pain and meant she was unavailable for compressed bookings."

"Good for her," Erik said, typing on the tablet once more. "One less beautiful American acting like an Ugly American."

"I don't even know if she's American," Katherine Bruce said. "Someone suggested she might be from England, but in the few words she ever spoke in my hearing, I didn't catch an accent. Maybe Canada."

"Why did you think she might be British?"

The fashion editor shrugged.

"Probably because of that damned book," she said.

"Which one—*Paddington Bear*?"

"Yes. I saw her in a T-shirt once with a picture of him on it, in his stupid black hat and his stupid blue coat with his stupid note pinned on it, and asked her if it was her favorite book or something. She smiled and said no, it just reminded her of home."

Erik looked up. "Oh? That sounds promising."

"Yes, yes it does, but it turned out to be nothing. When she first went missing, we did all kinds of looking into Paddington Bear. I'd never read the book before, but it quickly became my constant companion, if you can imagine that—me, carrying around a stupid paperback *kid's book* in a Coach bag. We cross-referenced the author, tore the book apart searching for clues—I even sent a private detective to the famous address where that damned bear supposedly lives in London in the books—#32 Windsor Gardens—but all we managed to do is scare the devil out of a poor old couple who lived near there, who were used to being hounded by children, not detectives, about Paddington. There is no such place, by the way."

The reporter suppressed a smile and continued typing on his tablet.

"When London crapped out, we even sent the private eye to 'darkest Peru'—where the bear supposedly came from. You can imagine what he came back with."

"Let me guess—nothing?"

"Nothing. Bupkis. Spent $1.2 million chasing an imaginary stuffed bear around the flipping world. And didn't find a whiff of the Doce Cheiro spokesmodel."

"And that's all you've got—a wild goose chase and a voracious reader of history books?"

"That's all I've got."

"Not much to go on."

Katherine Bruce blinked. "Wait, what am I thinking? There is one other twist to all this." She picked up a slate gray folder and dropped it on the desk in front of him. "This is the only contact Briony has had with the world since her final shoot, which was for Dior, in January of last year."

Erik opened the folder. It contained a thick stack of fashion photos, all from the same basic vantage point, but from slightly different angles, of many models, men and women in fall or winter clothing, walking the same runway. His trained eye told him the shots were impressive in their photographic quality, but nothing more. He looked up at the magazine publisher and raised an eyebrow.

"So?"

"These arrived, from her manager's office, at the end of March last year," Katherine Bruce said. "They're shots of the autumn/winter line at Milan's fashion week."

"But none of them are of Briony," Erik said.

"No." Katherine reached over and flipped the top photograph. "But her name is on every one of them."

Bryson looked at the stamp on the back. It was a plain ink logo, in a simple block font, reading BRIONY.

"What does this mean?" he asked.

Katherine Bruce leaned forward. "If it follows industry protocol, it means that Briony *took* the photos. If she did, I don't know how she managed to do it—she must have been in disguise or something—and I have no idea where she got press credentials. There was no request for payment, no explanation, and Hanoway Ltd. was utterly silent on the matter. I have no idea what any of this means. But it never happened again."

"Maybe she's decided she wants to be behind the camera instead of in front of it."

"That would be insane. The salary she made as a model has almost three more zeroes at the end of it than what a fashion photographer makes. If she's sick of modeling, she can write a book, get a TV or a movie deal, or pitch products on QVC—"

"Not everything is always about money, Ms. Bruce."

"You know, I think I may have heard that once. Nonetheless, no more photos from any other fashion week ever arrived. It's driving me mad."

The reporter stood and stretched. "I'll look into it, but I'm not promising you anything."

"Bring me Briony. Earn your reputation."

Erik's ice-blue eyes gleamed.

"I've earned my reputation every day since before I graduated from college, Ms. Bruce," he said coldly. "That reputation is for *investigative journalism,* which has mostly been employed ferreting out the bastards that pass intentionally bad legislation, grease the palms of drug lords and exploit powerless men, women, and children in ways that would make your blood run cold if I described them to you—well, maybe not yours, now that I think about it. I don't have time for this nonsense. So let me be clear with you—I will *bring* you no one, least of all Briony. I'm not a bounty hunter."

"Hmmm," Katherine Bruce said, rubbing her cheek. "Hadn't thought of that. Bounty hunter. Might be my next option if you don't come through."

"If I *do* find out what happened to her, I will bring you the story," Bryson continued. "And I will do what I can to get you in contact with one another. But if you ever again address me in a manner that makes you sound like a torturer from the Spanish Inquisition, that day will be the last blessed day you will ever see me. Do we have an understanding?"

The fashion editor stared at him frostily. Then she smiled with the same frost on her gloriously colored lips.

"Completely."

Erik snatched the photo of Briony's face from the desk. "All right. If your contact info is different than the text I received inviting me to this charming meeting, send me a better number or email." He shouldered his camera case and turned away, heading for the door. He opened it quickly.

"Goodbye, Ms. Bruce," he said.

"Mr. Bryson?"

Erik exhaled sharply. *"Yes?"*

Katherine Bruce looked him up and down.

"You have a very nice look yourself. The cool blue eyes, the dark, sexy, loose curls, the cut body—you could be a model, too, and make a good living at it. If you fail in this assignment, you'll need a new line of work anyway. Look me up if that happens."

Bryson swallowed. Then he cupped his ear with his hand.

"I'm sorry," he said dryly. "I didn't hear a thing you just said."

He closed the door behind him with a decided snap.

Katherine Bruce waited until she heard the bell of the elevator closing. Then she touched the call button on her smart phone.

"Are you ready?" she said to the voice that answered. "Good. He's on his way down now. Don't let him out of your sight until he's out the door. Then the pros will take it from there."

The quiet voice posed a question, and she smiled.

"Yes—his camera case and phone were successfully tagged at security. The tracking signal was confirmed to be working before he arrived at my office. Thank you for distracting him, Zoe."

Chapter 3

Geneva Cointrin International Airport, Switzerland

AT THE SAME moment Erik Bryson was getting his marching orders in Manhattan, Sarah Briony Windsor, the girl who had morphed from a pretty but gawky sixteen-year-old into a worldwide phenomenon in 2003, was poking at the flobby prosthetic chin she had attached to her face in the Geneva airport bathroom, deep within a stall where no one could see her.

The contortions she had undertaken to keep from dropping the rubber chin, her makeup case, the bottle of spirit gum adhesive, and her camera bag into the lidless toilet could have qualified her for a role in a Cirque du Soliel show, she thought, pressing her fingers into the squishy layers. When the spirit gum had finally set, Briony held up the mirrored surface of her foundation case and examined her efforts.

A woman she did not recognize stared back at her, jowly, middle-aged and dark-haired.

Briony suppressed a little squeal of delight.

Quickly she touched up her unflattering makeup, put

on her sunglasses, gathered her gear, and hurried out of the ladies' room, making her way to the gate.

At check-in she had a moment's nervousness when the gate attendant asked randomly for her passport.

"I did this downstairs, before I went through security," she protested.

"This is an international flight, madam," the young blond woman said curtly in accented English. "We check at will."

Briony felt her cheeks burn as the attendant, whom she imagined was around her own age—twenty-eight— looked quizzically at her wrinkled double chin and bad dye job, then at her birth date. Her name on the document was as ordinary as it was possible to be—Sarah B. Windsor—and finally the woman handed her passport back and nodded toward the jetway. Briony had waited until she was halfway down the hallway leading to the plane door before she allowed herself a slight smile at the attendant's clear disgust that a woman less than thirty had let herself go so terribly.

As she nodded pleasantly to the flight attendant and made her way to her seat, she thought back to what it had taken to get here, the first hurdle on her path back home.

Her assistant, Claire, an Englishwoman with impeccable manners in public and the salty tongue of a longshoreman over a glass of Pinot in private, had been skeptical of her insistence on a Coach seat.

"You have never flown anything but First Class, or at least Business, in your bloody *life*," she had said during their Internet conference a few nights before. "At least not since you were sixteen and I've been making your travel and security arrangements."

"You certainly have spoiled me," Briony had agreed, looking out the hotel window at the gorgeous Swiss landscape. "But First Class is just asking for trouble. It may be nice to deplane before everyone else, but then you are paparazzi prey."

"Most celebrities like it that way," Claire had said fondly, her green eyes twinkling.

"I know," Briony had replied as she prepared to hang up. "One of the many reasons I don't want to be one anymore. Thanks for everything, as always, Claire."

"Hmmph," said Claire. "Hope you have an extra couch for me to sleep on wherever you end up—without that celebrity status, I'm going to need to downsize my salary expectations."

Briony smiled at the memory now as she looked at her carry-on, and then at the storage compartment above her row. "Excuse me," she said to the flight attendant who was counting seats in the aisle next to her. "Would you be so kind as to get two blankets and a pillow down for me?"

The man, blond, thin-faced, and three inches shorter than her, looked at her for a moment, silently noting her superior height, then curtly complied.

"Thank you," Briony said breezily, ignoring the unmistakable annoyance in his expression. She tucked the camera case carefully under the middle seat in front of her and packed one of the blankets around it, wincing as a twinge went through her. She stood and stretched.

Suddenly she felt the wind knocked out of her as a

sharp blow struck her lower back.

Briony dropped the pillow and the remaining blanket and grabbed the back of the seat next to her as the world went black for a moment. Nausea rose up inside her, leaving her faint.

"Austin! I'm so sorry," said a young mother behind her in the aisle. The woman grabbed the rambunctious boy, seven or eight years old, who had just slammed his Tonka truck into her kidneys, and dragged him back, away from Briony. "Are you all right, ma'am?"

Briony nodded numbly, then folded herself into the window seat as the boy and his mother squeezed down the aisle toward the back of the plane.

"For goodness' sake, Austin, be more careful," she heard his mother admonish him. "You could have broken that poor old woman's back."

Yessssssss, Briony thought. *Victory.*

She settled in with the pillow, covering herself with the blanket, and mentally thanked Claire again for insisting on buying both of the seats next to her.

She was right about Coach, she thought as she half-listened to the cabin attendant's emergency instructions. *Oh well. Better get used to it.*

She was only able to stay awake long enough to bid the snow-topped peaks of the Swiss Alps in the distance farewell before sleep came for her.

"Goodbye, beautiful mountains," she whispered at the heavy plastic of the oval window. "I'll miss you—but not for long. Soon I'll be back in the Adirondacks, and then I will forget all about you." She pulled the window shade down and put her head against the pillow again.

"No offense," she whispered sleepily.

She awoke with a thump as the plane touched down at JFK.

It was an enlightening experience getting off the plane out of Coach. Briony had never waited more than a few moments to deplane before, escorted by assistants and security guards, being whisked through Customs and rushed to waiting limousines by men who talked into their earpieces. Instead, she now got to stand amid the great swell of humanity as passengers snapped open compartments all around and above her and pushed their way down the aisle. Briony decided that waiting was probably best all around, so she remained in her row until almost everyone had left the plane.

She smiled pleasantly at the crew, who returned her grin tiredly, and made her way through the airport to Customs, where her Sarah B. Windsor papers and insignificant belongings didn't raise an eyebrow. She followed the signs to the baggage claim area at the bottom of the large escalators, where Claire had told her an escort would be waiting.

Standing at the bottom of the escalator was the ever-present line of drivers holding signs with names printed discretely on them. Dead center of the line, very much out of place among the young and middle-aged men and women in blue uniforms, was a portly, elderly elf of a man, still in fine physical shape with a full head of glorious silver hair. He was dressed in a spiffy black suit and chauffeur's cap, wearing a pair of granny glasses and a broad grin, holding a sign that said DAKS OR BUST.

Briony laughed out loud, startling the woman checking text messages in front of her on the moving staircase and the man passing on the left at the same time.

It was all she could do to keep from shoving the whole line in front of her off the escalator.

Instead she waited impatiently, tapping her fingers on the hand rail. When she finally reached the bottom, she dashed to the elf-man and threw her arms around him, startling the other drivers and their passengers-to-be.

"Ed! Oh, Ed, I'm so glad you could meet me. Claire said the escort company already had you booked today."

Ed Hillenbrandt slid her carry-on bag off of her shoulder onto his own and returned her embrace, patting her affectionately on the back.

"Wouldn't have missed it, ma'am," he said.

"You recognized me?" she whispered into his ear. "Even with the dark hair and fake chin?"

Ed chuckled, equally quietly. "I'd know you anywhere, Miss Windsor."

"Shhh," Briony said. "And be careful with that bag—it has my cameras in it."

Ed bowed politely. "Indeed I shall. Come—I've already had your luggage wrangled. Let's get you out of here and off to those mountains."

Briony nodded briskly and adjusted her sunglasses, casting a quick look around her. No one was watching, as far as she could tell; traffic in the airport was steady this morning, mostly with business travelers, many of whom were trying to sort through their own drivers in the line.

She and Ed walked nonchalantly past the paparazzi and other wandering photographers looking for celebrities in the crowd. Most of them had already given up and were awaiting other flights, or had found marks among the first-class passengers. Briony let out a deep sigh, thankful again for her Coach seat, and followed her driver to where the modest black Cadillac sedan was parked amid a crowd of stretch limos and taxis.

Ed held the door for her, then got behind the wheel. "What'll it be for your singing pleasure, ma'am?" he asked mischievously as he waited to pull out of his parking space.

"You decide," said Briony. She opened her carry-on and checked her camera equipment. "I'll sing along to almost anything, as you well know."

Ed held up a battered disk. " 'Simon and Garfunkel in the Park?' One of my favorites—I was at that concert, you know."

"Perfect." Satisfied with the state of her gear, Briony zipped the camera bag shut and leaned back against the comfortable seat, wrapped in the thick blanket and full-sized pillow Ed had provided for her, and closed her eyes. "You do realize that concert took place before I was born, right, Ed?"

"You are one mean lady, ma'am."

"Trying my best." She stretched out, eyes still closed, and joined in with her driver's excellent tenor on *Mrs. Robinson*, singing Paul Simon's part to his Garfunkel.

She woke in what seemed like no time later, feeling the car turning and decelerating from the endless straight line of the highway. Briony sat up woozily.

"What—what's happening?"

"Bathroom stop. You may still be young and beautiful, but my bladder's sixty-five."

"Where are we?"

"Schenectady-ish. There's a very nice, clean Wendy's right up ahead."

"Well, you always were the expert on where all the good restrooms are." Briony hunted around for her purse, locating it after a moment on the floor of the car. "I need to go in, too."

"I need to make some gas and mileage notations for the service before I go in," Ed said as he put the car in park outside the restaurant. "You go ahead—it's early, and the parking lot's empty. I don't think you'll run into anyone."

"Oh, bless you," Briony said. She stepped creakily out of the car, then scurried into the side door of the building, opened the bathroom door and dashed for the single stall.

She was washing her hands at the sink, staring at the face she barely recognized in the mirror, when she heard a familiar pleasant tenor voice singing an Irish bar song which seemed to be approaching from outside the bathroom door.

It was getting disturbingly close.

Quickly she tore off a paper towel and dried her hands, then stepped hurriedly to the door.

Which opened, leaving her face to face with her driver as he crossed the bathroom threshold.

"Ed! What are you doing in here?" Briony demanded.

Ed blinked, then looked over his shoulder. He turned to face her again.

"You're in the men's room," he said.

He pointed to her right.

Briony looked. The urinal was in plain sight, big as day.

Ed stepped out of the way as she raced out of the bathroom and through the restaurant door, dashing across the parking lot. The car's lights flickered and bleeped as she approached; Briony looked back over her shoulder to see her driver standing at the restaurant window, laughing. He held up the car remote, then disappeared again.

She opened the car door and climbed into the backseat, mildly mortified.

A few minutes later, Ed was back in the car. He said nothing, but turned on the engine, put the car in gear and drove off.

After a long moment of silence, Briony leaned forward beside Ed's right ear.

"I'll give you ten thousand dollars if you never tell anyone what just happened," she whispered loudly.

Ed chuckled. "Keep your money. I would never have anyway."

"You're the best, Ed. No matter what everyone else says."

"May I make a suggestion?" Ed asked, turning back onto the interstate.

"Certainly."

"Lose the fake chin. It's really scary."

"Oh—oh boy." Briony tugged the latex appliance off her face, laughing, then rubbed the stinging surface of her skin where sticky trails of spirit gum remained behind. "I forgot all about it."

"Maybe having five extra pounds attached to your throat is the reason you were snoring from the George

Washington Bridge to the Thruway. That thing looks like skin harvested from a cow's udder."

Briony blinked. "Really? I was snoring?"

"Like a drunken sailor in a hammock belowdecks."

Briony blushed in spite of herself. "Oh dear. I'm so sorry."

"I'm just teasing," Ed said, chuckling. "You're far too young and pretty to snore, even when you're disguised as an old fishwife."

"Well, now that we're out of the airport I can throw that thing away," Briony said, moving it away from her on the seat. "It will be good to be home, to just be Sarah again. I intend to remain a brunette for the time being, however."

"What name are you using in your new career as a photographer?" her driver asked as they passed a truck loaded with hay bales.

"My fashion photos will go out under 'Briony' still, assuming I ever get hired on again after my anonymous shoot. I'm not sure about the other stuff I plan to do yet."

"You've got time," said Ed.

"Indeed. Nothing but time." Briony looked out the window again. The landscape had changed from the urban surroundings of the airport to the smaller buildings of the little riverside city. She stretched out and closed her eyes again.

"Wake me up when you can see mountains on both sides of you. And not before, please."

"You got it."